Date: 9/29/20

LP FIC MONROE
Monroe, Mary,
Across the way

ACROSS THE WAY

ACROSS THE WAY

MARY MONROE

THORNDIKE PRESS
A part of Gale, a Cengage Company

**LIBRARY OF CONGRESS CIP DATA ON FILE.
CATALOGUING IN PUBLICATION FOR THIS BOOK
IS AVAILABLE FROM THE LIBRARY OF CONGRESS**

ISBN-13: 978-1-4328-7855-9 (hardcover alk. paper)

Published in 2020 by arrangement with Dafina Books, an imprint of
Kensington Publishing Corp.

Printed in Mexico
Print Number: 01   Print Year: 2020

*This book is dedicated to
my beloved cousins,
Alice Curry and Donnie Ruth Franklin.*

ACKNOWLEDGMENTS

It is such an honor to be a member of the Kensington Books family.

Selena James is an awesome editor and a great friend. Thank you, Selena! Thanks to Steven Zacharius, Adam Zacharius, Karen Auerbach, Vida Engstrand, Lauren Jernigan, Samantha McVeigh, Elizabeth Trout, Robin E. Cook, the wonderful crew in the sales department, and everyone else at Kensington for working so hard for me.

Thanks to Lauretta Pierce for maintaining my website.

Thanks to the fabulous book clubs, bookstores, libraries, my readers, and the magazine and radio interviewers for supporting me for so many years.

To my super literary agent and friend, Andrew Stuart, thank you for representing me with so much vigor.

Please continue to e-mail me at Authorauthor5409@aol.com and visit my website at www.Marymonroe.org. You can also communicate with me on Facebook at Facebook.com/MaryMonroe; and Twitter @MaryMonroeBooks.

Peace and Blessings,

Mary Monroe

CHAPTER 1
MILTON

November 1939

What was this world coming to? I done heard — and told — a lot of outlandish fibs myself, but this one took the cake.

Me and Yvonne had a lot of enemies, but I never expected one to stoop low enough to finger us with a made-up story about a crime that could have got us lynched or sent back to prison for life. I still couldn't believe them peckerwood cops busted up the birthday party that me and Yvonne was having to celebrate Willie Frank's thirty-fifth birthday two nights ago and arrested us for setting up a white girl to be raped.

This was the *second* time I'd been busted on a bum rap. Thirteen years ago, one of my buddies invited me to go to a grill with him to celebrate my twenty-first birthday. Even though me and him had done a slew of robberies and broke into rich folks' houses together, he hadn't bothered to let me know that he was going to rob the place that night. The night cook always worked alone and had been robbed before, so he was prepared. As soon as my buddy pulled out his gun, the cook grabbed a gun from under the counter and shot him dead. I didn't have nothing to do with that crime, but nobody believed me. I spent the next eight years working on one of the most brutal prison chain gangs in the state. Yvonne had had her troubles with the law, too. Before we met, she'd spent a couple of years locked up for causing an old woman to fall and break her hip when she'd tried to detain Yvonne during a shoplifting incident at a candy store.

We had turned our lives around, got married two years ago, and started a bootlegging business. Prohibition had ended years ago, but a lot of folks still bought alcohol from bootleggers because it was cheaper so we jumped on that bandwagon right away. On top of going into a profitable business, me and Yvonne had even found Jesus. Being on the straight and narrow hadn't done us much good, though. Because here we was, back in trouble with the law again anyway. I could not believe it. What had I done to be in a pickle for the second time for something I didn't do? I wondered. God must have been punishing me for all them other crimes I'd got away with. I pushed that thought out of my mind because it was so unpleasant, it gave me a headache.

Two days in that nasty town jail had been hell. During that time, me and Yvonne had got roughed up something terrible by them punk deputies. Two of them nasty buzzards had even made a sport of Yvonne, raping her right before my eyes.

If it hadn't been for Willie Frank, a righteous white dude I'd met in prison, there was no telling what else might have happened to us. He was our best friend and business associate. To make a long story short, since we bought all the liquor we sold our guests from Willie Frank, he got his uncle Lamar to pull some strings to help us get out of jail. That old man owned a lot of land and his wife's sister's daughter was married to the district attorney, so he had a lot of pull in Branson, Alabama.

Lamar Perdue and Sheriff Orval Potts was close buddies and because of "lack of evidence" it had been easy for Lamar to get the charge against us dropped. It hadn't been cheap, though. Lamar had paid Sheriff Potts two hundred dollars, but he wanted us to pay him three hundred back. Me and Yvonne was already struggling just to get from one day to the next. We knew it was going to be hard for us to come up with that kind of money — and Lamar wanted it by the end of this month. That meant we had only about three weeks to get it. Even if I busted into a dozen houses and stole everything I could carry, there was no way I could come up with three hundred dollars in three weeks. Besides, I had stopped breaking into houses a long time ago. I had quit while I was ahead because I did not want to get arrested again. If I went back to prison, I could handle it, but Yvonne was too dainty to do another stint. I knew I'd have to do something real drastic to get the money we owed Willie Frank's uncle, and I didn't care what it was.

A few colored folks had issues with me and Yvonne being so close to Willie Frank because he was the lowest kind of white: a tobacco-chewing, snaggletooth, uneducated hillbilly that made his living running a still. We didn't care. He was still good people as far as we was concerned. Not only was he a lot of fun; he sold his liquor real cheap to us. But he made the other bootleggers he supplied pay full price. Even with his rag-gedy teeth, he was still a good-looking guy. He loved the ladies, and they loved him because of his fun-loving attitude, thick blond hair, and blue eyes. And he was a generous soul. He spent a lot of the money he made on colored women. Next to me, he was the second most popular trick that went to Aunt Mattie's whorehouse.

I felt so much better when Willie Frank drove us home from jail this afternoon. He'd stayed with us for a little while and then he drove over to Cunningham's Grill, a popular roadhouse on the outskirts of town, to let Mr. Cunningham know we'd be back tomorrow. I worked there as the head cook and Yvonne waited tables. Willie Frank was also going to spread the word among some of our regular guests that we was back in business selling liquor at our house.

He'd said he'd come back to our house tomorrow, but he returned half a hour later with more unpleasant news. "I hate to tell y'all, but Lyla Bullard and her cousin Emmalou told me they done got too skittish to come back over here. They was at the grill when I got there and told me as soon as I walked in the door." Me and Willie Frank occupied the living-room couch. Yvonne was slumped in a chair facing us, staring off into space one minute, sighing and fidgeting like a worm on a hook the next minute.

"I'm sorry to hear that we lost their business. A lot of colored men came to drink with us because of them," I replied. Lyla and Emmalou was two middle-aged white women who had come to the house on a regular basis. They had been present on the night of the arrest. I was going to miss them. Maybe it was for the best. Some of our colored female guests didn't like all the attention they got. For all we knew, it could have been one of them black-ass heifers that made the call to Sheriff Potts! If that turned out to be true, when me and Yvonne found out who they was, we was going to chastise them just as hard as we would a man. I gave Willie Frank a weary look and held my breath for a few seconds as I stroked the two-day-old bristle on my chin. I hadn't shaved or took a bath since Tuesday morning. I couldn't wait to get in the bathroom and freshen up. But I wasn't going to leave the room while Willie Frank was on the premises. His company was so important to me, I wanted to spend as much time around him as I could. Especially after all he had done for us this week. "I hope nobody else decides to stop drinking at our house. If *you* was to cut us off . . . ." The thought of losing Willie Frank was so distressing, I couldn't even finish my sentence.

He gasped and looked at me like I was

crazy. "Hush up! I can't believe you said that! You ain't got to worry about me deserting y'all!" he blasted as he wagged his finger in my face.

"Whew." I wiped off the beads of sweat that had bubbled up on my forehead. "I'm glad to hear that. But I had to bring it up," I said with a sheepish grin. "Now that that's out of the way, let me go on. I'll tell you one thing, I won't rest easy again until we chastise the devil that got us in trouble. When we find out who they is, we should break some limbs or give them a acid facial. I just might throw in a few knife wounds, and a death threat to boot."

Willie Frank was as anxious to get his hands on the culprit as we was. The look on his face now was so scrunched up in anger, it made me cringe. I hoped me and Yvonne never ended up on his bad side. Losing Willie Frank as a friend was the least of my worries. I couldn't figure out why such a farfetched thought even entered my mind in the first place. I couldn't think of nobody who looked out for us the way he done. As far as I was concerned, he was more like family than our real families was.

"Y'all know I'm ready, willing, and able to help," Willie Frank said. "We hillbillies believe in mountain justice. I suggest some-

15

thing more severe and permanent, like a shotgun blast to the head."

Yvonne gasped and sat up ramrod straight, with her eyes as big as pinecones. "Willie Frank, honest to God, you think we should kill somebody?" she asked.

He answered right away. "Yup. As long as that person can still breathe, he'd still be a threat. Now if y'all don't want to take a chance on something else happening, take my advice."

Yvonne looked at me with a curious expression on her face. When she raised her eyebrows, I nodded. And all three of us smiled.

CHAPTER 2
YVONNE

I never thought I'd be discussing murdering another human being. There was a few I'd locked horns with over the years that I would have loved to bump off, though. Like them three nasty dogs that got me pregnant and left me to fend for myself. But the person who had lied about me and Milton setting up a white girl to get raped had crossed a line. He deserved to die. Whatever Milton wanted to do, I'd go along with it.

After I thought a little more about Willie Frank's suggestion, I said in a flat tone, "If we going to kill somebody, I don't want to do it on no Sunday. That would be sacrilegious. I don't even cuss on the Sabbath."

"Sugar, like Willie Frank said, we got to do something so this bogeyman won't be a threat no more. And don't worry. I wouldn't stoop low enough to kill nobody on the Lord's day neither. But first let's wait until we find out who it is before we decide what

17

to do," Milton replied.

"Why would it make a difference who he is if we going to kill him?" I wanted to know. "Let's come up with a plan now."

"Well, it could be somebody we can't get at without no witnesses seeing us. Or they might have a gang and weapons and shit. This is one thing we need to think through real good. I just hope it ain't one of our friends." Milton suddenly looked so miserable, and I could understand why. The thought of somebody we was close to betraying us almost made me sick to my stomach.

"Swallow me a frog! If that's the case, he ain't no friend!" Willie Frank hollered with his eyes blazing with hate. "Don't spend too much time thinking this thing through. Lollygagging could be a big mistake. We don't want to give that booger enough time to do something fatal. Good God! I'd be devastated if y'all got killed. Ma, Pa, and all the rest of my folks done got so attached to y'all, they'd never get over it neither."

Hearing them ominous remarks must have got to Milton. He flinched and looked at me with a dazed and confused expression on his face. I didn't wait for him to respond to Willie Frank's outburst. I responded for him. "We won't waste too much more time.

18

I want to get this over with as soon as possible."

When Willie Frank left our house again, me and Milton cuddled up on the couch in our bathrobes. Even though we'd drunk two jars of moonshine apiece since we got home, we was still on edge. I could tell from the way he groaned every time he moved that he was still hurting from head to toe. I was, too, but he'd been beat up more than me and had more bruises. "My body been on hold for two days. I need to go sit on the commode for a while. After I relieve myself, I'm going to wash my hair," I muttered as I toddled up.

"Stay in the bathroom as long as you want, sugar. I'll just lay here and relax and organize my thoughts."

"I need to organize my thoughts, too." I sighed. "I got so many I don't know how my head can hold them all."

Half a hour later, I walked back into the living room with a towel wrapped around my head. Milton was hanging halfway off the couch. "I feel so much better," I said. I plopped down next to him and he leaned in to hug me. I flinched and scooted a few inches away.

"I'm sorry. I know that what them deputies done to you is still fresh on your mind."

19

I held up my hand and wagged a finger in his face. I was ready to put that incident behind me and stop talking about it. "Milton, I done almost forgot what it felt like." I was as mad as I could be about them deputies raping me, but I wasn't going to harp on it. I didn't want Milton to be no more upset than he already was.

"Oh. Well, the way you just reacted when I touched you —"

I cut him off right away. "That ain't the reason I flinched. I done that because I'm scared and I'm going to be scared until we collect them three hundred dollars to give back to Willie Frank's uncle." He hugged me again. This time I didn't flinch. "Milton, I want you to know right now that what happened to me in that jail cell could have been a lot worse. Let's be glad it wasn't. So, we don't never need to conversate about that no more."

"Oh?"

"I just want you to know that that episode won't have no effect on our lovemaking. Okay now. Let's talk about something else." I puffed up my cheeks and blew out some of the stale air I'd been toting around way too long. I'd rinsed out my mouth with salt and hot water a little while ago, but it hadn't done much good. The inside of my mouth

20

still tasted like I'd been chewing on an old shoe. "If I can get up enough nerve when we go back to the grill tomorrow, I might ask Mr. Cunningham to loan us some money. But that's only if he's in a good mood."

"And I'll start feeling Dr. Patterson out the next time I see him. Aunt Mattie is too unpredictable, but I'll approach her soon, too."

"That's good. While I was soaking in the tub, another idea came to me." I gave Milton a thoughtful look, and then a wide smile. He smiled, too. "What about Odell and Joyce Watson next door? They get free food, clothes, and all kinds of other things from her folks' store. All they got to pay is rent and a few other bills, so I know they got money to burn."

Milton groaned. "Humph. Tell me about it. That's why they such happy so-and-sos," he snarled with lips quivering.

"They can make us happy, too. On top of the money we need for Lamar, we should hit them up for as much extra as we can. Especially Odell." We had the goods on Odell, so he was ripe for the taking. When him and Joyce got married five-and-a-half years ago, her folks retired from running MacPherson's, the most successful black-owned country store in Branson. They had put Odell in charge right away. On top of the big bucks Joyce's parents was paying him, Joyce was making good money as a teacher's aide at Mahoney Street Elementary School, the top school for colored kids in town. Besides all that, Odell had a outside woman named Betty Jean and three little boys with her that he was supporting. They lived fifty miles away in Hartville. Milton had accidentally busted him a few months ago when him and a friend happened to stop for a snack at the restaurant where Odell and his secret family was kicking back. Odell gave us money not to blab, whenever we asked for it. Now he was going to have to pay us even more until we made up for the money we'd lost by being stuck in jail. "If we going to borrow a bunch of money anyway, we might as well get enough to treat ourselves to something good. Whatever we get from Odell and Joyce, we could take our time paying them back — if at all. If Joyce puts pressure on us to repay the loan, we'll borrow more from Odell without her knowing. We can pay off the first loan with the money from the second loan we get from Odell. She'd never know we was robbing Peter to pay Paul."

"Hmmm." I must have really struck a

nerve because Milton's eyes was sparkling like black diamonds as he stared at me. "I'm glad you brung that up, Yvonne. I been meaning to tell you that I had already thought about doing that. If we can scrape up enough extra from all the folks we planning on hitting up, I'd like to take you for a buggy ride." Milton tapped the tip of my nose with his finger and then he leaned over and kissed it. "We ain't done nothing that much fun since we visited that alligator farm in Florida on our honeymoon."

"Baby, I'd loved to go for a buggy ride. And I'd like to go gawk at them alligators again someday. But we need money for more important things first. If we get enough, I can buy some smell-goods. I'd like a bottle of that new French fragrance that just came out. I'm getting sick of splashing on vanilla extract."

Milton chuckled and gently pinched my arm. "Girl, what's wrong with you? Why would you want to spend money on something like a French fragrance when you can swipe it from MacPherson's like we do so many other things?"

"Uh-uh. They keep the smell-goods in a locked case, because for a long time that was the thing the other shoplifters swiped the most."

"All right then. Anything we can get over what we owe Lamar, we should pamper ourselves big-time. You can buy whatever you want with your cut. I'll use mine to get in a few crap and poker games."

I took in a sharp breath and shook my head. I didn't want us to get too carried away and sink into another black hole after we got out of the one we was in now. "Milton, you know I don't like you gambling too much." The puppy-dog look on his face made me feel like I was picking on him, so I backed off. "Well, one good thing about you gambling is that it helps keep your temperament under control."

"Thanks, baby. So, you wouldn't mind if I start gambling again every now and then with the extra money we get?"

I had a feeling he gambled — and lost — way more than he admitted. I'd been hearing rumors from some of the people who drunk with us that he was always looking for a game to get in. But since I didn't have no proof that his gambling was out of control, I let it slide. If I did get proof, I'd confront him then. "I do mind. But after what we been through, you can play poker or roll dice every day from now on if you want to — after you help me pay a few bills. Let's not get ahead of ourselves, though.

Everybody we plan on asking for money might turn us down."

Milton waved his hand. "Baby, don't worry your pretty little head about nothing. I got a feeling we'll get all we need . . ." He gave me a quick peck on the cheek and a pat on my shoulder. "We'll start with Odell and Joyce. But we should wait a few more days."

"Why?"

"Because they'll be surprised enough when they hear how much we need to borrow." Milton paused and widened his eyes. Then he snapped his fingers. "I just thought of something. Maybe we shouldn't bring Joyce into the mix too soon, if we do at all. She is such a pig in a poke. If she decides to be stingy, she might put a bug in Odell's ear and stop him from helping us out. When I decide the time is right, let's just deal with Odell. You cool with holding off on him for a little while?"

"Yeah, I guess," I muttered as I teetered up off the couch. "You sit here and get some more rest or go take your bath. I'll get supper started and fix us some drinks."

I didn't agree with Milton about holding off on Odell. But I wanted him to think I did. I had already made up my mind that I was going to approach Odell as soon as I could and hit him up for a few dollars to spend on myself. And I wouldn't tell Milton.

Friday was when Odell disappeared until Sunday evening, every week. For years, he had been feeding Joyce and everybody else a flimsy cock-and-bull story that he went to his daddy's house to help his stepmother take care of his sick daddy on weekends — and a few times during the week. The old man lived on the outskirts of town near the swamps. Odell had to drive down a long dark spooky road to get there and he claimed that it took a lot of time to do whatever he had to do, so he always stayed overnight. Brother Lonnie was in poor health, physically and mentally. He hardly ever left his house, but me and Milton bumped into him and his wife, Ellamae, at a fish market two months ago. He looked like he was ready to be embalmed, and nothing he said made much sense. When I brung up Odell's name, Lonnie gave me a blank look and had to think hard for a few moments to know who I was talking about. Ellamae was such a mean-spirited heifer, people was scared to visit them, so nobody could verify that Odell spent all that time at his daddy's house. Now that we knew about his business in Hartville with Betty Jean, it was plain as day that his "sick daddy visits" story was hogwash.

I was anxious to see how much I could get from Odell, and I had to get to him before he hit the road tomorrow evening. I couldn't wait to see his face tomorrow afternoon when he seen mine.

CHAPTER 3
YVONNE

When I got in bed, all I could think about was my meeting with Odell tomorrow.

I wondered what Milton would say if he knew I'd been blackmailing Odell, too. I didn't like to deceive my husband, and I probably wouldn't have if Odell hadn't told me that Milton had been blackmailing him behind my back since July. I had a feeling he'd been using his hush money to gamble with. I spent mine mostly on personal items and household expenses. Whatever I got from Odell tomorrow, which I hoped would be at least fifty or sixty bucks, I'd sock it away for when we really needed it. But first I'd treat myself to a new pair of sparkly ear-bobs and some rouge.

We left home to catch the bus to go back to work at the grill an hour earlier than usual on Friday morning. We wanted Mr. Cunningham to see how eager we was to get back on board. That was why we didn't want to miss another day, even though we could have both used more rest. But we needed the money more than we needed rest.

We didn't mind working hard because we'd been doing that since we was kids. Milton and I had worked on farms, and I'd even cleaned houses and done other chores for rich white women. There was no way in the world I wanted to go back to that kind of work. Our bootlegging business was a lot more fun, and we made a heap more money.

There was a bunch of other colored bootleggers and jook joints in town where folks could drink and have a good time. But in just two years, we was so popular, we had almost put them out of business. And it was no wonder. We served much better free snacks, we lived in a house with a indoor toilet — not a stinky outhouse like them others — in a safer neighborhood, and we always had the latest records for our guests to dance to. We had lured a heap of our customers away from them other bootleggers, which was the reason they hated us now. Them bad-mouthing us had backfired and most of the few customers they had left, was gradually trickling over to us. I was worried that our arrest had scared some of our customers off, though. But some of our regulars was so loyal, I expected a decent crowd tonight.

Me and Milton had left our house in silence. But when we got to Odell's car parked in front of his house, we couldn't hold back our comments. "He sure spends a lot of time and money keeping that car spit shined." I laughed.

Milton was quick to respond. "Humph. Prince Charming can afford it." That was the nickname we called Odell behind his back. We called Joyce Queen of Sheba. "Him and Joyce act like they got royal blood, but their shit is just as stinky as ours." I was about to laugh some more until I noticed the sad look on Milton's face as he gazed at the house Joyce and Odell bragged about so much. I knew he was thinking about how he'd bled like a stuck pig on their front porch last Tuesday on Halloween night.

Milton had been walking home by hisself after gambling with a few of his buddies when some unknown thugs chased and jumped him. The beating had been so brutal, he hadn't been able to make it all the way home. So, he'd flung open Odell's gate and run up on his front porch. He had laid there for quite a while before Odell eventually found him and brung him home for me to bandage him up.

"I bet him and Joyce sitting at their fancy kitchen table right now eating a breakfast fit for a king, like they ain't got a care in the world," Milton said.

"Pffft. With all that fancy furniture in their house, the money the store pulls in, a car, and everything else they got, they ain't got no reason to have a care in the world." My voice sounded so detached, you would have thought it was coming from another woman. We got quiet and stayed that way until we made it to the bus stop a couple of minutes later.

The bus was running late, so I started up the conversation again. "Milton, if Joyce and Odell don't come to the house this evening, should we go visit them and let them know we got out of jail?"

"If they don't already know, they'll probably know by the time we get off work. But today is Friday, so we know Odell won't be coming because he'll be leaving right after he closes the store to go 'visit his sick daddy' again." We laughed.

"Well, maybe Joyce will come."

"If she do, don't you say nothing about the money we plan on asking Odell for." Milton cleared his throat and went on.

31

"Um, baby, I been thinking. Maybe I should go up to Odell by myself."

"Why? I thought you wanted us to approach him together."

"I did. But the more I think about it, the more I think this should be between us men. If Joyce ain't going to be there, having you present might make Odell uncomfortable. Baby, you know as well as I do that this is a man's world. Men take care of the business, women take care of the housekeeping and babies. That's just the way things is."

"No, that's just a bunch of happy horse manure." I stamped my foot and punched Milton's arm.

"Oww! What you do that for? You know I'm still recovering from my injuries."

"If you don't stop talking crazy, you'll be recovering from some more injuries," I warned. "And being *de-balled* will be one."

"What did I say that's got you so fired up?" he grumbled, rubbing the spot where I had punched him.

I done a neck roll so extreme, it made my shoulders ache. "You think this is a man's world, huh? Where would you men be without us women? And, if it wasn't for us, y'all wouldn't exist in the first place."

"Um, you got a point there." Milton

32

giggled. He stopped abruptly and got serious again. "I didn't make the rules, sugar. The truth is, women and business don't mix. Some men don't think a woman is sharp-witted enough to do it proper. That's why there ain't no women running big businesses in this town."

I looked upside Milton's head, wondering what made his brain function. Whatever it was, it wasn't doing too good of a job. I didn't want to punch him again because it wouldn't do no good. And I didn't want to reopen none of his wounds. "Humph. What about Aunt Mattie? She got more tricks coming to her place than all them other colored whorehouses put together. And Mosella Cramden been running her restaurant without no help from a man as far back as I can remember. And . . . and what about Joyce's mama? She helped Mac make Mac-Pherson's a big success. Them three is the most successful colored businesswomen in Branson." I was talking so fast, I almost lost my breath. That was the main reason I hushed up when I did.

"Pffft." The way Milton waved his hand in my face, you would have thought he was shooing a fly. "They don't count. Husky old gorgons like them lost their female appeal so long ago, they might as well be men now."

I rolled my eyes. "All right then. You go talk to Odell without me. You just better make sure you lay out a good enough story about how we have to pay Lamar back for getting us out of jail. You have to make him feel sorry enough for us, he can't say no."

"Baby, I already got my speech ready."

"Okay, we'll see."

"You worry too much. You ought to know by now that I ain't going to let you down."

"I know you won't, and that's why I love you so much." We ignored the other people standing at the bus stop, and we kissed long and hard. My lips felt so good after he pulled away. But then he stared at me so hard I got nervous. "Why you staring at me like that? My breath stink?"

Milton sniffed and looked me up and down as he licked his lips. "Girl, if your breath smelled like cow dung, it wouldn't stink to me. I'm staring at you because you so beautiful. Look at them big baby-doll eyes, that long black hair, your flawless, high-yellow skin tone, and that tight little body."

I didn't want to smile because I wanted the conversation to remain serious. I smiled anyway. "I appreciate hearing that. I hope you didn't marry me just for my good looks."

34

"I didn't. But having a woman with your looks is sure enough easier to deal with than them baboons some men got. I'm glad I ain't Odell. I feel sorry for him. If I had to snuggle up in bed with a frump like Joyce every night, I'd become a monk."

"Well, Odell ain't stuck with just Joyce *every* night. He got Betty Jean to fall back on. And she is almost as pretty as me. So you ain't got to feel sorry for him." I laughed. Then I got serious again. "Milton, do you regret moving to this neighborhood? We been living over here for five months now. Sometimes I don't feel like I belong in such a nice house with pecan trees in the front and backyard, and that cute picket fence. We ain't got much in common with these smug folks over here, and we the only bootleggers operating in this part of town. Something tells me that this arrest thing will make some of our neighbors start avoiding us."

Milton's mouth dropped open and he eyeballed me like I'd sprouted a goatee. "What? You was just as hyped up as I was about moving away from that run-down neighborhood on the lower south side. You was itching to live among the colored doctors and lawyers and other uptown colored folks over here. And we done made some good friends over here. Like Dr. Patterson down the street. He invited us to have Thanksgiving supper with him and his family, remember?"

"He might not want us to come now," I whined. "We jailbirds."

"We was jailbirds when we moved here. And the way Joyce runs her mouth, I'm sure she done told everybody in the vicinity. Anyway, we ain't never tried to keep our past a secret. I done lost count of how many times I overheard Willie Frank mention to some of our guests who live in this neighborhood, that me and him met in prison. Them same folks still come to our house."

"Yeah, that's right. And to think that somebody tried to have us sent back to prison. It's . . . it's unspeakable. I never thought we'd be victims in such a messy situation. No wonder I'm feeling a little uncertain about our future."

"Yvonne, you can stop feeling uncertain about anything. Me and you ain't victims, we survivors. As far as the devil that set us up, we ain't going to stop until we find out who done it. By the time we get through with them, they'll wish they'd never been born."

We was even busier than usual at the grill.

Some of the folks who came to the house to drink with us came in for breakfast. They was happy to hear that the charge against us had been dropped, and that we was back in business.

Around ten a.m., I went into Mr. Cunningham's office and asked if I could borrow his truck to go into town on my lunch break. I told him I needed to pick up some medicine for the headache I had had since our release. His thick gray eyebrows lifted high above his cloudy, beady eyes, making him look more decrepit than he really was. He was such a sweet old man, I felt bad about lying to him.

"I declare, that's a long time for a headache. Don't you think you should go to a doctor and get checked out? Milton told me how them boogers manhandled y'all with them billy clubs and fists," he said, giving me a sympathetic look.

"Um, they didn't do too much damage. We got plenty of bandages and pills at home, and we feel just fine. Except for my headache. I need stronger pills than the ones we got."

"Well, you can use my truck. But my nephew borrowed it already and won't be back until later this afternoon. If you can wait and do your business in town then, you welcome to use it."

"Okay. Thank you so much." One thing I could say about our boss was that he was one in a million. He never disappointed us. When Milton had to take off time when he got that beating, Mr. Cunningham still paid him half his salary for each day. He had told us, and a few other people, that me and Milton was the son and daughter he always wanted. I didn't know how our money situation was going to turn out. But I knew we'd be able to count on Mr. Cunningham for something, if it came to that. It all depended on how much we got from Odell.

Milton had told me this morning that Willie Frank was coming to the grill to take him to see Aunt Mattie on his lunch break so he could ask her for a loan. He had decided to see how much we could get from her before we approached Dr. Patterson, Mr. Cunningham, and Odell. He didn't want me to go with him because he believed that a whorehouse was no place for a lady like me to be. I was flattered so I didn't argue with him.

I didn't want to be where them nasty hoochie-coochie women done their business nohow. But I didn't have no problem with Aunt Mattie and her girls coming to drink at our house. They always spent a heap of money and left good tips. At the end of the day, life for me and Milton was all about getting paid.

money and left good tips. At the end of the
day, life for me and Milton was all about
getting paid.

CHAPTER 4
ODELL

"Sugar, I forgot to tell you that I saw the
lights on in Yvonne and Milton's house last
night when I got up to go use the bathroom," Joyce said before we left for work
this morning. We was still eating the lavish
breakfast she'd cooked.

"Oh? I hope nothing else serious happened over there."

"Maybe it was their landlord nosing
around. Anyway, I didn't think it was important enough to wake you up and tell you."

"It was probably Willie Frank. I seen his
truck over there yesterday evening and a
few times before that. I guess he's keeping a
eye on the house," I said, buttering my third
piece of toast.

"I didn't see his truck last night."

"Joyce, maybe he forgot to turn off the
lights when he left. Or maybe he parked
down the block so nobody would know he
was over there. You know how nosy and

meddlesome some of our neighbors are. They might start up a rumor that he was over there stealing stuff."

"When I got up to go to the bathroom again a couple of hours later, the lights weren't on."

I swallowed a chunk of my toast and drunk a few sips of my coffee before I replied. "What's the big deal? Willie Frank could have come back and turned them lights off while we was sleeping."

"Maybe so." Joyce looked at my almost empty plate. "I'll be glad when my appetite is back to normal. I don't think my stomach is going to settle until we know how Yvonne and Milton are doing. I'm glad to see that nothing has affected your appetite . . ."

My breath caught in my throat. I had to keep reminding myself to put on a miserable face so Joyce would stop making comments about how I was acting. And it wasn't easy. I'd been so giddy last night, I'd drunk two glasses of whiskey and snapped my fingers as I listened to music on the radio until she gave me a funny look. I'd immediately changed my demeanor. "Um, that whiskey got me acting like a fool," I'd claimed.

"Then why did you drink it?"

"I'm as sick as I can be about Yvonne and

Milton. The whiskey numbs the pain." I spent the rest of the evening with a long face and making comments about how bad I felt for our neighbors. Joyce didn't mention nothing else on that subject after we went to bed because I climbed on top of her and pried her legs open. Sex worked on Joyce like a tonic. After I finished taking care of her, she slept like a baby.

When we woke up this morning, the first thing she said was, "Odell, I know you care about Yvonne and Milton. If whiskey helps numb the pain you're feeling, I think I'll have a few shots when I get home today."

"And I'll have a few more myself," I said.

Almost a dozen customers was already waiting in front of the door when I opened the store this morning. With so many folks planning to cook Thanksgiving feasts in a couple of weeks, they was picking up canned goods and other nonperishable items left and right. A lot of my customers wanted to start cooking early, so I had arranged for my suppliers to deliver the turkeys and other popular holiday meats such as hams, chitlins, and rump roasts, two days before the holiday. I planned to take a huge turkey and a ham to Betty Jean. I felt bad because she couldn't cook it until the day after the holiday, when I could be there. To make up for her having to delay the celebration every year, I took her a few extra boxes of other goodies and doubled her weekly allowance for that week. She had already started hinting about all the things she wanted Santa Claus to bring her and the boys next month. That was another holiday I wouldn't be able to spend with her this year. Since it was going to be on a Monday, we'd celebrate it the Sunday before.

Things was moving right along. I greeted and chitchatted with some of my regular customers, and every single one commented on how sorry they felt for Yvonne and Milton. By now everybody in town had heard about them letting a bunch of colored men rape a white girl in their house. It seemed like this mess was never going to die down. So that I wouldn't look uncaring, I played sorry right along with them.

Buddy Armstrong and Sadie Mae Glutz, my two elderly, busybody cashiers, had everything under control, so I skittered into my office around eleven a.m. to do a little paperwork. My "paperwork" always included some sneaky business. I got away with stealing money from the business by doctoring up invoices and creating a few for vendors that didn't exist. All that extra

43

money went into my pocket. My in-laws, bless their gullible hearts, had never questioned anything I did, so I was going to keep doing the same thing as long, and as often, as I needed to. Taking care of Betty Jean and the kids was a huge expense. It wasn't no big deal to me. In a good week at the store, there was so much money to be skimmed off the top, it amazed me. On top of that steady cash flow, I snuck merchandise from the store to give Betty Jean and the boys, not to mention her relatives and a few other folks in Hartville I had to be nice to. But I didn't care how much money I had access to, I didn't want to keep doling it out to Yvonne and Milton.

I couldn't stop patting myself on the back for coming up with the brilliant plan that had got rid of them two bums. With their greedy hands out of my pocket, I'd have even more money to live it up with. One of the first things I planned to buy to celebrate my new life was a new car. The Ford Model T I had now still ran pretty good. But the lights got only so bright — even though I had recently replaced the battery — and the tires was practically bald. I couldn't let that go on too much longer. It was important for a man in my position to showcase a prosperous image. A LaSalle was the vehicle

I had in mind. The only other colored folks in Branson that owned such a classy set of wheels was our doctors and other prominent folks. My first choice was a white one so I could show off my flawless coffee-colored skin.

I was also going to buy Betty Jean some new furniture and have a telephone installed. And eventually I'd move her and the boys to a bigger and better house. The boys could still share the same room, but I wanted the baby girl we'd been working on creating to have one to herself. When all the holiday activity died down, I'd take Betty Jean and the boys on a nice vacation to Miami. We would lounge on a beach for at least a week. In the meantime, I had to come up with a good excuse that would explain me leaving Joyce by herself for that much time. That was the least of my worries. I could tell her black was white and she'd believe me.

After I completed my paperwork, I propped my feet up on my desk and kicked back with the latest issue of *Weird Tales* magazine. I was in such a giddy mood, I couldn't keep my mind on what I was reading. I set the magazine aside and played a few games of tic-tac-toe. That didn't hold my attention long neither. I was so antsy, I could barely sit still. I couldn't wait for the day to end so I could go back to Betty Jean's house.

I had already loaded up my car with several boxes of stuff she'd requested. Gathering it was always a challenge. I had to swipe a thing or two throughout the day every time Buddy and Sadie got busy. I always parked behind the store on the days I took merchandise. Nobody had any reason to be snooping around my car, peeping in the windows. But I covered the boxes on the back seat with a tarp anyway.

Before I could haul the last two of the five boxes from my office to my car today, I had to stuff all of today's profits in a brown paper bag. I done this every Friday after I closed the store before I delivered it to Mac and Millie. My in-laws didn't trust banks to handle all their money. They only deposited enough to cover household bills and a few miscellaneous expenses. Since they'd put me in charge of bookkeeping, too, they had opened a separate checking account in my name only to cover employee paychecks and everything else related to the store. Long before I entered the picture, they had been storing their money in cardboard boxes that they kept in a windowless pantry behind their kitchen. Right there with canned goods, fishing poles, and other knickknacks. Like a lot of the elderly folks in our neighborhood, they didn't always lock the doors to their house. They trusted everybody and had even gave me a key. So, if they wasn't home on a Friday when I got there, I let myself in and put the money bags in the pantry.

On top of the cash in the pantry, there was even more in some burlap sacks that used to hold potatoes. It was money they had been socking away long before I came into the picture. They kept them sacks in their attic. I had no idea how much money that was. Mac had mentioned it to me right after they put me in charge of the store. I had never been in the attic and didn't want to go up there because I knew I would be tempted to start dipping my hands into them sacks, too. Especially after Mac told me they never touched that money because there was more than enough in the pantry to keep things afloat. Every cent they had would belong to Joyce, and *me,* when they passed on. I prayed a strong enough tornado never cut through Branson and leveled my in-laws' house and blew all that money away before they died.

I snorted and glanced around my office, beaming with pride. I felt so comfortable in

47

this room. Joyce had decorated it with live plants, curtains she'd made herself, and she'd got rid of the old metal desk her daddy had used for decades. She'd replaced it with a larger, more up-to-date one made of wood. I kept the chairs Mac had used and the same file cabinets, but only because Millie was sentimental about them. There was a great big wedding picture of me and Joyce on the wall facing my desk. The very first dollar the store had made was in a frame next to it. I had it made in the shade. I had my "job" so down pat, I could do it in my sleep. Before I knew it, I did doze off. The next thing I knew, somebody slammed the door shut and startled me. I thought I was dreaming until I opened my eyes and seen something that almost made me go into shock: *Milton Hamilton.*

"Hello, Odell. Did you miss me?" he said with a smirk as he strutted toward me. I had never seen such a smug look on his blunt-featured face. Even though it had been just a few days since the last time I seen him, it looked like he had lost several pounds off his short, pudgy body.

"What the hell —"

He cut me off before I could finish my sentence. "Surprised?"

I narrowed my eyes and scrambled out of

my chair. I couldn't believe how fast sweat started rolling down my face and how hard my heart was pumping. "W-w-when did you get out of jail?" I was so horrified and stunned, it was a wonder I didn't shit on myself. It took all of my strength for me to stay in control of my body functions.

"Yesterday afternoon." He stood in front of my desk looking as cold as a block of ice. When he seen the magazine I'd been reading, and the game I'd been playing, he snickered. "My, my, my. I see you hard at work, as usual."

"I was taking a break," I snarled. "As hard as I work, I deserve to lollygag every now and then."

"You sure do." He guffawed.

It was too far-fetched to think that Sheriff Potts would let a colored man, who'd been accused of masterminding a white girl's rape, out on bail. I had to ask anyway. "You out on bail?"

"Naw." Milton shook his head and hand at the same time. He had on the greasy smock he wore when he was working at the grill, so I assumed he'd come here from work on his lunch hour. "Sheriff Potts let us go on account of lack of evidence."

I couldn't believe my ears. Since when did them cracker lawmen need evidence when a crime involved a colored man and a white female? There was something real fishy going on and I needed to know what it was. I had convinced myself that my scheme to get him and Yvonne locked up was foolproof. "Oh? How did he figure that?"

"Because there wasn't no evidence of me and Yvonne setting up no rape. Whoever called the sheriff didn't tell him nothing to back up their story with. No names, no raped white girl, no nothing."

I took a deep breath and dropped back down into my seat. "I'm happy to hear he let y'all go. How is Yvonne holding up?"

Milton went on to tell me a few things I didn't want to hear, like them getting roughed up and them deputies having their way with Yvonne. The thing that really threw me for a loop was what he told me next. "Even with no evidence, we still had to pay off Sheriff Potts to drop the charge. Four hundred dollars."

My jaw dropped. "Where did you and Yvonne get that kind of money?"

"That's where you come in . . ."

"You just said y'all paid Sheriff Potts already."

"We did, in a way. See, Willie Frank got his uncle Lamar to put up the money. We have to pay him back by the end of this month."

"Hmmm. Well, I still owe you the hush money I wasn't able to get to you on Wednesday. That'll help, and I'll even throw in a little extra."

Milton shook his head. "Naw, naw. Them itty-bitty eight dollars and 'a little extra' ain't going to do this time."

My heart was skipping beats and my eyes was burning as I glared at him. My head felt like it was about to crack open. "This whole business with you and Yvonne is driving me crazy." I was surprised I was able to sound so calm.

He hunched his shoulders and told me, "It be's that way sometime, brother."

I heaved out a mighty sigh. "All right. Let's get this over with. How much do you want from me?"

"Four hundred dollars."

CHAPTER 5
MILTON

Odell stared at me so hard and long, I thought he was trying to look clean through me. And it was giving me the jitters. When he spoke again, his voice came out sounding so threatening, I feared for my safety. "Four hundred dollars? Hell no. What's the matter with you?" He had started sweating a few moments ago. Hearing the amount of money I wanted must have really shook him up because now there was so much sweat on his face, it was shining like a new penny. I hoped I would never find out, but I had a feeling that if he ever got mad enough to get violent, he'd break every bone in my body.

"Odell, why you getting all hot and bothered? I'm the one trying to get my life back together," I whined.

"Milton Hamilton, you can't be serious. I can't come up with that kind of money by the end of this month."

"Dagnabbit! I ain't playing with you, Odell! I need that money!" I gave him the stink eye and wagged my finger at him. "And you better give it to me!"

He moaned like somebody dying. His whole body shuddered, and his eyes rolled up in his head. I said a silent prayer that he wasn't having a stroke or something else that would put him out of commission. That was my worst nightmare. Odell wouldn't be no good to me and Yvonne if he was disabled. He let out a loud breath and composed hisself real quick. I was so relieved I wanted to jump up and dance a jig. I stayed cool and calm because I wanted him to know how serious I was. "Where do you think I'm going to get it from?" he whimpered.

"Borrow it. You got all them highfalutin white friends and in-laws with deep pockets. Besides that, you can always swipe from the cash register."

"I ain't never borrowed nothing from my white friends or Joyce's parents. And I only swipe a few dollars at a time from the cash registers. What I do take, I use it to support Betty Jean and my boys."

"If you can't get but 'a few dollars at a time' out of them cash registers, then you ain't got no choice but to borrow the rest."

Odell moaned again. As distressed and weak as he sounded and looked, I wondered how a stuck-up fake like him managed not to cry, too. If he did, I'd have even less respect for him. "You done pushed me close to the edge, man."

"Well, you got yourself in this fix," I reminded him. "All I care about is you giving me that money before you fall over that edge. Understand?"

He reminded me of a trapped animal: a rat caught in a trap he'd set hisself. "I-I-I understand," he stuttered, which I thought was a major sign of weakness in a man.

"Now look on the bright side, this could be even worse."

Odell gulped and put on a poker face that looked hard enough to bounce a dime off. "What could be worse than you asking me for four hundred dollars I ain't got?"

"Asking you for five hundred."

He groaned so loud, folks out on the street probably heard him. His eyes darkened and a scowl crossed his face that would have stopped a clock. "Listen and listen good. I would never give you that kind of money — not even in your dreams! Furthermore, I advise you to come to your senses before it's too late!" he blasted. The way his shoulders was drooping now told me he didn't have too much more steam left in him. He was so comical, I wanted to laugh. Instead, I stood there like a mute, staring at him like he was going straight-up crazy. Maybe he was, but nutcases didn't scare me. If anything, his crazy-acting outburst only made me more determined to get what I wanted sooner, in case he ended up in one of them asylums. That would have put him out of commission, too. "Knowing you, even after I give you the four hundred, you'll still expect them eight dollars I been paying you every week, right?"

"Yup. But there's another bright side to look at." I exhaled and puffed out my chest, proud of myself for being such a shrewd businessman and staying focused when it came to dealing with Odell.

"The only other bright side I can think of is you and Yvonne disappearing!" he yelled with his teeth clenched. It amazed me how fast his voice could rise so high. He was practically roaring at me. "And I mean *for good!*"

I laughed. "That ain't going to happen. We love Branson, so we ain't never going to move away and I doubt if we'll ever have to worry about Sheriff Potts locking us up again. If he do, I'm sure Willie Frank's uncle Lamar would come through for us again." I had accomplished what I had came for, so I was ready to end this visit. I figured the least I could do was throw him a bone before I left. "Now let me tell you another bright side. Since I didn't get my weekly payment from you on Wednesday, you don't have to give it to me today. You can give that to me when you give me next Wednesday's payment."

Odell stared at me for a few seconds before he spoke again. He looked so beat down, I felt sorry for him. "All right," he mumbled.

"What about the four hundred?"

"I'll get it. Now if you don't mind, get the hell up out of my sight. I got things to do."

"I'm going. I got things to do, too. But before I go, I have to tell you that I am very disappointed in you, Odell."

His jaw dropped so low, it looked like a soup ladle. "*You* disappointed in *me*? You got some damn nerve! You come into my office with this outrageous cash demand, and you *still* disappointed?"

"Not in you giving me my money, though. I know you'll come through. I'm hurt because you ain't showed no concern for my well-being after all I been through." I sniffled and rubbed my nose. "Them laws treated us worse than mad dogs. They

mauled us, cussed at us, we didn't eat nothing, and we slept only a few hours at a time
the whole two days."

"What did you expect? You just better be
glad they didn't do nothing more serious to
y'all before Lamar stepped in. What do you
expect from me, other than my money? If
you thought I was going to run up and hug
you when you walked through that door,
that's something I'd never do in your case. I
will admit that I'm glad you and Yvonne
got let out of jail, and I'm sorry for what
Sheriff Potts and his deputies put y'all
through. And for the record, me and Joyce
actually got down on our knees and prayed
for y'all."

"Oh? I swear to God, I appreciate you telling me that. It means a lot to me, right
here." I stabbed at my heart with my finger.
"Well, I better leave before I get emotional."
I started inching backward toward the door.
Before I put my hand on the doorknob, I
stopped. "Can I ask Buddy or Sadie to give
me a pig foot? I didn't have time to eat
nothing before I came here." He didn't
answer my question. He just gave me another mean look, mumbled some cuss
words under his breath, and rudely waved
me away. I didn't want to get my feelings
hurt no worse, so I spun around and left his

office. When I got back to the main floor, I went straight up to Sadie's counter. "Odell said I could have a pig foot."

"Okay," she said, already leading me to the meat section.

"It's a good thing you asking for one now. We ran out right after noon yesterday. Odell had me set out some more this morning. I ate one a little while ago and this batch is so tender, the meat is falling off the bone," Buddy yelled, even though he was ringing up a customer.

"Buddy's right. You don't want but one?" Sadie grinned.

"Well, Sister Sadie, since you asked, make it two. I'm real hungry. Me and Yvonne didn't eat nothing the whole time we was locked up."

"Oomph, oomph, oomph." She patted my shoulder, gave me a pitiful look, and shook her head. "How come they turned y'all loose on such a serious charge?" I told her the same thing I'd told Odell. I didn't see no reason to tell her or anybody else that Lamar had paid for our release. Even if Sheriff Potts still thought we was guilty, money meant more to him than us getting convicted. Lamar proved that money talked, which was one thing I'd known all my life. Unfortunately, when the money was mine, the only talking it done was to say "bye-bye." I chuckled to myself because I knew that I'd lose that extra hundred bucks from Odell in a crap or poker game. I was already seriously thinking about asking him for another lump sum — *five hundred bucks* — in the very near future. If I decided to go through with it, I knew he'd give that to me, too.

CHAPTER 6
MILTON

When me and Sadie got to the meat counter, there was three huge jars sitting side by side, filled almost to the brim with plump, pickled pig feet. They was nice and pink, so I knew they was fresh. She opened the first jar, speared two with a fork, and wrapped them in a napkin and handed them to me. I didn't waste no time biting a plug out of one. Being a cook, and a good one at that, I knew good food like I knew the back of my hand. These was the most scrumptious pig feet I ever ate. If Sadie hadn't been standing next to me, I would have been gnawing like a beaver. But since I'd met Odell, I had picked up some of his good manners. Because of him, I didn't even belch or pick my teeth with broom straws in public no more.

"Sister Sadie, I just love coming in this store!" I exclaimed. "I declare, Odell got it running like a babbling brook."

"Aw, you just saying that on account of

you and him is such close friends, ain't you?"

"No, I'd feel the same way even if we wasn't."

"All I can say is that you should thank God every day for leading you and Yvonne to Odell and Joyce." Sadie stopped talking and looked me up and down with that pitiful look still on her face. "Um, Milton, you know I'm a Christian, but I do believe in a eye for a eye. Whoever lied on you and Yvonne need to be taught a lesson. I'm pretty sure it started out as a prank, but it got way out of hand. Who would have thought that y'all would end up in jail?"

"Well, when we find out who fingered us, what we going to do to them won't be no prank."

I didn't have no more time to waste because I had to pick up Willie Frank. He had come to the grill and loaned me his truck. When I got to Aunt Mattie's whorehouse, where I'd dropped him off, two well-dressed men was rushing in, and one in overalls that looked like a farmer was strutting out smiling and brushing off his shirt sleeves. Right after I parked across the street in front of a sumac tree, Willie Frank stumbled out the front door. He was smiling, too. "Did Odell come through for you?"

61

he asked when he crawled into the driver's seat.

"He said for me not to worry. He'll get back to me after he goes over his finances."

"Good, good. I just hope y'all come up with enough to pay Uncle Lamar back. He ain't the kind of man to play with when it comes to his money."

"Well, your uncle ain't got to worry. I can count on Odell. Our friendship is too important for him to let me down. If he can't give me the money out of his own pocket, he'll get it from somebody else. I prayed about it last night. I feel so much better today. Especially now that I done talked to Odell."

"See there, I told you to turn it over to God." Willie Frank started up his motor and the truck shot off down the street. I snorted and looked at the side of his face, which had two different shades of lipstick on his cheek. "By the way, you look like you got right frisky this time," I teased. "If your grin got any wider, the top half of your head would fall off."

We guffawed like hyenas. Willie Frank had to cough to catch his breath. "Yup. I got right frisky this time. My regular sweetie, Sweet Sue, had back-to-back tricks, so I had to pester that midget gal, Tiny."

We had just reached the dirt road that led to the grill. "I just hope and pray that nary one of them heifers get drunk or mad enough to put a bug in Yvonne's ear about my visits."

"Pffft. I wouldn't fret about that. Yvonne is like most other women I know; if they really love you, they'll believe anything you tell them."

"Well, that's the best kind of woman. But . . ."

"But what?"

"I just hope Yvonne ain't fooling around with other men behind my back. It would break my heart."

"Why would she? If you treat a woman good, she ain't got no reason to fool around. And that's a fact. I'll give you a good example. You know yourself Odell treats Joyce like gold. I seen a few of your men guests looking at her long legs with a hungry eye. I bet she wouldn't give them the time of day. As long as Odell is true to her, she'll be true to him. You remember my words the next time you even think about Yvonne getting it on with another man. Hear me?"

"I hear you."

Yvonne was busy finishing up with one of our regular customers when I got back to work. About two minutes later, she came up to me in the kitchen while I was wiping off the counter with a dishrag. I was glad I was by myself so we could talk in private. "What did Aunt Mattie say, Milton?"

I gave her a puzzled look and shrugged. "Huh? About what?" I laid the dishrag on the counter so I could give her all my attention.

Her eyebrows lifted up and her jaws started twitching. That made me jittery. "You done already forgot why you went to see her? I want to know what she said about the loan you went to ask her about!" she boomed.

I had lied to Yvonne so much, every now and then I let my guard down and almost got myself in a pickle. Being that I was such a pro, I always managed to catch myself in time. "Oh that. Well, sugar, she was busy and I didn't get a chance to ask her."

Yvonne didn't look so distressed now and her voice got gentle. "All right then. I guess you'll have to go back when she ain't busy." She cleared her throat and rubbed the back of her head, like she was trying to figure out the right words to say next. "Look-a-here, I wasn't going to tell you, but I don't like lying to you. Um . . . when I take my lunch break, I'm going to drive Mr. Cunningham's truck into town to pay Odell a visit. I'm going to ask him for a few dollars to tide us over until our finances is in better shape."

I reared my head back and gave Yvonne a serious look. "Oh? Well, that can be took care of when we get home from work. You ain't got to make no special trip to town for that."

"Him and Joyce don't even know we out of jail yet."

I folded my arms and glared at her. "Humph. With all the long tongues we know, I'm sure somebody will tell them soon, if they ain't done so already. If not, we'll visit Prince Charming and Queen of Sheba on Sunday when Odell gets back home from visiting Betty Jean and let them know ourselves. But I don't think we should take a chance on asking him for money in their house where Joyce might hear us. Her ears is almost as big as her head. She and Odell ain't a team like me and you. There ain't no telling how she'd react if she knew from the get-go what we need. When Odell gets comfortable with the idea, he can tell her. Shoot."

"Milton, Odell got Joyce in the palm of his hand. Whatever he agrees to, she'd probably go along with it. She might not be such a pig in a poke after all."

"I don't care. This is too serious. We can't take a chance on getting Joyce involved too soon. She could hurl a monkey wrench into our plans, and we could end up with nothing. Now you be patient." I sighed and picked up the dishrag and started wiping the counter again.

"Put that rag down and talk to me," Yvonne ordered, stamping her foot.

I stopped wiping and used the dishrag to mop sweat off my face before I laid it back on the counter. "I'm sorry, sugar. Keep in mind that even though Joyce is way more educated than us, she is naïve as hell. We got street smarts, so we might be able to hoodwink her in some way — behind Odell's back of course — and get a few bucks from her, too. Shoot. She can afford it. If she don't give us nothing, we ain't lost nothing. But we can't risk losing a jackpot from a sure thing like Odell. That would be a stupid move and we ain't stupid."

Yvonne dropped her head. When she looked back up at me, there was tears in her eyes. "Baby, I've enjoyed being on the same team with you. Before I met you, my life was so humdrum, I couldn't tell one day from another. But . . . I . . . I have to come clean about something. You'll probably find out sooner or later anyway. And I don't want you to think less of me."

"What is it you want to come clean about?"

"See, I know what a big fish Odell is and I wanted to take advantage of it. There ain't no telling when or if we'll ever stumble upon another gold mine like him. Um . . . I been getting hush money from him ever since you told me about him and Betty Jean."

I held my breath and narrowed my eyes. "Say what?"

Yvonne gave me a exasperated look. "Don't even try to act surprised. If you think we such a good team, you need to come clean, too. He told me you been getting money from him since July. Eight dollars a week every Wednesday."

My face felt like I had leaned over a bonfire. "I'm sorry. I didn't tell you because I didn't want you to think I was greedy."

"Pffft." Yvonne waved her hand. "I didn't tell you for the same reason. Things is different now. We got to work together to find out who set the law on us, and we can't do that by hoodwinking each other with a bunch of lies. That ain't the way Christians behave."

I glanced around to make sure we was still alone. "That's right, sugar." I licked my lips

67

and snorted. "Well then, I guess I'm duty-bound to come clean, too."

"Oh yeah? About what?" Yvonne asked with both eyebrows raised.

"See, the truth is, I didn't go see Aunt Mattie today like I told you. I dropped Willie Frank off there so he could pester her prostitutes, and I used his truck to go see Odell. I figured if I didn't ask for no money today, he wouldn't get so upset. When I told him what we needed by the end of the month, he didn't like it. But he said he'd give us the whole amount we owe Lamar."

"Three hundred dollars? How long will he give us to pay it back?"

"We ain't going to pay it back. Shoot. With all the dirt we got on his prissy black ass, he ain't fool enough to try and make us."

Yvonne's eyes lit up like fireflies. The next thing I knew, she hauled off and kissed me so hard, she almost bruised my lips. When she pulled back, she was grinning like a clown. "We don't have to pay him back? Milton, that's good news. Now we don't have to ask Aunt Mattie, Mr. Cunningham, and Dr. Patterson."

I done a double take. "Why not? We still need some money to make up for the time we was in jail and couldn't work at the grill or entertain no guests. And what about the 'extra' we talked about getting so we'd have money to have some fun? After I get the three hundred, I'll go back to Odell a few days later and ask for more. Fifty or sixty would do. We deserve it for all them times him and his Queen of Sheba made us feel lowly, with their hoity-toity behavior. Humph. I'm still pissed off about them serving us elderberry wine when we go over there, instead of that expensive whiskey they admitted they give only to their 'special friends.' We just as special as anybody else."

"Milton, you know I agree with you. But let's not get too far off the subject. Now, back to what we was talking about." Yvonne let out a loud sigh before she went on. "Keep in mind, that whatever we get from Aunt Mattie, Mr. Cunningham, and Dr. Patterson, we'd have to pay back. We'd be out of Lamar's debt, but we'd still be in a hole. If we don't have to pay Odell back, we'll have a little breathing room. I hope you will be able to get another fifty or sixty from him. Goodness gracious. I was only going to ask him for a few dollars today. You got him to agree to give us the whole three hundred."

"Yup." Despite what I'd just said about coming clean, there was no way I was going to tell Yvonne that I had demanded a extra hundred from Odell for myself. It made sense for me to get while the getting was good. "Shoot for at least twenty from him today," I suggested.

"Okay, sweetie. Mr. Cunningham's nephew brung his truck back a little while ago. I'll be taking off in a minute." Yvonne tucked some loose strands of her hair behind her ears. She looked at me like she was so proud, it made me almost bust open. It had been a long time since I seen so much love and admiration in her eyes. She looked downright dreamy. "But before I go, I want to tell you something else."

"What?" I gazed at her from the corner of my eye. That dreamy-eyed look was still on her face, so I knew that whatever she had to tell me wasn't going to be too bad.

"Milton, I knew the day I met you that we was going to do well, so long as we worked as a team. I ain't never met a man as focused as you."

I hoped she didn't praise me too much more. I didn't want to get giddy and say or do something that would embarrass me. It was a good thing I was cool and calm enough to stay cool and calm. Her compliment embarrassed me a little anyway. I wasn't nowhere near being shy, but I sounded like I was when I replied. "Thank you, baby. And you know how I feel about you. As a partner, you right up there with Willie Frank." There was something about being humble that made me feel good about myself.

"I can't get no higher than that," she squealed. Then she let out a little giggle and kissed me again before she whirled around and skittered out the door.

CHAPTER 7
YVONNE

During the ride to town, I started thinking about all the recent setbacks me and Milton had gone through. On top of our arrest, a few other things had caused us some grief. One was the beating on Halloween night last week that Milton had got from some unknown devils. A few days after that, as I was walking down the street on my way to pay Odell another visit, I'd had a hostile encounter with Lester Fullbright, my ex. I'd left him because I had caught him pleasuring a woman who had called herself my best friend at the time. The same day I moved out of his house and into Milton's, I'd also stole the money Lester had been saving for years. When he stormed Milton's house and attacked me, Milton helped me whup his ass. Because I'd stole Lester's money, he got evicted because he couldn't pay his rent. He had to move in with his mama, so he'd threatened me that day I seen him on the street.

Another thorn in my side was the fact that we still had to be concerned about rival bootleggers causing us harm because we'd stole so many of their customers. Me and Milton and Willie Frank assumed that my ex, or one of them bootleggers, had made the call to Sheriff Potts. We didn't have nothing to go on that would lead us to the right culprit. I was confident we'd soon find out who the back-stabbing bastard was. But right now, getting money was what I needed to concentrate on.

When I got to MacPherson's, I parked directly across the street. I sat still for a couple of minutes and scanned up and down the street to make sure none of my enemies was close by. I didn't want to get accosted by nobody who would slow me down and interfere with my plans. I didn't see nobody, so I piled out of the truck and rushed into the store. I whizzed by Buddy and Sadie so fast, they didn't have a chance to bother me with none of their silly gossip and nosy questions.

The door to Odell's office was closed, and I didn't bother to knock. I opened it and waltzed in like it was my office and wasn't surprised to see him reared back in his chair behind his desk, sleeping like a baby. I

73

coughed and cleared my throat to get his attention. He opened his eyes and sat straight up so fast, his chair almost tipped over. "Hello, Odell." I shut the door and strolled up to the front of his desk.

He didn't waste no time making me feel unwelcome. "Doggone it! I figured I'd be seeing you again soon!" he blasted.

"I figured the same thing," I said with a sniff.

"You want to sit down?" He waved me to the chair facing him.

"No thanks. I'm only staying a few minutes, so I ain't going to beat around the bush. I need money. Willie Frank's uncle Lamar paid Sheriff Potts to drop the charge and turn us loose. Now we need money to pay him back."

"So, I heard. Milton told me when he came by here a little while ago. Four hundred dollars is a heap of money."

Four hundred dollars? Milton had lied to me again. He was planning on getting a extra hundred for hisself. Well, two could play the same game. No matter how much I got from Odell today, the most I'd admit to Milton was twenty dollars. "I'm sure Milton told you we got until the end of the month to scrape up that money we owe Lamar. In the meantime, we need a few bucks to tide

74

us over. How much can you give me today?"

"I don't know. I been trying to hold on to my money. Me and Joyce got to buy a lot of Christmas gifts next month. Not to mention all my regular expenses," he grumbled.

"Regular expenses? You mean like Betty Jean and them kids?"

His face tightened. "That ain't none of your damn business, so don't you be bringing them up." He blew out a loud breath and glared at me like I was a roach. "The most I can give you today is twenty or thirty dollars."

"Is that all?"

He leaned forward and dipped his head, still glaring at me. "W-what did you have in mind?"

"At least a hundred."

Odell groaned and shook his head. "Look, woman. I ain't made out of money. I'm just a working soul, like you and Milton. I'm practically broke now until I get paid again."

"Puh-leeze." I rolled my neck and swirled my finger in the air. "Don't lie to me."

"What makes you think I'm lying?"

"Pffft. You can get money at all times from more than one source. On top of pilfering from them cash registers, you can borrow from Joyce and her mama and daddy."

Odell gasped. "Woman, you must be

crazy. Do you seriously expect me to steal or borrow money to give y'all?"

"Ha! If you can do it for Betty Jean, why not us?"

"I'm going to tell you the same thing I told that fool husband of yours: Y'all done pushed me close to the edge with all this blackmail mess." Odell was talking so fast he choked on some air. After he cleared his throat, he stood up and pulled out his wallet. "All I can spare today is fifty." He pulled out two twenties and a ten and handed them to me.

"When can I get the other fifty?" I stuffed the money down in my brassiere.

"What other fifty?" Odell's shoulders slumped and he gave me a stunned look. You would have thought that by now, he would be used to my behavior and demands. "I just told you all I could spare was fifty."

"And I just told you I wanted a hundred. So, when can I get the rest of it?" It was fairly cold outside. The wind was blowing so hard, the window behind Odell's desk was rattling. I was glad I had my winter coat on over my work smock. But even with the chill in the room, he was sweating bullets. "Odell, I wish you would stop fidgeting and sweating. You making me nervous."

"Yvonne, if I make you so nervous, why

do you keep coming here?"

I snickered. "To get money. Now, when can I get the rest of what you owe me? I was really counting on getting a hundred bucks today."

"I don't know. Milton wants the eight dollars I didn't give him this week, and his regular payment come next Wednesday. And if he expects me to come up with four hundred dollars by the end of this month, I'll have to pray for a miracle."

Four hundred dollars. I wanted to say, "Don't you mean three hundred dollars?" If that extra hundred bucks was important enough to Milton for him to lie to me about it, I'd let it go. He had so many other good qualities, me fretting over him being a liar was petty. "I'm going to pray that your miracle will include another fifty for me. But do you think you could give it to me sooner? I don't want to wait until the end of the month."

"I'll do what I can. Now is there anything else we need to talk about?"

"Just one more thing. We'd like to get back up on our feet as soon as possible. Them two days we spent in jail really put a damper on our bootlegging business. On top of that, some of our regulars might be skittish and not come back for a while, if they come back at all. If they hear you and Joyce is back in the mix, that'll ease their concerns."

"I'm sure Joyce will be glad to hear y'all got out of jail, and she'll want to come over. Maybe even this evening." His tone had got soft and he didn't look so mean now. "But, as you know, I'm usually away from home every week from Friday evening until Sunday . . ."

I chuckled. "Yeah, I know. Visiting your sick daddy," I said with a smirk.

"I'll make sure Joyce comes over tonight, though."

"That's nice. I can't wait to see her. Now you have a blessed weekend." I rushed back out the store faster than I had rushed in.

I had to get some gas before I got back on the road. Because I hadn't ate no lunch, I stopped at a chicken shack and got a sandwich and a root beer pop. While I sat in the cab of the truck and ate, I thought a lot about how well I had handled my latest meeting with Odell. I had no idea it would be so easy to collect fifty dollars from him today — especially the way Milton had been putting the bite on him since July. I decided to wait until next month to ask him for the other fifty I couldn't get today. I'd use it to buy some Christmas gifts, including something for Joyce and Odell. As much as we'd come to depend on the money we got from Odell, it was the least we could do.

When I got back to the grill, Milton immediately motioned for me to join him in the kitchen. We went to a corner in the back of the room. "Did Odell give you them twenty dollars I told you to ask for?"

"I got thirty." I pulled out one of the twenties and the ten and waved them in his face. "And he didn't even fuss at me too much."

Milton gazed at the money like it was something good to eat. "Holy moly. Now I wish I had told you to ask for fifty. Well . . . what else did y'all discuss? I guess he told you I paid him a visit today, too, huh?"

"He told me. But he was so anxious to get me out of his hair, he didn't want to talk about nothing else." I noticed how nervous Milton was acting and I knew why. He was wondering if Odell had told me the exact amount he'd asked for. "He told me he agreed to give you a big payout by the end of this month. He didn't tell me how much, though. I guess he didn't want to tell me that because he might have thought I'd ask for more."

"Um . . . just three hundred like I asked him for."

"That's perfect." I handed Milton the twenty-dollar bill. "You take this and go pay our light and water bill tomorrow."

He snatched it so fast, I was surprised it didn't tear in half. "We don't owe this much, and since I didn't get no money from Odell today, I'll keep the change."

"That's fine. I'll keep the other ten for myself."

CHAPTER 8
ODELL

My day had started out so good. I had got up and put on one of my favorite suits, rubbed some pomade on my hair, and splashed some aftershave on my neck. Joyce had cooked a scrumptious breakfast and I'd ate like a hog at a trough. Just recalling it made me feel a little bit better.

Now here I was a few hours later, beside myself with anger. I called Joyce at work to let her know that them two lowlifes was out of jail because that rape charge couldn't be proved. "Praise the Lord!" she boomed. Her voice was so loud it irritated my ear. "Who told you they got released?"

"They came to the store this afternoon to let me know." Just saying them words made my stomach turn.

"Hmmm. I wonder why they didn't wait to come to the house this evening? That way they could have told us at the same time."

"Uh, baby, today is Friday. They know I

always have other commitments right after work and won't be at the house," I reminded. "I'm sure they'll come see you as soon as they can."

"I hope so. If they don't come over this evening, I'll go over there. I won't stay long because they're probably still trying to get their bearings back." Joyce paused and let out a loud breath. "I just wish you could be with me. Can't you visit your daddy later tonight, or tomorrow morning? We could at least spend an hour or so with Yvonne and Milton first. Afterwards, I'll even go to your daddy's house with you. It's been a while since I was out there and I'm over how nasty your stepmother was to me that day."

"That sounds nice, sugar. But when I was out there last weekend, I told Daddy I'd get there today in time for us to go fishing for a couple of hours while it's still daylight. You know how him and Ellamae go to bed as soon as it gets dark."

"I haven't gone fishing with you in a while. I don't mind doing that, either."

"Joyce, I appreciate you offering to go with me. But Ellamae likes to know in advance when she needs to cook extra food. The last time I showed up with you, she wasn't too happy about me bringing a guest without letting her know in advance."

"Guest? Odell, I'm your wife!"

"I know, sugar. But you know how set in her ways she is. Daddy, too. And to be honest with you, I'm not in the mood for a lot of fussing. With all that's happening with Yvonne and Milton, it's been a real stressful week. Besides that, my canned goods vendor is going to be late with our order, and I had to lock horns with a few more shoplifters, twice this week," I griped. "If I go next door this evening, I wouldn't be good company. The last thing Yvonne and Milton need to deal with today is my long face and dreary attitude. We'll spend time with them on Sunday when I get home from Daddy's house."

"Okay, baby. Anyway, I'll go over there by myself tonight. I'm sure they'll understand why you couldn't come."

"Good. Now let me get off this phone and get back to work. I'd like to get up out of here on time."

"I got one more thing before you hang up."

I moaned under my breath and rolled my eyes. "What else?"

"I know tornado season is over, but I heard some thunder a little while ago. Judging from those dark clouds, it'll probably rain this evening and all the roads will be slippery with mud puddles all over the place. You be careful driving on that windy dirt road to your daddy's house."

"Joyce, I been driving on bad roads in the rain for years and I ain't never had no accident. You worry way too much about me and you need to stop that," I scolded. "Now you have a blessed evening."

After I hung up, my head started aching and my chest was so tight it felt like I had on a corset. Getting visited by Yvonne and Milton in the same day had me so rattled, I had a hard time concentrating on anything else. When my egg and milk vendor came around three p.m., I didn't even check to make sure he'd brung everything I'd ordered. I signed the invoice and shooed him out the door so fast, he looked at me like I was crazy. Maybe I was and just didn't know it. Right after he left, I got a call from one of my meat suppliers. When he told me he would be three days late delivering next week's orders because of a clerical mix-up, I didn't even fret. I knew I'd catch the heat from some of my regular customers who always expected to get everything they'd ordered on time. But I didn't care. I was facing a much bigger dilemma with Yvonne and Milton.

The rest of the afternoon, I only left my

office to duck out the back door to get some fresh air and use the toilet. I didn't go back out on the main floor until a few minutes before closing time. Sadie had already put on her coat, collected her purse from under her counter, and was about to walk out the door. "Odell, you all right?" she wanted to know. "We ain't seen you since Yvonne left, and now you look upset."

"I guess you still feeling emotional about them getting arrested, huh?" Buddy asked as he pulled a black-and-red knitted cap over his head.

"Yeah, th-that's it," I blubbered. "I got so shook up when they got arrested, I didn't know what to do. Now that they out of jail, seeing them threw my emotions off-kilter."

Sadie started to back up with a woeful look on her face. "Poor Yvonne and Milton. It's a good thing they wasn't locked up but a couple of days. Just think how much more upset y'all would be if they'd been sent to the county jail, or worse. They still fairly young and strong. But as serious as the mess they went through, it might take a while for them to bounce back to normal. You and Joyce being their close friends and next-door neighbors, I know y'all will give them a heap of support."

Support? That was a joke. If Sadie and

Buddy hadn't left when they did a minute later and continued to go on and on about "poor Yvonne and Milton," I probably would have snapped. Them two mangy, hustling dogs might finish ruining my life after all. I went back to my office and sat for a few more minutes, stewing like a pot roast. All kinds of ominous thoughts and ideas was swirling around in my head. The main one was, I had to get Yvonne and Milton off my back *permanently*. And the only way I could do that was to kill them.

Each day after I closed up, I pulled every single bill out of the cash registers and put it in a box that I kept in my office. Then I set the box on the floor in a corner next to a mountain of old magazines, discarded merchandise, and other odds and ends. I piled two or three other boxes on top of it. There was so many other items on the floor, my desk, and everywhere else in the room, if a thief broke in, he'd never find the money. Getting burglarized was the least of my worries. Except for the usual shoplifters — and me — MacPherson's had never been looted. The next morning I'd take out enough cash for us to make change for the day. Each Friday I collected the bulk of our profits and put it all in a brown paper bag. I delivered it to Mac and Millie before I went to go visit Betty Jean. They trusted me so much, they never counted the money before I left.

My in-laws wasn't home when I got there around five thirty this evening. I let myself in and went directly to the pantry. The bag I brung today was almost twice as heavy as the one I'd delivered last Friday, thanks to all the holiday sales this week. I was slap-happy about that. Because of Yvonne and Milton's new demands, I had to keep a heftier wad than usual.

I didn't waste no time getting back into my car and on the road to Hartville. For one thing, I didn't want to run into Mac and Millie. They was old, but they was good at recognizing when somebody was in distress. And I was as distressed as I could be.

When I got to Betty Jean's street, she and the boys was waiting for me on her front porch. Just seeing them lifted my spirits. When I got close enough, they all started hugging and kissing on me. "Daddy, what you bring us?" Daniel asked, pulling on my arm. He was four and a half now, and the only one who looked like me. Jesse was almost two and a half, and Leon had turned a year old back in September. They both

87

had Betty Jean's light skin and keen features.

"I got a load of stuff in the car. I'll bring it all in after I rest up and eat some supper," I said.

"Baby, come on in. I already got a tub of warm soapy water ready for you to soak your feet," Betty Jean told me.

"Did you bring us some money?" Jesse asked as he patted my pocket. I doled out money every time I visited. But one of the kids, or Betty Jean, asked me the same question every time I came.

"Yeah, I brung money." My voice sounded so tired, and I was, physically and mentally. I gently pushed my sons to the side and dropped down on the couch like a sack of potatoes. I looked around the neat, clean-smelling living room. Betty Jean had very good taste, so the furniture was even nicer than what me and Joyce had.

The boys piled up on the couch beside me, punching and pinching each other to see who'd sit the closest to me. As usual, being the baby, Leon started bawling. The older two backed off and let him flop down in my lap. Daniel and Jesse scooted as close as they could on each of my sides. We gave our sons equal amounts of discipline, guidance, and love because we wanted them to grow up and be responsible adults. The only thing I hoped was that they wouldn't be too much like me. I prayed that they'd marry women who'd be enough for them. Then they wouldn't have to do what I was doing. Keeping up with two lives was so stressful, some days I didn't know if I was coming or going.

Betty Jean squatted down, rolled up the legs of my pants and pulled off my shoes. She massaged my feet before I plunged them into the warm soapy water in the foot tub she had set on the floor in front of me. It didn't take long for me to relax. I was glad the boys had settled down. Now me and their mama could conversate without them interrupting us. "Odell, how was your day, sugar pie?" she asked, scrubbing dead skin off the sides and bottom of my feet with a butter knife.

"Oh, it was the same as usual," I replied. I closed my eyes and leaned my head back. I was enjoying all the attention and pampering. It was moments like these that made me feel so good. There was nothing better than spending quality time with my other woman and our children.

"Did you have any problems with the shoplifters this week? This is the time of year when they really get busy."

"Tell me about it. A couple of them crooks

tried to swipe a few things yesterday and today. But my cashiers caught them in time."

"That's good. You done worked too hard to make MacPherson's the success it is. And with you being such a generous soul, I'm surprised some of your customers don't try to take advantage of you by asking for credit and handouts. I'd hate to see them mess up things for you so bad that your in-laws put you back to stocking shelves like they had you doing before you married Joyce."

"Baby, that ain't never going to happen. I got my in-laws in the bottom of my hip pocket."

CHAPTER 9
JOYCE

When Odell called me up at work this afternoon to tell me that Yvonne and Milton had been let out of jail, I was surprised and relieved. I shared the news with my coworkers, and they felt the same way. Some of them had never visited a bootlegger's house and wasn't too thrilled to know that there were colored folks brazen enough to do something so illegal. But colored people in the Deep South had so much going against them, we had to support one another no matter what crime they'd committed — unless it was something serious like murder. I would never support a person if they killed somebody.

We dismissed the students at three thirty p.m. each day. I rarely left before five, though. I enjoyed hanging around to help tidy up the classrooms, plan the activities for the next day, and sometimes just to chitchat with my coworkers. Today I was anxious to get home so I could visit Yvonne and Milton. They were nothing like Odell and me, but they were fun and entertaining. Like some of the offbeat characters in the novels I read, I had grown attached to them. Besides that, they were so woefully ignorant, they made me feel smarter. The thing I didn't like was that every time I talked down to Yvonne, she responded by saying something that made me feel bad. I didn't let that bother me because Odell and I were way above them in so many ways.

As I was about to gather my things and leave, our principal wanted to have a short meeting to discuss our upcoming Thanksgiving program. Patsy Boykin, one of the other teacher's aides, couldn't stay because one of her kids was sick. Whenever she couldn't give me a ride to and from work, I either walked or took the bus. I didn't feel like walking today. And knowing how much Odell had on his plate, I didn't want to call him back and ask him to give me a ride home before he went to visit his daddy.

Immediately after the meeting ended at four fifteen, I collected my purse and coat from the cloakroom and left the building running. Since I am six feet tall, my legs are so long it didn't take but a couple of minutes to get to the bus stop four blocks away. Now all I had to worry about was walking past my parents' house to get to mine on the same street a few blocks away without them seeing me. I didn't want them to slow me down. Mama and Daddy spent so much time gazing out their living-room window, one of them would see me for sure. That was the reason I took the back way to get home after I got off the bus. I rushed down the alley behind the houses on our block, proud of myself for outsmarting my nosy parents. The moment I reached their house, Mama pranced out onto her back porch.

"Joyce, why you walking so fast and coming in through the back way? You know about all them lizards and weevils hiding in them tall bushes along the way this time of year," she yelled, shading her eyes and looking at me like I was crazy.

I stopped and started shifting my weight from one foot to the other. "Um, taking this way gets me home a few minutes earlier," I explained.

"Why you in such a hurry to get home on a Friday when you know Odell ain't there?"

"I know. He called me at work and told me that Yvonne and Milton had been let out of jail. I wanted to go see them right away and let them know how concerned we were about them," I panted.

"So I heard. Sadie called here a little while ago and told me that they'd come to see Odell this afternoon. I wonder why they was in such a rush to see him?" I didn't like the way Mama screwed up her face every time Yvonne's and Milton's names came up.

"I don't know, Mama."

"And they didn't show up together."

"They didn't?" I wondered why Odell hadn't mentioned that detail.

"He visited Odell around noon, she came later. And the whole time they was with him in his office, the door was closed . . ."

I wondered why Odell hadn't mentioned *that* detail, either. "Well, they probably came separately because they couldn't get away from the grill at the same time. And maybe they wanted to talk to him about something personal, so they closed the door. I'm not even going to ask Odell about something that petty."

"Whatever. I just hope and pray you and Odell don't get no closer to them than y'all already are. Oh well." Mama shrugged. "Life goes on, I guess. Oh, by the way, Odell left that pretty red-and-green muffler here that you knitted for him last Christmas when he dropped off the money bag a little while ago. It must have slid off his neck before he left. He loves that thing, so he'll probably come back to pick it up before he go to his daddy's place. It's real windy and chilly out there. Me and Mac is fixing to leave directly to go have supper with some folks from church. We might not be home if he was to come back to get it. Why don't you come in and wait for him, in case he do? That way you and him can go visit them bootleggers together. It ain't fitting for a woman to be over there on her own." I almost laughed when I thought of what Mama would say if she knew how often I visited "them bootleggers" on my own.

"That's all right, Mama. Odell and I had a long conversation when he called me today. I even asked him if he wanted to go with me to see them before he went to see his daddy. He said something about them going fishing before it gets too dark, so that's why he headed out there right after he dropped off this week's profits. If he comes back to get his muffler before y'all leave, make sure he wraps it around his neck real good so it won't fall off again. You know how he always catches colds quicker than anybody else. And he's been feeling under the weather enough lately."

"I will. Well, you just be careful over at that place. Me and your daddy sure would hate to read about you in the newspaper.

Before we come home after supper, we'll swing by your house to make sure you made it home in one piece."

"Mama, stop worrying about me. Y'all don't have to come check on me tonight. I'll be just fine."

"Joyce, you spend so much time by yourself, how can we not worry about you? If only you had some kids to keep you company . . ."

I rolled my eyes and sucked in a deep breath. I knew where this conversation was going. My head started throbbing as soon as Mama started talking again.

"Joyce, your marriage won't be complete until you give Odell a child."

"I know, Mama," I muttered with a heavy sigh. I wanted to get off this subject as fast as I could, so I blurted out, "Some of us just need more time. You were in your late forties before you got pregnant with me — after trying for *decades*." That shut her up for the time being. But I knew the subject would come up again real soon. Her words were still ringing in my ears as I started walking faster toward my house.

I was concerned about the toll being fatherless was having on Odell. My poor sweetie never complained about it, but I knew he was disappointed in me. Whenever he was around other folks' kids, he got downright giddy. Children loved visiting the store because they knew he'd give them free play-pretties, candy, and anything else they wanted. But Odell was more patient than my parents. I was confident he would give me a little more time to fulfill his biggest dream.

Everybody knew how badly I wanted to have a child. Especially Yvonne. Her three young children by three different men lived with her overly religious aunt and uncle in Mobile. They didn't like Yvonne's lifestyle, and weren't going to let the children know she was their real mother until they reached adulthood. Yvonne didn't like that arrangement, but she'd gone along with it. She owed the aunt and uncle a lot because they had raised her when her parents lost their lives in a tractor accident when she was a little girl. She loved her kids and knew what a blessing it was to be a mother, so she was sympathetic to my situation.

Back in August, my period hadn't come the week it was due, and I'd gotten real hopeful. When it came the following week, Yvonne was just as disappointed as I was that I was not pregnant. I cringed every time I recalled the conversation we'd had that afternoon on my back porch. I had been cleaning chitlins when she showed up and plopped down on the bannister. "If you really want to get pregnant, try standing on your head for ten minutes after you and Odell make love."

"I've never heard anything so ridiculous in my life." I'd laughed. "How could standing on my head help me become pregnant?"

"With you having such a long body, by the time Odell's jism reaches your baby-making equipment, it's too weak to do the job. Standing upside down right after y'all finish making love — not five or ten minutes later — would send it in the right direction while it's still fresh and potent."

"Pffft. If it was that easy to become pregnant, there wouldn't be a childless woman in this state. Who told you that? And how come you're just now telling me?"

"I just heard it myself last week from June Ann Lawson, a lady from my old neighborhood. She and her husband came to the house to celebrate her first pregnancy. She is six months along and they been celebrating ever since they found out. They finally got around to visiting me and Milton to let us know. They been married longer than you and Odell and been trying the whole time. She didn't tell me who, but somebody told her standing on her head would help her get pregnant. So, I'm telling you. She only had to do it six or seven times."

"And you believed her?"

Yvonne hunched her shoulders. "Why wouldn't I? June Ann is definitely pregnant and proved it to me by letting me feel her baby kicking around in her belly."

I stared at Yvonne. I wanted to laugh again, but she looked so serious, I didn't. "Well, I'm happy for June Ann," I said with a sniff. "But she shouldn't be drinking if she wants to have a healthy baby."

"June Ann ain't crazy enough to jeopardize her baby's health after it took her so long to make one. Her husband drunk up a storm, but all she had was three root beers."

I gave Yvonne a thoughtful look. "Thanks for sharing that with me, but I don't think head-standing is something I'll be trying."

"Suit yourself." She shrugged and started walking off the porch. "I'm just trying to help fix your problem. Call me when them chitlins get done so I can come back and get me and Milton a plate."

CHAPTER 10
JOYCE

It was hard for me not to think about having a child of my own because in addition to Yvonne and Mama, other people brought up the subject. Like Yvonne, one even tried to help me "fix" my problem.

A week after I'd had that conversation with Yvonne on my porch, I ran into Clarabelle Tucker on the bus. We'd attended the same teacher's aide training program together and had once been very close. She lived on a farm on the outskirts of town now, so I only saw her a few times a year, if at all. And every time we bumped into each other, she was pregnant with a new baby. This particular day, after she'd bragged for a few minutes about how well things were going for her, she started up on me. "I hear you and Odell still trying to have a baby," she'd said with a pitiful look on her moon face.

"That's true," I'd muttered as I'd fidgeted

in my seat. Despite the fact that this subject made me uncomfortable, I was still willing to discuss it. "I guess it wasn't meant to be. I would have made such a good mother."

"You poor thing you." Clarabelle gave me an impatient look this time as she waved her hand. "Girl, you need to stop whining and do something about it."

"What do you think I've been doing since I had that miscarriage? Odell and I make love several times a week — and have been doing so ever since we got married."

Clarabelle looked around before she continued in a lower tone. "I'm talking about something more serious than just doing the nasty."

"What are you talking about? The last time I checked, making love with a man was how a woman became pregnant."

"That's still true, but it's not the *only* way."

I stared into Clarabelle's eyes a long time before I replied. "If you know something, tell me now. My stop is coming up in a few minutes and I don't know when I'll see you again."

Clarabelle looked around some more and leaned closer to me. "Aunt Mattie gave me some stuff called *neipee*. It worked."

"Neipee? What is it?"

"It's a white powder to mix half a teaspoon in a glass of milk and drink once a night when you want a baby. I started using it right after my husband threatened to leave me if I didn't give him a child. The doctor had told me there was no reason why I couldn't conceive, but he'd been telling me that for *eight* years. A woman from my church finally told me to get some help from Aunt Mattie, so I did. Six weeks after I started drinking that potion, I found out I was pregnant. I had my first son the following year." Clarabelle paused, rubbed her belly, and continued with a wall-to-wall smile on her face. "The one I'm carrying now is number five and I hope it's a girl. Four boys is enough for one family. I declare, that neipee is some powerful baby-making batter. I turned two of my cousins on to it and they got pregnant right away too."

I wanted to laugh, but I knew better. Whether I believed in hoodoo or not — and I wasn't sure if I did or didn't — I knew that it was not something to make fun of. I'd heard too many stories about folks who had done that and suddenly developed mysterious ailments. And I couldn't ignore the fact that one of the teachers I worked with told me she had visited a hoodoo man in Lexington last year when nothing she got from her doctor helped get rid of headaches she'd been having off and on for several weeks. After two visits, her headaches stopped and never returned. Clarabelle's claim had really piqued my interest. "What does that powder taste like?"

"It's just a little bitter, and you can't even smell it."

"Hmmm. Did you ask Aunt Mattie what was in it?"

"Pffft. What's wrong with you, Joyce? You and I are the same age, so we've been around long enough to know that you don't ask hoodoo folks their business. It might upset them. If you make one mad enough, they are liable to put something on you a doctor can't take off."

"Yeah, I know. But what you just told me sounds so farfetched. How do you know that getting pregnant wasn't God blessing you?"

"Oh, He had a hand in it. Before my first pregnancy, I'd prayed and flat out challenged God to help me. When I got up the next morning, something told me to go see Aunt Mattie. So, God led me to her."

"Pffft. I believe in prayer, but I don't know about Aunt Mattie's mumbo jumbo," I'd protested, dismissing Clarabelle's testimony with a wave of my hand.

"You can keep praying all you want. But you need to open your eyes and mind and realize when you getting a response to a prayer. There is a reason I ran into you today and this subject came up right off the bat. God's trying to tell you something through me."

"Well, I'll keep praying because I do believe God answers all prayers. But . . . um . . . maybe I'll try that white powder someday anyway."

Someday came sooner than I expected, about a month after my conversation with Clarabelle. I was too skittish to approach Aunt Mattie or any of the other hoodoo folks in the area. I went out to Clarabelle's house and gave her the fifty dollars required to get me a generous supply of that powder from Aunt Mattie. I'd made Clarabelle promise not to tell Aunt Mattie it was for me, and not to blab to anybody else.

When I got home, I put the neipee in a jar and set it on a shelf in the pantry. It looked so much like flour and baking powder, it blended right in with the rest of my condiments. That same night, I drank the first glass. I did that for the next five days and all I got was the runs. I tried it for six weeks and didn't get any results, so I put it on hold. In October, I tried Yvonne's suggestion. Immediately after Odell and I had finished making love one Sunday night after he'd come from visiting his daddy, I ducked into the bathroom, closed the door, and stood on my head. I had nothing to lose, and everything to gain — if it worked. But I felt like a fool propped upside down against the wall. In less than a minute, there was a crook in my neck, a charley horse in my leg, my back almost went out, and Odell walked in.

He gasped and rushed toward me. "Joyce, what in the world do you call yourself doing? Have you lost your mind?" Then he laughed. If he hadn't done that, I would have told him the truth.

"Huh? Oh! Yvonne told me that standing on my head was a good way to get rid of a headache," I said as I somersaulted myself into an upright position. I had never felt so nutty and embarrassed in my life.

Odell stopped laughing and grabbed my arms. He held me in place until I was able to stand up straight on my own. "You got a headache? Baby, if you had told me you wasn't feeling good, I wouldn't have pestered you tonight." He embraced me and started stroking my back.

"I was fine then. It started all of a sudden

105

after we finished." I sniffed and rubbed the side of my head.

"What about them pain pills you been taking all these years?"

"I ran out," I lied.

"Well, I'm going to bring home a big supply from the store tomorrow." He released me, put his hands on his hips, and shook his head. "I can't believe the most educated colored woman I know would stand on her head to get rid of a headache. How could you believe such a cockamamie thing — especially coming from a dimwit like Yvonne? In the first place, a woman your size, standing on her head could lose her balance and hurt herself and have to go to the hospital. Lord! If I hadn't walked in here when I did, your name might have ended up in the newspaper. Can you imagine what folks would say if they found out you'd done something so stupid and had a freak accident? Especially them folks you work with at the school and them students' mamas and daddies. Not to mention how it would make *me* look."

"I know and I'll never do it again."

That was three weeks ago. Since I hadn't used up all of that neipee powder Clarabelle had given me, last night I decided to start drinking it again. While Odell was taking a bath, I mixed enough for two glasses. When I went to sleep, I dreamed I had given birth to a child that had the same sparkling black eyes, high cheekbones, and thick curly hair as Odell.

The concoction hadn't given me the runs this time, so I decided to use it until I ran out. But I would never attempt to stand on my head for ten minutes again. If God hadn't blessed me with a baby by the time I ran out of that neipee, I'd give up.

I sighed and shook those thoughts out of my head.

Twenty minutes after I got inside my house, I happened to look out the front window and saw Yvonne and Milton walking by. I didn't waste any time running out to my front porch to greet them. "Hellooooo. I heard Sheriff Potts released y'all. Praise the Lord." They stopped and stared at me with blank expressions on their faces. After what they'd been through, I was surprised they didn't look more cheerful now that they were free. "It's wonderful."

"No, it's Jesus. Without Him, we might never have seen the light of day again," Milton said in a serious tone. He finally smiled and a split second later so did Yvonne. "We got out yesterday afternoon but was too tired to come over last night to let y'all know. Besides that, we got a few scrapes, knots, and bruises during the process."

"They beat y'all, too?"

"Yup. But not as bad as they could have," Milton added, sighing with relief.

I shuddered. "My Lord. I can't imagine what being in jail is like. But since y'all spent time locked up before, I guess y'all knew what to expect." They stopped smiling as I went on. "I hope y'all learned your lesson and will be more careful about who you let come to your house. Jesus might not come through the next time. I'm glad those roughneck deputies didn't break any arms and legs." I was talking so fast, I had to pause and catch my breath. "We don't carry anything in the store to treat injuries that serious. But I'll have Odell bring y'all some salve that'll help heal those other injuries. He told me Sheriff Potts didn't have enough evidence to keep y'all."

"That scoundrel didn't have no evidence at all!" Yvonne blasted. Now they looked upset and hostile enough to cuss out the world.

"I declare, y'all look so worn out. Go home and rest. I'll come over in a little while. It'll be nice to be around folks and have a few drinks again," I gushed. I thought it would help if I kept up a cheerful attitude, but they still looked upset and hostile.

"We'll be glad to have you, Joyce," Milton muttered, glancing toward the street and then at my front door. "I hope Odell will come over when he gets back from his daddy's house Sunday night . . ."

"He will. But I'm sure he'll be thinking about y'all the whole weekend. He's probably on his way to his daddy's house as we speak." I looked over their drab gray work smocks. "I'm glad to see that y'all went back to work at the grill already."

"We couldn't afford not to," Yvonne said in a bone-weary tone.

"It's a shame y'all couldn't take off today just to rest and heal. But I understand about the money situation. I'll talk to Odell and see if we can give y'all a hundred dollars. And it'll be a gift, not a loan."

I couldn't believe how quick their demeanor changed. Now they had wall-to-wall grins on their faces. I was surprised they didn't do cartwheels. Especially Milton. He actually danced a five-second jig. "A hundred bucks would make us right happy." He turned sharply to look at Yvonne. "Ain't that right, sugar?"

She was grinning so hard now, I was

surprised her jaws didn't lock. "Sure enough. I'm so happy I could wrap it in eggshells," she squealed, bobbing her head up and down like a woodpecker. "Joyce, we'd be lost without you and Odell."

"I know," I agreed.

CHAPTER 11
MILTON

Dr. Wilbur Patterson, the sharp-featured general practitioner from down the street, and his plain, pigeon-toed wife, Eloise, moseyed in our front door ten minutes after me and Yvonne got home. They was the first guests to show up Friday evening. "Milton, I hope we aren't too early," Mrs. Patterson said, with a apologetic look on her face. "I tried to get this man to wait an hour or so to give y'all time to get settled. But he was champing at the bit and couldn't wait any longer. So, here we are."

"Y'all right on time. We been itching to get back into the swing of things," I assured her.

"That's what I wanted to hear! I was so happy when I saw y'all walking up the street. I'm glad everything is okay, because I'm itching to do some socializing," Dr. Patterson tossed in.

The four of us laughed and group hugged.

"Wilbur and I didn't think Potts could make a case," Eloise said in her high-pitched voice. "We were here Tuesday night and we sure didn't see any teenage white girl on the premises. I hope y'all can still join us for Thanksgiving."

"We'll be there with bells on," Yvonne replied with a firm nod. "We got much more to be thankful for now."

"Y'all find a seat and I'll get some drinks," I piped in. "I'll talk to y'all some more directly."

The Pattersons plopped down in chairs facing the couch and I brung them large jars of white lightning right away. "If we hadn't missed work this week, I'd let y'all have these drinks on the house. But . . ."

Dr. Patterson held up his knotty hand. "We don't want to make matters any worse for y'all. We know how tight money is going to be for a while," he said. I grinned, but I didn't comment. Now that I knew how sympathetic he was, I had a feeling he'd give us a loan if we had to ask.

Within a hour, half a dozen more guests had came. We usually had twice as many folks on Friday night, but we was making good money anyway. Aunt Mattie waltzed through the door wearing some of her best jewelry. Her gray hair was covered up under a thick black hairnet, and she had on enough nut-brown face powder and blood-red rouge to paint the side of a barn. But I could still see the wrinkles and liver spots on her used-to-be-pretty face. The ankle-length, buttoned-up navy-blue coat she had on looked more like a choir robe. Under the coat was a low-cut blue dress that a woman her age didn't have no business wearing.

All five of the women who prostituted for Aunt Mattie trailed behind her. Tiny, one of my regular pieces of tail, gave me a wink and made a slurping noise with her mouth. But the other four didn't do nothing to acknowledge my romps with them, which was the way it was supposed to be. I was a very happy married man and I wanted to stay that way.

Aunt Mattie was pleased to be back in the mix. She couldn't stop grinning and flutter-ing about like a butterfly. Four of her regular customers was in the house. Each one was grumbling and giving her mean looks. I as-sumed they was disgruntled about having to delay whatever romps they had previously scheduled for tonight. I knew that when Aunt Mattie and her girls left, them horny devils would follow them back to the whore-house. I had a itching to drop in myself in the next day or so.

I gave Aunt Mattie a one-armed hug. Then I took her by the hand and led her to the couch. We dropped down at the same time. "I know this arrest thing done cost us a few customers, but I am so glad it didn't scare you off," I told her in my sweetest tone.

"This time. I don't know about the next time, though." She chuckled, but I knew she was serious. Her top moneymaker was a short-haired beanpole with a baby face named Wanda Sue Boggs. Everybody called her Sweet Sue. She had already hemmed Willie Frank up in a corner and was whispering in his ear. He was glassy-eyed and lapping up her words like the juice on a hambone. "Just look at that." Aunt Mattie chuckled again. "I ain't never seen a white man so fixated on a colored woman as Willie Frank is with that bald-headed hussy."

"Me neither," I agreed. He had raved so much about Sweet Sue's bedroom talents, I recently had to check her out myself. He was right. But, to me, that still didn't seem like enough to have a man like Willie Frank acting like a fool over her. Aunt Mattie blinked as I went on. "I appreciate you shutting down business tonight so you and all the girls could be here to help celebrate me

114

and Yvonne's release. I hope you have such a good time, you won't mind missing out on all the good money y'all won't make tonight."

"Look-a-here, young man. Me being born a slave was bad. I still have nightmares about what I went through before Abe Lincoln set us free. But the slavery experience taught me some valuable life lessons. One is that good friends is way more important than 'good' money," she said in the gentlest tone I'd ever heard her use. "I remember when you was a little bitty boy how often I had to chase you and your scalawag play-mates out of my yard with a switch when y'all stole pecans off my trees and deviled my hound dogs. You turned your life around when you found Jesus while you was in prison. You must be one of the most righteous colored men I know. I'm pleased to call you and Yvonne my friends. There ain't no other place I'd rather be tonight."

My poontang tab with her was late again. If she said anything about it, I would remind her of what she just said. "I declare, you treat me more like a grandson than both my grandmamas done," I said with my voice cracking. "Knowing you is a double blessing."

Despite what I'd just said, I cringed when

Aunt Mattie's gnarled hand cupped mine and squeezed it. I cringed even more when I seen a big wart on her thumb. My mama had raised me to believe that warts was contagious. But I was more concerned about all the stories I'd heard about her using hoodoo hexes to get back at people when they offended her. She also claimed to have psychic powers and could see into the future. All that was far-fetched, but I wasn't stupid enough to do or say nothing to find out firsthand if any of it was true. There was enough normal enemies causing us stress. We didn't need to add no witch doctor. With that in mind, we bent over backwards to stay on her good side.

I was anxious to get up and mingle, but I sat as stiff as a tree limb while Aunt Mattie continued. "I can't tell you how scared I was for you and Yvonne, not to mention myself. When them laws busted in here Tuesday night, they shook me up so bad I thought I was having a heart attack." Aunt Mattie shuddered. "That's why I couldn't make it to the back door like everybody else. Hiding in your broom closet until things died down wasn't no picnic," she said with a groan. She leaned closer and whispered in my ear, "By the way, with all that's done happened, I'll let you slide on your tab. You

116

can catch it up when you get back on your feet."

I whispered back, "Thank you. I hope you don't get mad, because it might be a while before I can get caught up. Money don't grow on trees. In the meantime, can I still visit your girls? Until I get my bearings back, I'll need a little something extra to take the edge off me . . ."

Aunt Mattie gave me a exasperated look and a neck roll. But she still told me what I wanted to hear. "I guess you can. Only once or twice a week until you get caught up on your tab. Poontang don't grow on trees neither. Do you hear me, young man?"

"Yes, ma'am," I muttered, with my head bowed like a contrite puppy.

Yvonne was entertaining a bunch of guests on the other side of the room. Joyce occupied the spot on my other side. She was busy chatting with one of the men who worked for the railroad. When he walked away, Aunt Mattie reached across my lap and tapped her arm. "Joyce, where is Odell at tonight?" she asked, blinking her beady black eyes. "Is he out in the boondocks taking care of his sick daddy tonight?" There was a suspicious look on her face. I didn't think she knew Prince Charming was spending his weekends with another woman. But

I had a feeling she suspected he was doing something other than taking care of his sick daddy.

"Yes, ma'am. That's where he's at." Joyce rattled off the words in such a dry, low tone, I could barely hear her. She hadn't said too much since she walked in the door half a hour ago. "He said we'd come back over here when he gets home Sunday night."

"Uh-huh." Aunt Mattie jabbed my side with her bony elbow, and added with a sneer, "With Odell living just one house over and being such a close friend, I'm surprised he didn't come to welcome Milton and Yvonne home as fast as he could, like the rest of us. His daddy can't be *that* sick . . ."

Joyce was sitting so close to me, I felt her body stiffen. At the same time, a mild gasp slipped out of her mouth. "Yvonne and Milton went by the store today. He's already welcomed them home," she said, looking at me. "Milton, I'm glad you and Yvonne were thoughtful enough to do that. Otherwise, we wouldn't have known y'all was out until I got home. And I wouldn't have been able to share the news with Odell until he got back home Sunday."

"Well, everything is hunky-dory now. Joyce, is your drink strong enough?" I asked, eyeing her half-empty jar.

"Yeah, it's fine." She gave me a tight smile before she went on. "So, do you and Yvonne have any idea who made that telephone call to Sheriff Potts?"

"Not yet," I replied with my teeth clenched. It was a struggle to keep my anger under control. "I'm sure we'll find out real soon."

"I sure hope so!" Joyce's tone was so loud people on the other side of the room looked at her. She gave me a apologetic look, and lowered her tone. "I can't tell you how surprised I was when I heard that somebody had called Sheriff Potts at home and told him such a barefaced lie."

"Surprised ain't even close to what I was when I heard the news. I was downright mortified," Aunt Mattie snarled. "If I ever find out it was one of the men that come to my house to do business with my girls, I'm going to put a spell on him a magician can't take off."

I looked from Aunt Mattie to Joyce with a question shooting through my head like a bullet. *How did Joyce know Sheriff Potts had been called at home?* "Joyce, who told you that? I thought he'd received the call at the jailhouse." I held my breath waiting for her to respond.

119

A smug look crossed her face. She puffed out her chest with so much pride you would have thought she really was Queen of Sheba. "Maybe the person couldn't reach him at the jailhouse, and that's why they called him at home." She took a big gulp from the jar in her hand. She was on her second large drink, so she was more than a little drunk. That was the only reason I gave her the benefit of the doubt. She could have been talking off the top of her head and didn't know what she was saying.

There was only one way to find out. I took a deep breath before I asked. "But how did *you* know the call was made to Sheriff Potts at his house?"

"Odell told me," she answered.

CHAPTER 12
JOYCE

About forty-five minutes after I'd arrived next door, Yvonne motioned for me to follow her into the kitchen to get more snacks. I sliced pieces off a large chunk of hog-head cheese and put them on a tray. She loaded hush puppies and pickles onto a large plate. "Yvonne, I want you and Milton to know that Odell and I are going to do all we can to help y'all readjust."

She turned from the counter with a curious expression on her face. "You already said y'all was going to give us a hundred dollars. You talking about something else now?"

"We'll still give y'all some money. But what I meant just now was, if they hadn't let y'all out, Odell was going to get some prayer chains going. He was going to approach our preacher and have him start the first one. Then he was going to go to your preacher and make the same request. Do you think y'all still need that much spiritual assistance?"

"No, we'll be all right, so long as y'all give us that money. We'll save the prayer chains for another time, in case we get in another pickle." Yvonne paused and gave me a thoughtful look. "I wonder why Odell didn't mention that when we seen him at the store this afternoon?"

"I don't know. I'm sure he'll mention it later. But I wanted you to know now."

"I appreciate hearing that, Joyce. And when I see Odell again, I'll let him know that, too."

When I got back to the living room, I danced a couple of times with two other men before Willie Frank pulled me out on the floor. As usual, he hopped around like a rabbit. I lost count of how many times he stepped on my toes and ankles with his steel-toe brogans. And when a slow song came on, he wrapped his arms around me and pressed his body so close to mine, I felt a hard lump between his legs. I was several inches taller than him, so it poked the top of my thigh instead of my crotch. It was so disturbing. Another man's hard-on was something I hadn't experienced since I met Odell. I was glad Willie Frank didn't smell like tobacco or snuff for a change. His longish blond hair was so clean, I could smell the vanilla-scented shampoo he'd used. "I hope Sweet Sue doesn't get mad at me for slow dancing with you," I teased.

He looked up at me and snickered. "Aw, shuck it. You ain't never got to worry about her getting on your case about me. She ain't the jealous type, and she knows she's the only woman for me." The only time I ever heard him speak in such a mushy tone and act so cheerful was when he was talking about Sweet Sue.

Even though Odell and I had the perfect relationship, I didn't like to judge other folks who weren't as blessed as we were. But I felt sorry for Willie Frank. Something had to be wrong with him. What white man in his right mind would fall in love with a colored prostitute? "What about all the men she's with at Aunt Mattie's house?"

Willie Frank waved his hand and rolled his eyes. "Oh, that's just business. It ain't easy to find work nowhere these days. Folks have to take whatever they can get." He didn't seem so cheerful now. "The thing is, I'd still love that gal to death even if she robbed banks for a living." He stopped talking and glanced toward the back of the room where Sweet Sue, decked out in a skimpy green dress, was hugging a man with each arm. "And she loves me. I don't know what I'd do if I lost her."

"I know exactly what you mean. I feel the same way about Odell. We are more in love than we were when we got married. My life would be empty if I lost him."

"Well, you'd still have your ma and pa."

"God willing." I sighed.

"Plus, you ain't no swamp frog. You'd get another man eventually."

"Yeah, but nobody could replace Odell."

"Cheer up. You'd still have Yvonne and Milton and me, too. I know a busy lady like you got a mess of other friends to socialize with. You won't be lonely. The bottom line is, you'd still have a heap to be thankful for — with or without Odell."

"Thank you for those kind words, Willie Frank."

I didn't want to leave early, but I had to in case Mama and Daddy did stop by my house on their way home from the restaurant. I left right after the second slow dance with Willie Frank ended. Another reason I left was because I didn't want him to keep trying to convince me I'd be all right if something happened to Odell.

My parents were entering my front gate when I got there. Daddy owned a Ford Model T. It was only a few years old and he loved to drive it. But since they didn't like to park close to "them bootleggers" one house over from me, they had taken the car home and walked. Even though they lived only a few minutes away, I didn't think it was such a good idea for them to be roaming around on foot at night. Especially after those thugs attacked Milton last Tuesday. On top of our nice, quiet neighborhood no longer being safe, Daddy's arthritis was so bad, he had to walk with two canes. Mama dragged along with gouty feet and stiff knees, and she complained about a few ailments I'd never heard of. I worried about them as much as they worried about me.

"I see you didn't waste no time falling back in with them bootleggers," Daddy griped in his booming voice. He had lost every strand of his hair years ago, but he still waxed his head with pomade every day. I had inherited his small black eyes, narrow face, and height. Mama's best features were her pearly white teeth and big brown eyes. Even though they were at least seventy pounds overweight each, they were still attractive for elderly people.

"Oh, Daddy, don't start up on that again," I scolded. "Y'all come on in and have some elderberry wine."

"Buttermilk would suit us better. We

drunk enough wine at supper with Sister and Brother Blake," Mama said with a grimace and a mighty burp.

When we got inside, Daddy started looking around. "Girl, don't you get lonesome spending weekends by yourself?" he asked, dropping down into the wing chair facing the couch. His massive weight made the chair legs squeak and wobble.

"You've asked me that a thousand times before," I complained.

"So, now it's a thousand and one times," he snapped, wagging one of his canes at me.

"I'm used to Odell spending the weekends with his daddy. When I do get lonesome, I visit my neighbors."

"Joyce, why don't you get a cat or a dog to keep you company?" Mama suggested. She plopped down on the arm of the chair Daddy occupied and it squeaked and wobbled some more. She snorted and added, "Then you won't have to spend too much time with them bootleggers."

"Mama, Daddy, how many times do I have to tell y'all that they are two of our closest friends? They just got out of jail. I had to go over and let them know I was concerned about them. If Odell and I were the ones arrested, I'm sure they would have done the same thing for us."

"You and Odell ain't crazy enough to be bootlegging or doing nothing else to get arrested!" Daddy yelled. This time he wagged both of his canes at me. "My Lord. Them going to jail for letting a bunch of fools rape a white girl in their house should have spooked you enough to keep you home."

"That whole rape thing was a lie. That's why they got out of jail," I pointed out.

"Humph. They might not be so lucky the next time," Daddy said. "Do they have any idea who called the law on them?"

"No. But I'm sure that whoever it is, they won't be coming around again. So there is nothing to worry about," I predicted.

"How do you know that? You ain't no prophet!" Mama barked.

"Odell thinks the same thing. And he's always right," I defended.

"Oh well. You a grown woman and we can't keep telling you how to live your life," Daddy admitted.

"Then I wish y'all would stop trying to do that," I grumbled.

Mama gave me a dismissive wave and snickered. "Girl, quit whining and go get us that buttermilk. And turn on some heat before we all catch pneumonia."

When my parents ran out of things to fuss about, which took almost an hour, they left.

I immediately went to bed. There was so much on my mind, I couldn't go right to sleep. I kept claiming I wasn't lonesome when Odell was gone, but I was. Not enough to accompany him to his daddy's house more often, though. I preferred Yvonne and Milton's company.

If it hadn't been so late, I would have got up and gone back over there.

CHAPTER 13
YVONNE

Our house was jumping. I had just brung out the fourth serving of hush puppies and deep-fried pork skins. Several folks had a drink in each hand. It tickled me to death to see them get sloppy drunk on our booze, which was probably only half as potent as it was when Willie Frank delivered it. The reason for that was, every night we poured leftover drinks back into the jug they came out of. Throwing away booze was the same as throwing away money and we wasn't that stupid. We sold some of the same recycled stuff two or three times and nobody never knew the difference.

A man who used to perform a tap-dance routine at a popular speakeasy in Birmingham, had recently moved to Branson. He had everybody clapping and egging him on when he put on a show for us.

We rarely had problems with our guests, but every now and then somebody got too rowdy. A cute, plump woman wearing a red wig-hat, got upset when she seen the man she'd come with paying too much attention to Sweet Sue. When she went up to Sweet Sue and slapped her, I jumped in between them. Sweet Sue was one of them back-woods, roughneck women you didn't mess with unless you wanted to get your face sliced with the straight razor she carried in her brassiere. I gently pushed her to the side and told her to tell Willie Frank to give her a drink on the house. Then I grabbed the other woman by the arm and ushered her into the kitchen. She was so stunned, she stumbled, and her wig-hat turned sideways. "Look-a-here, woman; me and Milton is the only ones in this house allowed to hit somebody," I told her, shaking my fist in her face. "If you misbehave again tonight, I'm going to beat you like you stole some-thing, and ban you from coming here!"

"I'm sorry, Yvonne. I didn't mean no harm. But me and Pete just got engaged. He promised me he would never look at another woman," she said with a pout and a sniffle while she adjusted her fake hair. "I won't slap nobody else." She sounded sincere. When she gave me a hug and a smile, I let her off with just that warning.

Even with all the commotion taking place

in the living room, Milton had got real quiet and grim-faced, almost immediately after Joyce left a hour and a half ago. She was the last person I had seen him talking to. I wondered if she had hurt his feelings again with one of her insensitive comments. She had done it so often it never seemed to bother him that much no more. But something was bothering him now. Every night, he was the life of the party. He had stopped drinking and when I put on some of his favorite records, he didn't dance or sing along the way he usually done. His dark mood and silence was making me worry.

While I was conversating with a couple of guests, Milton abruptly left the living room and shuffled into the kitchen. I couldn't wait no longer to ask him what was going on. A few minutes later, I followed him. My heart skipped a beat when I seen him staring out the side window at Joyce and Odell's house, mumbling cuss words under his breath. "Milton, what's the matter with you tonight?"

He took his time turning around. When he did, there was a woeful expression on his face. "There ain't nothing wrong with me," he claimed, barely moving his lips.

"Hogwash! Spit it out. I know when something is bothering you. You ain't been this distressed-looking since we was in jail." I massaged his shoulder and softened my tone. "Sugar, did Queen of Sheba say something to upset you?"

Milton blew out some air and gave me a weak nod. "You could say that."

I folded my arms and squinted. "What did she say this time?"

He nodded toward the living room. "Let's go in there and get Willie Frank. We all need to talk."

"Well, he was fixing to leave, so we better go stop him." We dashed back to the living room, but it was too late. Willie Frank had already left. I looked out the front window and seen him and Sweet Sue getting in his truck. "He'll be back tomorrow. The three of us can conversate then. In the meantime, don't you want to discuss it with me?"

"Naw," he snarled. "Now leave me be."

I straggled back into the crowd and practically had to force myself to act normal.

When our last guest left, Milton immediately went to bed. I didn't want to deal with his bleak mood. I decided to lag behind and clean up some of the mess our guests had made. I took my time, hoping he'd be asleep when I got to the bedroom. When I got there half a hour later, he was laying on his back staring up at the ceiling.

132

I was so exasperated by now, I stomped across the floor and stopped by his side of the bed with my hands on my hips. "Milton, whatever Joyce said must have been pretty bad for you to be looking so miserable. Now I ain't going to let you go to sleep until I know what she said."

"Yvonne, put on your nightgown and get in this bed. I don't want to talk about that yet. Besides, I could be wrong. If I am, I'd rather you didn't know what she said." Milton turned his face to the wall. When I got in the bed and snuggled up to him, he felt like a log.

"Sugar, remember what we talked about last night?" I said in the sexiest tone I could manage. I thought it would soften him up.

Me cooing like a dove didn't work. When he responded, his voice was so harsh you would have thought he was talking to somebody who had swiped his wallet. "We talked about a mess of things."

"I mean when we was in bed. You asked if we could make love tonight. I told you we could . . ."

"Not tonight, baby. Now let me get some sleep."

When I woke up Saturday morning at seven, Milton was still snoozing. I was tempted to get dressed and go next door and feel Joyce out, hoping she'd tell me what she'd said to him last night that had him acting so odd. But she ran her mouth so much about subjects I didn't care nothing about, I probably would have had to stay with her all morning to hear what I needed to hear. I put that notion out of my mind.

An hour later, I heard Willie Frank's truck pull up outside while we was eating breakfast. He had his own key, but I ran to open the door for him anyway. "I'm so glad to see you," I squealed, giving him a hug.

"Huh? Hell's bells. You just seen me a few hours ago." He snickered. I noticed he had on the same blue flannel shirt and black pants he'd wore last night. His eyes had dark circles and was red and puffy. I knew he hadn't been home or got much sleep. "I can't stay long. I was so anxious to get Sweet Sue back to her playpen last night, I forgot that plug of chewing tobacco I left on the windowsill." He strolled over to the window to get his tobacco.

"Willie Frank, we need to talk," Milton said in a gruff tone as he strode into the room, still in his pajamas. "I think we got another mess on our hands."

"Oh? This involve a legal issue?" Willie Frank asked.

"Something like that. And I don't like it one bit," Milton griped. He was squinting so hard, it looked like his eyebrows had merged.

"Whatever the hell it is, I want to know before I go crazy," I snapped as I stamped my foot and glared at Milton.

He stood in the middle of the floor tapping his foot, looking from Willie Frank to me and back. "Y'all ain't going to like what I'm fixing to say," he warned.

"Uh-oh. I better take a seat then." Willie Frank shuffled over to the couch and eased down. Milton plopped down next to him, and I stood in front of him with my arms folded.

When Milton started talking again, he sounded even more serious. "Willie Frank, do you know where Sheriff Potts received that bogus telephone call at?"

"That's a odd thing for you to be concerned about. Why do you need to know?" Willie Frank asked with a confused look on his face. Then he glanced at me and shrugged. I shrugged, too.

"Just answer my question," Milton ordered.

"They called Sheriff Potts at his house."

"You sure they didn't call him at his office?" Milton asked.

"Yeah, I'm sure. That's what he told me and Uncle Lamar."

"Do you think they mentioned it to somebody else?" Milton's voice cracked, and that scared me.

I unfolded my arms and plonked down on the couch arm next to him. "Baby, what is it you trying to say?" I asked.

I could tell by the way Willie Frank was shifting in his seat that he was getting agitated. He didn't give Milton time to answer my question. "Milton, who would they mention it to? And, before you ask, I didn't mention it to nobody neither. And why is it important where the sheriff got the call at?" Willie Frank said.

"Because if Sheriff Potts, and you and your uncle, didn't tell nobody else where that call came in at, only the person who made it would know. Am I right?" Milton dipped his head and gazed at Willie Frank so hard, he stood up.

"Look, the main thing is, y'all got off. That's all we need to be concerned about," Willie Frank pointed out. Then he got a faraway look in his eyes. He bit his bottom lip and suddenly looked real sympathetic. "What is it you ain't telling me and Yvonne . . ."

"Joyce knows Sheriff Potts got the call at

his house," Milton blurted out through clenched teeth.

CHAPTER 14
YVONNE

The room got so quiet, you could have heard a gnat sneeze. My head started spinning and my tongue felt like it had blew up twice as big as normal. I didn't know what to say. *"Joyce?"* me and Willie Frank hollered at the same time. If Milton had told us she had tried to shoot President Roosevelt, I couldn't have been more shocked. She was a odd duck, but there was some things I never expected to hear her say, or even know.

I sat stock-still with my heart beating against my chest like a mallet. "Milton, what did you say?" I asked, slapping the side of my head as I gazed at him with my eyes bugged out.

"You ain't deaf. You heard what I said," he replied.

When my head stopped spinning and my tongue shrunk back to its normal size, I got up off the couch arm and went and stood

138

next to Willie Frank. Me and him both stared at Milton with our eyes wide and our mouths hanging open. A split second later, my head started spinning again. I got so woozy, a baby bird could have blew me down. If Willie Frank hadn't held me in place, I would have slid to the floor. "Baby, who told you that?" I asked.

Milton didn't waste no time answering. "That big-mouth heifer said so herself while she was rattling on and on last night. I was so outraged, I wanted to slap somebody."

Willie Frank waved his hands in the air and shook his head. "Milton, I'm in a tizzy. What I want to know is, who in the world told Joyce a detail like that?"

Milton took his time answering this time. He crossed his legs and leaned back in his seat. The suspense was killing me. "Didn't you hear what Willie Frank asked you? You the one deaf now?" I hollered.

"I heard him," Milton replied, speaking real calm. Then he blurted out in a loud, cold tone, "Odell told her!"

I was too shocked to do anything other than just stand there as stiff as a pine tree. Willie Frank gasped and done a double take. "Milton, you sure that's what Joyce said?" he asked.

"I know what she said," Milton shot back.

He wobbled up off the couch and put his hands on Willie Frank's shoulders. "Now think hard. I know your uncle and Sheriff Potts both shop at MacPherson's. Odell is one of the few colored men they respect. Is there a chance one of them let that piece of information slip out while they was over there?"

Willie Frank looked puzzled. Then he shook his head. "Well, I don't follow them around so I wouldn't know. I do know that Uncle Lamar couldn't have told him. Right after he left the jailhouse on Thursday, he drove to Huntsville to visit his girlfriend. That's where he's been ever since. And even if Sheriff Potts went in the store and got to talking to Odell, that don't sound like a subject they'd discuss. I can ask him if you want me to. That way, we could clear this up. Odell is the last person I'd suspect of making such a deadly telephone call."

"Look, my man. If you, your uncle, and the sheriff didn't tell Odell, he had to find out another way!" Milton blasted. "And I can't think of but one other way: He made that call."

"Milton, hush up and bite your tongue!" I screamed. "Do you know what you just said?" My whole body was shaking. The thought of us being betrayed in such a

140

deadly way by somebody we thought was our *friend* was almost too much for me to stand. I was surprised I hadn't fainted by now.

"Hell yeah, I know what I just said," Milton snarled. "I wouldn't say nothing this crazy unless I knew what I was talking about."

"I can't believe what I'm hearing," Willie Frank muttered, slapping the side of his head.

"Maybe Sheriff Potts mentioned it to one of his deputies, and they ran into Odell in the store, or somewhere else, and told him," I suggested. The last thing I wanted us to have to deal with on top of everything else, was a Judas goat. I knew Odell was a lying, cheating dog, but I never thought he'd stoop low enough to try and get us sent back to prison — or killed. But that was what it sounded like he'd done. The reality hit me like a ton of rocks. "Lord have mercy," I mouthed, shaking my head so hard a bobby pin fell out of my hair. "Well, the only way we can know for sure is to ask Odell."

"Pffft. If he did do it, do you think he'd be man enough to admit it? Lying is all part of being a backstabber!" Willie Frank barked, swirling his finger in the air. In all the years we'd known him, I had never seen

141

him this upset and angry. "I'm going to get to the bottom of this mess. I'll pay Sheriff Potts a visit and fish around and see if I can get him to tell me what he told Odell."

"Then what?" Milton asked.

"If the sheriff says he didn't, then we'll decide what to do about it." Willie Frank sucked in a deep breath and rubbed the back of his head. "We can't accuse a upstanding man like Odell of something that serious. Y'all was innocent, so y'all know how much it hurts to be blamed for something you didn't do." Willie Frank reached in his pocket and pulled out the keys to his truck. "I'm going to go to the sheriff's office right now and ask him flat out if he mentioned where he got the call to somebody else. Y'all want to come with me?"

"Hell no!" I boomed. I stamped my foot so hard, the lamp on the end table rattled. "We'll stay put until you get back. We must be the last colored people on the planet that cracker wants to see these days."

"All right then. I'll be back directly." Willie Frank looked toward the door. "Uh, if Odell was to slide through here while I'm gone, don't let on that we know nothing."

"Oh, we ain't got to worry about him coming today. This is Saturday. He'll be with his sick daddy until tomorrow," I said with a sneer.

"Yeah, that's right." A preoccupied look crossed Willie Frank's face. "I swear to God, Odell's devotion to his daddy proves he's got a heart. I don't know of a man or woman who would give up so much time to be a caregiver to a man married to a able-bodied woman like Ellamae. She used to be a nurse, and ought to be taking care of Lonnie on her own. Odell's been burdened with that responsibility since before I met him. We *got* to be wrong about him."

"We'll find out soon enough," Milton mumbled. He shot me a knowing look and I nodded.

When Willie Frank left, me and Milton stayed on the couch, perched like crows on a fence. I got up a couple of times and peeped out the front window, hoping Joyce would come over. If she did, I would ask her what all Odell had said about the call. She was so dense, she never would have guessed that I was fishing for information.

Milton got so jittery, he drunk two glasses of home brew and had to use the toilet twice in less than fifteen minutes. When he sat back down on the couch, he couldn't sit still. I couldn't either, for that matter. We was still on the couch fidgeting when Willie Frank came rushing back through the front door thirty minutes later. The frantic look on his face told me that he was going to tell us something we wouldn't like.

"What took you so long? And what did the sheriff say?" Milton asked with his hands outstretched. Me and him stood up at the same time.

Willie Frank raised his hands. "He wasn't in his office. I had to go to his house. Now y'all stay cool and calm until I finish," he advised. After a few deep breaths he went on, talking with his tongue snapping over each word. "I didn't want Sheriff Potts to start asking me no nosy questions about why I wanted to know about that call. I had to chitchat about a bunch of other mundane things before I got to the point. Anyway, after discussing his health issues, his dogs, his hardheaded wife and kids, that widow woman with them four kids in Lexington he's been fooling around with for ten years, I eased in the question of that phone call he received. Sheriff Potts swore that he didn't mention nothing about where he got the call to nobody else. Not even his deputies. He said his wife answered the phone first and handed it to him. While I was standing there, he called her in the room and asked her if she'd told anybody about the call. She said she hadn't. I declare, that means only

one thing —"
I cut Willie Frank off and finished his sentence. "Odell is definitely the one who tried to get rid of us."

145

CHAPTER 15
ODELL

I couldn't imagine how much worse things would be for me if Yvonne and Milton knew I was the one who had called Sheriff Potts on them. I wasn't going to worry about it too much because nobody would think I had anything to do with it. Even though it had backfired, I was glad I'd done it because it shook them up and disrupted their business. What I was more concerned about now was how I was going to get that money to Milton by the end of this month.

I had enjoyed this weekend's visit with Betty Jean and the boys. We'd ate supper at Po' Sister's Kitchen Friday and Saturday evening. After supper on Saturday, me and my two oldest boys had went fishing. Then we'd visited with one of Betty Jean's cousins who lived about a mile down the road. We had got back home two hours later than I'd told Betty Jean we would. Me and the boys sat on the front porch making slingshots to shoot rocks at some of the pesky squirrels and coons that hung out around our house. I gave that up when Betty Jean started complaining about all the work she was doing by herself. So, I mopped all the floors for her. Just like I done with Joyce when she got overloaded with housework. Last week after I'd mopped every floor in our house, I cleaned out the kitchen closet, pantry, and the attic. Later that same day, I went out and got Joyce some roses and came home and cooked our supper. That had really impressed her. "Odell, if you'd been born a woman, you'd make the perfect wife. But I'm glad I got you as the perfect husband." Her comment had made me feel so guilty; I'd slunk out of the room with my head hanging low. I couldn't have asked for two better women than Joyce and Betty Jean.

Despite all the fun I'd had in Hartville this weekend, I was glad when Sunday evening rolled around. I was anxious to get home so Joyce could fuss over me. When I pulled up in front of our house a few minutes before seven p.m., she opened the front door and trotted out onto the porch before I even finished parking. "Come on in and give me some sugar," she purred as I piled out of the car.

"Baby, I'm so glad to be home," I told

her, rushing up the porch steps two at a time. She took me by the hand and pulled me into the living room. "I swear to God, Daddy almost drove me up the wall this time," I complained.

"I'm sorry to hear that. How did Ellamae treat you?"

I groaned as we sat down on the couch. "Same old, same old. She even went fishing with us Friday evening. Just when the fish started biting, a daddy longlegs spider crawled up her leg and she almost fainted. A few minutes after that, a frog hopped into her lap while she was sitting on the ground baiting a fishhook." I threw my head back and laughed. "That was enough for her. She got so hysterical, we had to leave right away. Me and Daddy couldn't stop laughing. When we got back to the house, she cussed a blue streak at us for putting her life 'in danger.' When it was time to go to bed, she made me sleep on the living-room couch instead of in their spare bed."

"I'm not laughing because there is nothing funny about a woman being attacked by a spider and a frog. I've had my share of encounters with weevils and lizards, so I know how traumatic things like that can be. It sounds like Ellamae was really mad at you."

"Well, I guess she was. She wouldn't have been spooked by them creatures if I hadn't took her and Daddy fishing. Me and him laughing about it made it worse. But she claimed I had to sleep on that rickety couch because they was airing out the mattress on the spare bed. Long as my legs is, I had to lay with them hanging over the top of the couch arm. My legs is still stiff," I complained.

Joyce caressed my cheek. "You poor thing. It sounds like you had the weekend from hell." She finally laughed. "I'm glad I didn't go with you, and I don't plan on going anytime soon. I hope you don't mind."

"Sugar, I don't care if you never go back out there with me. Daddy understands."

"Well, I can't overlook my responsibilities as a Christian. I need to be a little more tolerant, but I don't want Ellamae to ruin my holiday spirit. I'll go out there with you after the first of the year. Now remember, I'd like to spend Thanksgiving alone with you like we planned. And I told Mama and Daddy we'd spend Christmas with them."

"Let's talk about all that later. I'm too tired and wore out to deal with it now," I protested, patting her knee.

"I hope you're not too tired to go next door for a little while."

I froze. Bile rose in my throat so fast, I had to hold my breath for a few seconds. "Next door?"

"Yes. Yvonne and Milton were a little disappointed because you didn't stop and say hello to them before you went to your daddy's house on Friday. I told them we'd come over when you got home this evening. We need to keep reassuring them that we are still in their corner."

I could feel a knot forming in the pit of my stomach. Somehow, I managed to keep a smile on my face and my tone gentle. "Joyce, I told you they came by the store Friday afternoon. They know I'm in their corner."

"I know. But you should have a little more sympathy. You know how pitiful they are. We've been setting a good example for them. Let's not stop now." Joyce got silent and stared straight ahead for a few seconds. When she turned back to me, there was a distant look in her eyes. "I'm going to pray that they don't get into more trouble. I mean, we can only put up with so much before we have to stop associating with folks that might make us look bad. I hope that doesn't happen because I had fun with them this weekend, and I'm not ready to give that up yet."

"That's nice, sugar. Did they have a big crowd?"

"Uh-huh. But a few of their big-spending regulars were missing. Willie Frank told me some of those folks said that they're too scared to come back."

"That's too bad for Yvonne and Milton. Their bootlegging profits will be shy, and they'll have more money problems."

"Oh, I'm sure they'll make up for it." Joyce slid her finger through my hair. "Um . . . I hope you don't mind, but I already told them we'd help them with some money. I think a hundred dollars is a good amount."

My chest tightened. The way my body was feeling, it was a wonder I didn't keel over. I looked at Joyce like she'd just turned into a toad. "You told them we'd give them a *hundred* dollars?" I couldn't believe my ears. I had just gave Yvonne fifty bucks on Friday. I had to come up with four hundred to give Milton, plus his weekly blackmail payment. Now Joyce was telling me she had promised them another hundred!

"Odell, don't look so surprised. We can afford it. We are blessed to have so much, it'd be a shame not to share more with the poor folks."

"We do share. What about our cash donations to the church fund that Reverend Jessup started for the poor colored folks when the Depression first hit a few years ago? We still contributing to that."

"Well, I think we need to chip in a little more."

"Joyce, be reasonable. I don't think our church fund was set up to line the pockets of *bootleggers.*"

"Odell, I am not talking about using the church money. I'm talking about our personal fund. So what if Yvonne and Milton are bootleggers? They still need to eat and pay bills. Besides, they are our neighbors, and two of our closest friends."

"Milton already borrows money from me often enough —"

She cut me off. "I told them they wouldn't have to pay us back. Now if you want to be stingy, you go ahead. I'll take it out of my money. And to save face when I give it to them, I won't let them know you didn't contribute anything . . ."

It was a good thing I was sitting down because I got so flustered, I had to take a bunch of deep breaths to compose myself. "Joyce, I'm sorry. I ain't never let you down and I ain't about to start now. I'll give you the whole hundred dollars when I get paid."

"Good. I'm sure that'll make them very

happy." Joyce smiled and gazed at me like I was something somebody had served up to her on a silver platter. "We have more money than we need. And when Mama and Daddy pass on, I'll inherit the store, all the money they leave behind, and their house — which is completely paid for. We'll be the richest colored couple in Branson." Joyce's words was really rattling me. Her stroking my arm didn't help none. "And —" She abruptly stopped talking.

"And what?"

"Well, I'll probably sell the store once it becomes mine."

I gulped and almost choked on my words. "Sell the store?" There was such a confused expression on Joyce's face, you would have thought I was speaking a foreign language. "How do you know the new owner would let me keep managing?"

"It won't matter. I'm going to sell the house, too. With the money we already have, and whatever we'd get from the sale of those two properties, we won't have to work anymore. Or at least for a very long time. How many colored folks our age can retire while the country is still in an economic slump? We'd have enough to live the good life — and not in a one-horse town like Branson."

"You . . . you want to move, too?"

"Why not?"

"To a big city like Birmingham or Mobile?"

"Uh-uh." Joyce shook her head and scrunched up her face. "That's still the South. We'd be just as limited there as we are here. Every time I see a WHITE FOLKS ONLY sign when I go shopping, I feel less than human. I'd like to live in a place where I can eat and reside wherever I want, and not worry about getting arrested for saying something to a white person that might offend them. I'm talking about cities like Detroit and Chicago. Colored folks are moving to places like those in droves. And from what I hear from the relatives they left down here, they are living like kings."

My whole body felt like it was going to break up into a million little pieces. I was not about to leave Betty Jean and my sons behind. I did not want to uproot them, no matter how much property and money me and Joyce inherited. Besides that, Betty Jean was too close to her family, her friends, and her church. I knew there was no way she would agree to move to one of them cold Northern cities.

"Joyce, please don't talk about your mama and daddy dying, and us letting white folks' antics chase us away. That kind of talk depresses me. And just so you know, I do not want to live where it snows. You know how much I love managing the store, and we both way too young to retire. I'm only thirty-six. I have a lot of good years left. I want to be doing something productive, not sitting around waiting to die. Shoot. If you sell the properties, with my lack of education, the only other jobs I'd be able to get would be on somebody's farm. Or doing handyman work again at Aunt Mattie's whorehouse. Don't you think we done come too far to end up like that?"

Joyce held her hand up to my face. "Don't get too riled up, sugar." She giggled. That eased my discomfort a whole lot. I realized she wasn't as serious as I thought. "I'm sorry I started a conversation on this subject. Now that I know how you feel, we'll leave things the way they are. You can manage the store as long as you want. If I do sell it, I'd get the new owner to put it in writing."

"Good. Now let's change the subject." I was so relieved, I grabbed Joyce's hand and kissed it. Then I kissed her lips. I was still holding her hand when we stopped kissing. I was glad she giggled again. "Let's move on to something more pleasant."

"How about supper? Do you want to eat before we go visit Yvonne and Milton? I cooked some frog legs, collard greens, and macaroni and cheese."

"Woo-hoo!" I rubbed my palms together. "I been craving a scrumptious meal like that for days. Besides, I should put something on my stomach before we go next door. Drinking on a empty stomach makes me queasy." When I rose, I pulled Joyce up by her hand. She squealed and got as giddy as a lovestruck teenager when I lifted her off the floor and carried her into the kitchen.

I scarfed down as much food as I could. But when we got next door, I immediately felt sick to my stomach. There was at least two-and-a-half-dozen folks present. Dr. Patterson was standing by the door. He clapped me on the back and kissed Joyce on her cheek. "Odell, it's good to see you and your lovely wife again," he said in a low tone.

"Did Mrs. Patterson come with you to-night?" Joyce asked.

"Uh-uh. Eloise is at her sister's house do-ing her hair. She's coming directly, though. She and I are going to help Yvonne and Milton get over this mishap as much as we can."

"So are we. Right, Odell?" Joyce said, giv-ing me a pleading look.

156

Before I could answer, Milton strutted up to me and gave me a bear hug. He looked like a avocado with a face, in the dark green suit he'd charged to his account at the store last month. "Odell, my man! I'm so glad you made it!" he boomed.

"I . . . I'm glad I made it, too," I mumbled.

He ushered us to a corner in the back of the room. "I'm sorry there ain't no seats left. Y'all don't mind standing, do you?" he asked, looking from me to Joyce.

"I don't mind at all," Joyce chirped.

"Odell, I don't mean to be rude, but I need to keep mingling with my guests and taking more drink orders. Me and you can chitchat a little later. I . . . uh . . . need to discuss something," Milton told me with a sly wink.

Joyce rolled her eyes. "Don't worry, Milton. If you want to talk to him about the money I said we'd give y'all, I've already mentioned it to him. He's all for it. We'll give it to y'all soon," Joyce blurted out, grinning from ear to ear. "Now go get us some drinks."

CHAPTER 16
MILTON

It wasn't easy for me and Yvonne and Willie Frank to act normal around Odell until we decided his punishment. The minute he walked in the door Sunday night, I wanted to gouge his eyes out.

"I think we need to confront and chastise Odell as soon as possible," Willie Frank whispered in my ear. He glared at Odell as he stood at the other end of the room, a few inches away from Sweet Sue. Him and her both was grinning like hyenas.

"Not yet. Me and Yvonne need him around long enough to get what we can from him so we can pay your uncle back on time," I reminded.

"Yeah, that's right. But it'll be hard to keep my hands off him! Just look at the way he's sizing up Sweet Sue!" Willie Frank blasted. "I'm glad I don't have to worry about him visiting her at Aunt Mattie's house. He is so dazzled by Joyce, he wouldn't look sideways at another woman." Willie Frank's last sentence made me choke on some air. He had to slap me on the back to help me catch my breath. "You all right, buddy?"

"Yeah. I'm good." I wanted to laugh my head off. I didn't know if me and Yvonne would ever tell Willie Frank about Betty Jean. If we did, he'd laugh his head off, too. "Um, I'd better do some more mingling." I said a few words to a couple of other folks until Yvonne ushered me into the kitchen. When we got to the corner in the back of the room next to the pantry, she whirled around and narrowed her eyes. "Why you looking so distressed?" I asked.

"Because I'm fit to be tied."

"What's wrong, baby? Did one of them jokers out there disrespect you, or try to get in your bloomers?"

"It wasn't nothing like that. It's worse." Yvonne paused and let out a loud breath. "Milton, listen to me, sugar. I know for sure now that it was Odell who made that call to Sheriff Potts," she said with her lips quivering.

"I know that, too. We done already discussed it. Is that what's got you so riled up?"

"Until a few minutes ago, I still had just a little bit of doubt about Odell calling the sheriff. I don't have no doubt no more."

"Why? Did you hear something else?"

"I overheard Odell conversating with Dr. Patterson. He didn't know I was less than a foot behind him. He said something to the doctor about 'that troublemaker' calling the sheriff *at his house.* So, his own words confirmed what Joyce said."

"Oh yeah?"

"Guess what else he said that he shouldn't have known?" Yvonne didn't let me answer, which I couldn't have done nohow. "He said the sheriff arrived *eight* minutes after he got the call. How would he know that?"

Her words made my ears ache. I massaged them and shook my head. "That no-good sucker. Yvonne, don't you move." I rushed back to the living room and brung Willie Frank into the kitchen.

"What's up?" he asked, looking confused.

"Yvonne, tell him what you just told me," I ordered. She repeated it almost word for word.

Willie Frank's jaw dropped. "Good God! We was right. There ain't no doubt about it now. There is only one way Odell could know how long it took Sheriff Potts to get here, too. He's got to be the lying blabbermouth that made that call!"

"Exactly. What he said put the last nail in

160

the coffin," Yvonne growled.

"*His* coffin," I added. "I hope he don't stay here too long tonight. I'm scared I won't be responsible for my actions."

"Now hold on, Milton. We can't do nothing for a while. In the meantime, we have to keep acting normal. The last thing we want is for Odell to get suspicious of us," Willie Frank said. All of a sudden, he got a strange look on his face and he scratched his head. "I can't imagine what y'all done to make him do such a thing."

"I can. It ain't nothing but straight-up jealousy," I declared.

Willie Frank and Yvonne looked at each other, then at me with confused expressions on their faces.

"All right now. Y'all don't need to look so confused." I cocked my head to the side and nodded at Yvonne. "I got the best-looking Red Bone woman ever born. Look at all that long straight hair, that slim little body, and them baby doll features on her face. She look more like twenty-two than thirty-two. Every colored man in this town wish they was in my shoes, and in my bed." I winked at Yvonne. "Odell is stuck with a woman I wouldn't be seen with at a sideshow. Hell, she is a sideshow." I laughed and was glad Yvonne and Willie Frank did, too.

"Well, Joyce is mighty plain, and looks rather long in the tooth for a woman of thirty-five. But she ain't that bad," Willie Frank defended. "She do got some saving grace: a big inheritance coming to her someday."

"It don't matter that she'll be rolling in money when her folks kick the bucket. She still won't be half as mouthwatering to look at as Yvonne."

"I don't know, y'all. There has to be more to this situation than Odell being jealous," Willie Frank said. "Y'all swipe a lot of stuff from the store — a heap more than anybody else. He could have got wind of it, but was too skittish to confront his close friends and neighbors. But he's losing money left and right and decided to put a stop to it."

Willie Frank's theory sounded good to me so I ran with it. "You could be right. Odell ain't never caught us stealing, but how do we know him or Sadie or Buddy didn't see us taking stuff? That's a good reason for him to want to get rid of us. And him being such a big shot muckety-muck in this town, he didn't want to look like a bully by accusing small fries like us. I bet that's what it is!" I hollered. "That and him being jealous of me having a woman like Yvonne . . ."

"Aw, Milton. You making me feel embarrassed," Yvonne said shyly, turning one shade of red after another. "Seriously, if lusting after me and us stealing merchandise was all it took for Odell to try and get rid of us, he is too dangerous for us not to do something."

"Thank you. That's why we have to be careful what we say and do so he won't suspect nothing," Milton advised.

"Sure enough," Willie Frank agreed.

"If he do get suspicious, what could he do? Leave town?" Yvonne asked.

"I doubt if he'd do that. He got it too easy living here. But if he figures out that we on to him and might want revenge, he could make hisself so scarce we'd have a hard time getting our hands on him when the time comes," Willie Frank pointed out.

"It wouldn't be easy to get him at work, or on the street. That joker is too sly to get ambushed." Yvonne was talking so fast, spit was flying out both sides of her mouth.

"And another thing. I been thinking; we shouldn't kill him," Willie Frank said with a grimace.

"What? You was the one who said we should blow his head off with a shotgun," I reminded him.

"You done chickened out now, Willie Frank?" Yvonne asked.

163

He shook his head. "No, it ain't nothing like that. I mentioned the shotgun thing before we knew who it was. Odell ain't just another colored man, he's a big wheel in this town, see. If somebody was to kill *him,* there ain't no telling what might happen. I can just see one of them agitating, do-gooder politicians cooking up a speech that would cause a ruckus. I got a better idea. We can fix him in a way that would cause him enough pain, he'd never try to get back at y'all again."

"Yeah, right. If we don't want him to lie on us again, we'll have to cut his tongue out. But a slick sucker like him would probably write something on a piece of paper," Yvonne hissed.

"I got it." Willie Frank snapped his fingers. "We could rob the store and his house and sell his property for some big bucks. Or, we could pour molasses in his gas tank —" He abruptly stopped talking and shook his head. "No, that ain't mean enough. He'd buy all new stuff and get his car fixed in a heartbeat. Instead, we'll steal his car and push it in a sink hole. He is so attached to that old jalopy, losing it would hit him real hard. Whatever we do, we'll let him know we done it because we know he was the one that called the sheriff on y'all. And I'll let him know that if he does something to get at y'all again . . . *I'll turn the Ku Klux Klan loose on him.*"

"Hmmm." I pressed my lips together and caressed my chin. "Willie Frank, you just hit on something. Since you brung up the Klan, we could lynch him ourselves instead of doing any of that other stuff. A lynching would definitely point the finger at the Klan."

"Hmmm. A lynching just might be the solution. Let me think on it." There was a hopeful look on Willie Frank's face.

Me and him started walking out of the room. We stopped when Yvonne stamped her foot and cussed under her breath. "I'll be glad when we get this over with. I'm sick of living next door to, and entertaining, a low-down, funky black devil like Odell!" she blasted.

I raised my hands in the air. "All right. We done said enough about this for now. Let's get back out there and go on about our business."

Ten minutes after we returned to the living room, Joyce came up to me while Odell was talking to Aunt Mattie. "Milton, we would love to stay longer, but we'll be leaving in a few minutes."

"Already?" It was hard for me to sound

disappointed, but I done my best. I even frowned.

"Odell is tired and itching to go home and get in bed. His daddy and stepmother really gave him a run for his money this weekend," she explained with a apologetic expression on her face. "Poor Odell was so beat when he got home today."

"I bet he was. Poor Odell . . ." I muttered. It was so hard not to sound sarcastic. But even when I did, Joyce didn't pick up on it.

"I don't know how much longer he can keep going out there to help take care of Lonnie. I might take a notion and go talk to that old man about moving in with us. We'd have to make sure Ellamae is out of the picture first, though."

"Well, she is long in the tooth. A woman her age could have a stroke or heart attack and drop dead any day now. Then y'all wouldn't have to worry about her no more."

Joyce's mouth dropped open. "Sweet Jesus, Milton. That's not what I meant, and I hope she doesn't pass on anytime soon. Odell told me she keeps threatening to get a divorce and move to Atlanta and live with one of her nieces. That's what I'm hoping for."

"Oh. Well, I'll pray for things to work out for y'all with Lonnie. I'm sorry I brung up such a ghoulish subject." I exhaled and went on. "Now before you leave, let me ask you one thing: When do you think we'll be able to get that cash gift from y'all?"

"Huh?" I had no idea why she looked surprised. She was the one who had brung up them giving us some money. Now she was standing in front of me looking like a thunderbolt had hit her. "Oh! The hundred dollars? Don't worry. Y'all will get it soon. I'll make sure of that."

I was so relieved. "And we'll be glad to get it." If Joyce hadn't been such a fright to look at, I would have kissed her.

CHAPTER 17
YVONNE

This Sunday night had been good for us. We'd made a decent amount of money and had a lot of fun. Nobody would guess that we'd been involved in so much turmoil lately.

After our guests left, me and Milton snuggled up on the couch. His arm was around my shoulder. It felt good, but I didn't think I'd ever relax completely until we settled the score with Odell. "Baby, I don't say it enough, but I want you to know that I really and truly love you," I told him.

Milton chuckled. "I got a good memory. I hear that from you often enough. You don't need to keep telling me."

"I hope you still love me . . ."

Milton cocked his head to the side and looked at me with a curious expression on his face. "What's wrong with you, girl? Why you talking out the side of your mouth?"

"Well, I just want to make sure you know

where I stand with you. And that I ain't never going to change."

"Baby, you seem a little bothered. Did Prince Charming and Queen of Sheba say something to upset you tonight?" Milton asked. *"Again,"* he tacked on.

"Not really. The minute Joyce started bragging about Odell, I pretended I had to rush to the toilet." I laughed.

Milton didn't look the least bit amused. He looked preoccupied now. He took his arm from around my shoulder and let out a long, loud breath. "Things won't be the same after we . . . uh . . . do our business with Odell."

"I know they won't. But we ain't got no choice. He got it coming. I wonder what will become of Joyce, though."

"That all depends on what we do to Odell. Whatever that is, I just hope one of us don't let nothing slip out to the wrong person so it'll come back and bite us on the ass," Milton replied in a worried tone.

"You know I wouldn't let nothing slip out. And Willie Frank wouldn't neither."

"Look, as smart and slick as Odell is — or thinks he is — he let it slip out about that telephone call. Do you think when he done it, he thought he'd say something to the wrong person?"

"As far as we know, the only person he told is Joyce."

"Exactly. She was the *wrong* person. She turns around and tells me in front of some of our guests!" Milton fired back. "One of them nurses from the colored clinic was standing close to me. She could have heard something. How do we know she ain't out there repeating what Joyce said?"

This conversation was wearing me out. "I didn't think about that," I mumbled in a tired tone.

"And another thing, what about that comment he made to Dr. Patterson that you heard about how long it took Sheriff Potts to get here after he got that call?"

I dropped my head and stared at the floor. When I looked back up at Milton, I was surprised and mad to see so much contempt in his eyes. "Why you looking all crazy at me? We on the same side."

His gaze immediately got soft, and so did his tone. "I'm sorry, sugar." He rubbed the back of his head. "Let's go to bed." We went to bed and made love for the first time since our arrest. I didn't flinch or think about how I'd been raped just a few days ago.

After we finished pleasuring each other, Milton went to the bathroom to clean and dress some of his wounds. The ones on his face didn't look so bad no more. And they would heal up quicker if he'd stop fiddling with them scabs. The real damage was the footprints on his back where them deputies had stomped him. My arms was still sore from them grabbing me and pinning me down on the ground. They'd busted my bottom lip, but I'd covered the bruises with plum-colored lipstick.

When Milton came back, I turned on the lamp on my nightstand, puffed up my pillows, and propped myself up against the headboard. I was comfortable, but I didn't like how ominous our shadows looked on the wall. Tonight was the first time they looked so *black* . . .

"You all right, sugar?" he asked, sliding back under the covers.

"Yeah." I didn't want to call attention to them shadows if I didn't have to. Milton was superstitious enough. "It's been two days."

"Two days since what?"

"Since you told Odell how much money we need."

"So what? We still got more than two-and-a-half weeks left to pay Lamar."

"I know, but maybe we shouldn't cut it too close. What if we wait until two or three days before the month ends, and find out

Odell couldn't come up with the full amount? You know that white man ain't going to let us off with a partial payment. We need to have three hundred dollars in our hands by the deadline he gave us."

"What about the money Joyce said they'd give us?" Milton asked with a yawn.

"Odell could change his mind about that. Or what if he will only let us have ten or twenty dollars? And even if they give us a hundred-dollar gift, how do we know we'll get it anytime *soon*? We can't count that until it's in our hands."

"Look, baby. Odell said he'd give me what we owe Lamar in time! That's all we need to be concerned about!" Milton hollered, clawing at his face.

"You right. I should know better. Calm down and leave them scabs alone before you bust open one."

"They itch like mad when I get upset," he griped.

"Itching ain't going to kill you. If you get a infection, you'll have to take off more time from work. Now back to Odell. I was just making a point, in case things with him don't go as planned."

"I'm sorry. I ain't itching that bad. And I didn't mean to raise my voice at you," he mumbled. "Anyway, I don't see no reason

172

why Odell can't get all that money for us."

"I don't neither. But something could come up that would make it umpossible for him to pay us. He ain't no magician who could wave a magic wand and pull cash out of a hat."

"Ain't nothing 'umpossible' for Prince Charming. He don't need no magic wand." Milton let out a sharp laugh. "You think he would still be supporting that woman and them kids all this time if he had a problem getting money?"

"When he comes over here on Wednesday to give you your weekly payment, you should try and get a little extra."

"I'm already getting 'a little extra' from him, Yvonne."

"Oh?" For a moment, I thought Milton was going to confess that he'd put the bite on Odell for a extra hundred. I was wrong.

"I told him he got to pay me for missing last Wednesday's payment because we was locked up. He is going to give me a double payment this coming week."

"That'll be only sixteen dollars. I'm talking about a lot more than that. If we space it out better, say a hundred this week and next, he shouldn't have no problem giving us the other hundred the last week in the month. Now when you meet with him, you

173

let him know that we the ones in charge. Do you hear me?"

"I hear you."

"Good night, Milton. I'm fixing to turn off the lamp."

"Why? We usually sleep with at least one on in here."

"I know. But I don't like the way it's making our shadows look tonight." I nodded toward the wall on Milton's side.

He looked over his shoulder and shuddered. "Damn! I see what you mean. Them shadows look like black ghosts," he said with his voice cracking. "And they so deformed, we don't even look human."

A cold chill shot up my spine when I turned off the lamp. I clicked it back on a hour later when I went to the bathroom, and our shadows looked normal so I forgot all about it . . .

CHAPTER 18
ODELL

I hadn't had no peace of mind since I left Betty Jean's house this afternoon. I had no idea how I was able to be in the company of Yvonne and Milton for a couple of hours tonight and not go crazy.

From the minute me and Joyce had entered their living room, I went out of my way to avoid them as much as I could. But every time I looked up, one of them devils was gazing at me. Especially Yvonne. While me and Dr. Patterson was conversating, she'd looked at me with a curious expression on her face, which made me suspect she was trying to eavesdrop. I didn't think I was saying nothing she would be interested in, so I wasn't worried. Other than the price of produce, some fishing information, and a few news items, that was all me and Dr. Patterson talked about. But toward the end of our conversation, he'd brung up Yvonne and Milton's arrest. Without giving my response much thought, I'd said that Sheriff Potts had came only eight minutes after that anonymous person called him. I didn't think about what I'd said until after I'd said it. It wasn't no big deal, though. If Dr. Patterson repeated my words to somebody else and they asked me about it, it wouldn't be hard for me to come up with a answer. I could say that Sheriff Potts, or one of his deputies, mentioned it when they was shopping in the store recently. That idea didn't stay with me long because it suddenly dawned on me that none of them had been in the store since before the arrest. Shoot. If I did say one of them told me, and somebody asked them about it, I'd be up shit creek. All I could do now was hope that Dr. Patterson had forgot what I told him.

I put that damn subject out of my mind until me and Joyce got home and went to bed. And she was the one that brung it up. "Odell, I've been meaning to ask you something." I was laying on my back. She was on her side, facing me.

"Okay. Ask me 'something.' "

"How did you know that the person who tried to get Yvonne and Milton in trouble called Sheriff Potts at home?"

I froze. "Huh?" It was a few moments before I could go on. "Um . . . I can't

176

remember off the top of my head who told me. Why?"

"I was just curious. Friday night when I mentioned it, Milton gave me a strange look."

I froze even more. If the house suddenly caught on fire, I wouldn't be able to move fast enough to get out. "Did he ask you about it?"

"Yes, he did. He just wanted to know how I knew that. But he didn't make a big deal out of it," Joyce replied with a yawn.

"What did you tell him?"

"I told him what you told me." I was glad we had turned off the light because it would have been hard for me to explain the stunned look and sweat on my face if she seen it.

"What did he say?"

"Like I said, he didn't make a big deal out of it. He went on about his business and never brought it up again." The next thing I knew, Joyce started rubbing my thigh. I hoped she wasn't trying to get me hot. I'd made love to Betty Jean so many times today, my pecker felt like it had been deboned. It was as limp as a wet dishrag.

"Joyce, if you don't mind, I'd like to go on to sleep. It's been a long, tiresome weekend. I don't want to be too wore out in

177

the morning when I open up the store."

"All right, sugar." She stopped rubbing on me and moved closer to her side of the bed. After a loud sigh, she went on. "Since you brought up the subject, I've been feeling more worn out than usual myself lately. My stomach has been queasy off and on for several days. I took some pills this afternoon. I hope neither one of us is coming down with something serious."

"I think we just working too hard. Just keep taking them pills. That's what I been doing. I feel better than I felt yesterday, and the day before."

We had so much business Monday and Tuesday, I couldn't even take a call from Joyce when she called Tuesday morning, two hours after I'd opened up. I didn't get a chance to call her back until half a hour later. "Sadie told me you called. Sorry I couldn't talk then. The smell-goods man was here and I was going over my order with him. Right after he left, the toilet over-flowed, and I had to cover Buddy's cash register while he fixed it and mopped up the mess." I done my best to sound exasperated and rushed, so she wouldn't talk long. "This is the first chance today I had time to slow down and catch my breath."

"I was calling to see if you wanted to have lunch with me today. I sure would like some of that fried chicken at Mosella's."

"That would be nice, but I can't do it today. If you had asked sooner, I could have planned my day better. I'm so busy I don't have time to come pick you up."

"I can take the bus over there."

"No, I don't want you to do that. Today is not a good day, period. I wouldn't be able to be gone long enough for us to enjoy a nice leisurely lunch. Maybe we can go one day next week. My toy man is supposed to come this afternoon and show me his catalogue with all the play-pretties his company is offering for Christmas. And I got other vendors coming in this week that I need to meet with if I want everything delivered on time. If I ain't got enough merchandise for folks to buy for Christmas, it won't be a merry Christmas for me." I laughed.

"Oh, okay then. Before I forget, when do you think we can give that money to Yvonne and Milton? I was hoping we'd do it this week."

Just thinking about the extra money that was going to them dogs made me sick to my stomach. I had to hold my breath and count to five in my head to keep myself

179

from exploding. "We'll give it to them this Friday when we both get paid."

"Oh? You're going to go with me so we can give it to them before you go to your daddy's house?"

"Naw. I'll swing by the house and drop off my part of the money. You can take it to them. I don't want to go over there because you know how long-winded they can be. I like to drive to Daddy's house before it gets dark."

"Okay. Oh! Before I let you go, Milton said something about seeing us again tomorrow. I told him I wasn't sure." Joyce chuckled. "He said that if we didn't come over there, they might come see us."

"I'd rather go over there," I said dryly. "The less time they spend in our house, the better."

Joyce let out a long, loud breath. "Odell, don't be too hard on them. They can't help how crude they are. They haven't been home a week yet, so they must still be in shock. Please be a little more sympathetic."

"Joyce, they got other friends besides us. You act like *we* need to be babysitting them. I don't feel that way. For all you know, they don't neither. The last thing we need to do is make pests of ourselves. Milton probably wants to spend some time alone with

Yvonne. And I think that's what he would have been doing since they got out, if they didn't need the money so bad and had to host a bunch of drunks every night."

"That's a good point."

"We'll visit them again tomorrow, I guess. If you can donate twenty dollars out of your paycheck without it hurting, I'll add thirty. Fifty dollars should be enough. You can give it to them on Friday."

"Sweetie, I already told them we'd give them a hundred."

"Say what?"

"Odell, I told you that already. We discussed it last Sunday. Don't you remember?"

I gulped so hard I almost choked on some air. "Oh yeah, I remember now. I just wish you had talked to me before you made such a generous offer. That's a heap of money. They expect it now. We'd look bad if we didn't give them that amount."

"Then only give me the thirty you just offered. I'll chip in the rest. Giving up seventy dollars won't kill me, I guess . . ." I could just picture the pout on Joyce's face. "Never mind. I can give them the whole hundred myself."

I wanted to scream. But I said in the calmest tone I could manage, "Joyce, you don't

181

have to shell out nothing. Keep your money in case you want to do some shopping this weekend. I'll give them the whole hundred out of my pocket." The reason I was so calm now was because I suddenly decided to swipe the hundred bucks from one of them paper bags in her folks' pantry. So, in the long run, Joyce would be "chipping in" the whole amount.

"Odell! That's so generous of you!" she yelled.

"Well, I know my Bible, so I know that being generous is a virtue."

CHAPTER 19
JOYCE

The weather had gotten a lot cooler in the last couple of weeks. The days were getting shorter, and they seemed to be rolling by faster than usual. Thanksgiving was only eight days away and Odell and I were looking forward to it. I had already started planning the menu for the lavish supper I was going to prepare. We hadn't invited any guests, and if somebody showed up anyway, we'd probably not answer the door. Odell had made it clear that he wanted me all to himself that day. I had even bought a sexy negligee to wear later that night. I laughed to myself when I thought about how fast Odell would take it off me.

We went next door a few minutes past seven tonight. The door swung open as soon as Odell started knocking. "Come on in and get loose!" Sweet Sue greeted. "I was wondering where y'all was at."

Every time I saw Sweet Sue, I wondered

183

why men paid her to go to bed with them. Not only was she the thinnest woman I'd ever seen, she didn't have enough hair on her head to even need a comb. According to Buddy's and Sadie's gossip, she made more money turning tricks than any of the other prostitutes, so she was Aunt Mattie's favorite. Sweet Sue was nice enough to me, but I didn't like being around her that much. I had a hard time understanding how she — or any woman — could have sex with men for money and have the nerve to consider it a job. She gave me a quick one-armed hug. To my disgust, she hugged Odell with both arms long enough to make him squirm. I didn't like that one bit. My husband wasn't even attracted to pretty women, so I wasn't worried about him looking sideways at a plain Jane like Sweet Sue. "Find a seat and get off your feet," she told us. "Yvonne and Milton went to the backyard to help Willie Frank skin a possum to go in the stew Yvonne is cooking this evening."

We seated ourselves on the couch, and Sweet Sue skittered into the kitchen to get us some drinks. "I'm going to go in there and make sure she gives us clean glasses," I whispered to Odell. "The last time she gave me a drink there was a gnat floating in it."

When I got to the kitchen, Milton was standing next to Sweet Sue, watching as she filled our glasses all the way up to the brim. "Hey, Joyce. Good to see you again. Everybody missed y'all these past couple of nights," he said in a sugar-sweet tone. In a split second his tone turned gruff. "I just need to make sure Sweet Sue don't overfill the glasses like she been doing."

Sweet Sue made a hissing noise with her mouth, rolled her eyes, and cocked her smooth head to the side. "Then you need to get your black ass in here and fill them yourself," she growled.

Milton gently mauled the side of her head with his fist and gave her a threatening look. "Look-a-here, *Rapunzel;* you can talk to Willie Frank like that, but you can't talk to me that way in my own house."

"No, you look-a-here, Milton. You don't want to mess with *me,*" Sweet Sue responded, with a neck roll so exaggerated it looked like she was made of rubber. "And you know why . . ." I didn't want to hear any more of this conversation, so I was glad Willie Frank and Yvonne came through the back door before Sweet Sue finished her sentence. Milton looked so relieved. He rushed over to the sink next to Willie Frank, and they started washing possum blood off their hands.

Yvonne was carrying a big bowl filled with the carcass they'd cut up. The creature's head was on top, face up. "Hi, Joyce," she greeted as she dumped the meat into a big pot of boiling water on the stove. "This was one tough critter. Worse than that alligator we sliced up last month. We broke two knives!" she complained with a frown.

"Are you going to cook the head, too?" I asked, wincing because the possum's eyes were staring straight at me.

"Heck yeah!" Milton yelled. "Don't you?"

I winced again. "Uh-uh. *Never.*"

Milton laughed. "You ought to try it. The eyes taste like grapes. If you want us to, we'll save the head for you and —"

I held up my hand and cut him off. "That's all right. Odell is very particular about what he puts in his mouth."

"I bet he is," Milton said with a snicker. He was so ignorant and uncouth. Whenever he made comments like the one he'd just made, I could never tell if he was trying to be sarcastic or funny.

Willie Frank gave me a sideways glance before he said anything. "Speaking of Odell, did he come with you tonight?"

"He's in the living room, itching for somebody to bring him a drink," I replied. I didn't know if it was my imagination or what, but tonight it seemed like Milton and Yvonne were uncomfortable around me. And I had no idea why. Milton was shifting his weight from one foot to the other. Yvonne was blinking nervously and clearing her throat. They had never behaved this way in front of me before. The only thing I could think of was that we hadn't given Yvonne and Milton the money we promised, and they were getting antsy. There was only one way to fix that. "Milton, Yvonne, can I talk to y'all in private for a minute?"

Before they could respond, Willie Frank grabbed Sweet Sue by the hand. "We can take a hint," he said with a grin that seemed forced. He led her out of the room, and I waited a few moments before I said anything else. Yvonne and Milton were standing side by side, gazing at me with curious expressions on their faces.

"What is it, Joyce?" Milton asked.

"I know how close y'all and Willie Frank are. But I didn't think it would be smart for me to say too much in front of him. Or Sweet Sue."

Yvonne and Milton looked at each other, then back to me. "Joyce, spit it out," she ordered. "I need to get this possum stew cooked."

"And I need to get back out there and tend to our other guests," Milton tossed in.

I took a deep breath and told them what I knew they'd been waiting to hear. "This Friday is payday for me and Odell. I'll bring the hundred dollars when I come over that night." I couldn't remember the last time I saw them smile so fast and wide.

"Joyce, I am so glad to hear that." Milton danced a jig and clapped his hands. "Tonight, you and Odell can drink on the house."

"That's nice of you and thanks. But we don't mind paying for our drinks." I sniffed and rubbed my nose. I didn't like the way the room smelled, so I leaned over the pot on the stove and sniffed some more. "Ewww! I hope that possum tastes better than it smells." Then I gave Yvonne a stern look. "Girl, I know I've mentioned it to you before, but don't put the salt in that stew until it's almost done. And the next time, before the water starts to boil, put in a few drops of vinegar to cut that unholy stench."

"Thanks for giving me more cooking tips, Joyce." Yvonne glanced toward the living room. Milton snickered again.

"And another thing," I continued. "I don't think y'all should trust Sweet Sue to pour drinks. She puts her mouth in some strange places, if you know what I mean. So there is no telling where her hands have been." I lowered my voice. "By the way, I'd appreciate it if y'all didn't mention to anybody about our cash gift. We don't mind sharing, and we've loaned money to a lot of folks. But if they find out we gave y'all some money free and clear, they'll come out of the woodwork with all kinds of sob stories so they can jump on the bandwagon."

"Joyce, I swear to God, we ain't going to say nothing. When I get a chance tonight, I'm going to let Odell know myself just how much I appreciate his help," Milton declared.

"Good. You do that. One more thing, and please don't take this the wrong way. Odell and I still think that we can lift y'all up to our level of class, spirituality, and sophistication. We know we've got our work cut out for us and it's going to take a lot of time and effort on our part. But we are very patient." I put the most caring expression I could manage on my face.

From the blank looks on Yvonne's and Milton's faces, I had no idea what they were thinking. Had I just offended them? I wondered. I realized that wasn't the case when Yvonne smiled. "Joyce, I appreciate hearing that."

Milton smiled, too, and said, "I am so pleased God led us to you and Odell. You just made our day."

They looked and sounded so humble, I was impressed. Maybe they weren't so crude after all.

CHAPTER 20
MILTON

When I got back to the living room, Odell was all up in Dr. Patterson's face, grinning like a fool. The way he was kicked back on the couch with his legs crossed, a tall drink in his hand, and his head cocked to the side, he must have been spinning another one of his brags. As soon as he seen me, his face froze up like a sheet of ice. He set his drink on the coffee table, got up off the couch and walked up to me, dragging his feet like they weighed five pounds apiece.

"Hello, my man!" I greeted, gently punching the side of his arm. I added in a low tone, "Today is Wednesday. I hope you got my weekly payment."

He immediately showed his contempt for me with a frown so severe, it would have scared Satan. "I brung it," he snarled.

Odell probably despised me with a passion by now. That wasn't no big deal because a lot of folks hated me. Especially them other colored bootleggers, gamblers I'd cheated, and folks I had stole from. If I didn't let them roughnecks faze me, I sure was not about to let a sissified, uppity joker like Odell do it. "Why you giving me the stink-face?" I teased.

He didn't answer my question, but he tried to sound tough. "Look, I don't want to stay too long. Can we go somewhere to talk?"

I hunched my shoulders. "Yup. Let's go in the kitchen." When we got there, he pulled out his wallet and took out a bunch of dollar bills and handed them to me. "Bless your soul, Odell. Thank you." I bumped his shoulder with my fist. I counted to make sure it was the eight bucks for this week, plus the eight he missed last Wednesday. "Now, how you coming along scraping up that four hundred you owe me?"

"Look, I told you I'd get that money to you by the end of the month. I'm sick and tired of repeating myself. I don't want you to mention this matter to me no more until then," he snapped.

I gaped at him with my jaws tightening up so much, they ached when I spoke again. "What is your problem, Odell? People come here to have a good time. You looking and acting like you got a lemon stuck in your mouth. You ain't got no reason to be getting all hot and bothered with me — especially in my own house."

Odell gasped so hard he let out a hiccup. "How in the world can you say that after all you putting me through?"

"Well, with all due respect, you ought to be used to my requests by now."

He glared at me even harder. "Ha! I got news for you. I ain't used to being black-mailed and I never will be!"

I hunched my shoulders again. "Suit yourself. Believe it or not, I got some good news for you. I know a way I can help you, so this won't be too hard on you."

"Humph! I'd sure like to hear what that is! If *you* got good news for me, I know it's something that'll benefit you and Yvonne more."

"Well, you right. Let me lay it out for you short and sweet: If you want to, you can give me the four hundred in installments."

"What do you mean?"

"Since Joyce is bringing us that hundred-dollar gift this coming Friday, you can start making installments for the four hundred next week. Say fifty bucks one day, another fifty a couple of days later, more the next, and so on until you pay the whole amount."

"How is paying you off in bits and pieces

going to help me? You can forget that. Either way I'll be out the same amount of money this month. I'll give all the money to you at the same time!"

"All right then. That's fine with me. You ain't got to blow a fuse. I was trying to make it easier for you. We'll be cool with you so long as you give us that money and get us out of Lamar's debt. We ain't got no choice and you ain't neither."

"You greedy, low-down buzzard," Odell said with his teeth clenched.

My stomach knotted up. "Man, please don't low-rate me," I whined as I rubbed one of the scabs I still had on the side of my face. "I'm still trying to get over that beating I got on Halloween night, and the sheriff hauling me and my wife to jail. My emotions is still fragile. I know you got a big bee in your bonnet, but the least you could do is show me a little more compassion. I got feelings like everybody else."

Odell looked like he wanted to chew up my face. He blew out a harsh breath, waved his hand, and shook his head. Then he whirled around and rushed back to the living room.

Before I could leave the kitchen, Willie Frank stormed in with a wild-eyed look on his face. My sidekick was as white as he

194

could be, but when he got excited his face turned various shades of red. This time it was the color of a cherry. "What did you say to Odell? He looks mad as hell."

"Um . . . a few unexpected expenses came up that he need to take care of. So, he ain't too thrilled about lending us some money," I explained.

"How much did you ask him for?"

"Well, um, I told him to let us borrow as much as possible. He still don't know yet how much he can let us have. In the meantime, we still might have to hit up Dr. Patterson, Mr. Cunningham, and Aunt Mattie."

"Aunt Mattie? Didn't you tell me you was behind again on your pussy-cat tab at her house?"

"Dagnabbit! That's right!" I gave Willie Frank a frantic look. "Man, I can't ask her for no money until I bring my account up-to-date!"

Willie Frank gave me a thoughtful look. "Let me worry about that. I'll borrow what I can from her and give it to y'all. Just don't let her know about it."

"I won't. But what makes you think she'll lend you some money?"

"For one thing, I ain't never been late paying my tab. For another thing, I done sent her a heap of business. Half of the men in my family, and a lot of other white men I know wouldn't be going over there frolicking with her girls if I hadn't encouraged them. Besides, she was charitable enough to let me borrow the money I needed for the down payment on my truck."

"Willie Frank, I would love it if you'd do us that favor."

He shrugged. "That's what a friend is for." He grinned.

When everybody left, me and Yvonne poured the drinks folks hadn't finished, back into the jugs they'd come from. "I'm too tired. We'll clean up tomorrow when we get home from the grill. Let's go to bed."

When I got up Thursday morning around seven, I was pleased to see that Yvonne had already set breakfast on the kitchen table. "How come you got up so early?" I asked, wrapping my arms around her from behind while she wiped grease and crumbs off the counter.

She turned around and gave me a quick kiss before she answered. "There was too many things on my mind, I couldn't sleep no longer. I'm just worried about Odell."

"Why?"

"Milton, if we don't kill him, what if all

196

that other stuff we said we'd do don't work? He could be cooking up another scheme right now and do something else against us before we get him."

I didn't have nothing ready to say to that. I just stood there with my face froze up like a mask.

"Standing there looking stupid ain't helping none. I'm surprised at you. You supposed to be the one with all the smarts." Yvonne rolled her eyes and pulled out the chair in front of me. "Sit down and eat them grits and bacon before they get cold." She eased down into the chair across from me.

"One thing I want to say is, you ain't got no more on your mind than I got. So, get off my case." I bit into a piece of bacon and started smacking. Then a idea popped into my head that I couldn't wait to get out. I swallowed my food and took a long pull from the cup of coffee she'd set in front of me and let out a froggy belch. "If we don't kill him, I just thought of something we could do that would make him wish he was dead! Something much worse."

"What could be worse than us killing him?"

I winked at Yvonne. "Hear me out. After we get the money, we could tell Joyce about Betty Jean. If we make him lose everything he got now, his life wouldn't be worth a plugged nickel. Remember how all them rich white folks jumped off bridges, and in front of speeding trains, blew their own brains out, and whatnot when the economy dropped so low and put them in the poorhouse?"

"Suicide?" Yvonne screwed up her lips like that word had a nasty taste to it. I couldn't understand why. It was another form of murder. "Do you think Odell would be so distressed he'd take his own life?"

"Wouldn't you if you was in his shoes? I know I would. That would be the sweetest revenge, and we wouldn't have to get none of his blood on our hands!"

"Well, we did want him dead at first. And like Willie Frank said, as long as he's breathing, he'll be a threat. You know something, sugar; if he don't take his own self out, I definitely do believe he'd lose his mind and end up in that nuthouse permanently, where some of them other folks went when they lost everything. That's almost as bad as being dead, maybe even worse. No matter how you look at this situation, Odell's goose is cooked."

"To a crisp," I added, laughing so hard my sides ached.

198

CHAPTER 21
ODELL

Friday evening after Buddy and Sadie left for the day, I took all the money from the cash registers and carried it to my office. I locked the door when I got inside and dropped the money on top of my desk so I could admire it. "Lord, this is getting better and better. Every day is Christmas," I said to myself out loud as I stared at the cash. Despite all the misery Yvonne and Milton was putting me through, I was still a very happy man.

After I set aside enough money to put back in the registers for us to make change on Monday, I took my cut off the top and put what was left into a paper bag.

It had been raining off and on most of the day, and it was pretty windy and chilly when I left the store. The excitement of gazing at them dollar bills before I left my office had wore off. Now my mood was almost as gloomy as the weather. The next thing I knew, I was so mad I was about to bust open because I had agreed to give Joyce money to take to them greedy pigs next door, this evening.

When I arrived at my in-laws' house to drop off the week's profits, Mac and Millie was sitting on the living-room couch listening to the radio when I walked in. "Evening, y'all. This was another good week." I grinned as I waved the bag in front of them.

"Good! I know so long as we got you running the show, we'll always have a good week — even when we have a bad week!" my father-in-law yelled, laughing and clapping his hands like a seal. It wasn't even dark yet and he was already in his pajamas. There was a stocking cap on his head to keep the pomade he slathered onto his scalp from messing up Millie's pillowcases.

"Odell, you know where to put it," Millie piped in. "Put this week's profits in one of them bags that ain't too full. It's getting pretty crowded in that pantry." She gave me a warm smile. "Son, you such a godsend. I don't know what we'd do if you was to up and quit."

I done a double take. "Me quit? Only a crazy man would leave a job like mine. God knows I ain't even half crazy!" I insisted.

"I'm glad to hear that. Listen here, me

and Mac been thinking about one change we'd like to make. And I hope you'll be willing to go along with it."

Millie's words made me nervous right away. I could already feel my blood pressure rising. I held my breath and watched her face. She was still smiling, so it didn't seem like she was leading up to something that would disrupt the good thing I had going. "I . . . I hope it ain't too big of a change. I am so happy with everything the way it is."

"Oh, it ain't no big deal," she assured me. "What we might do in the very near future is have you take the profits home every Friday, or every day if you'd prefer. You and Joyce can store the money in your pantry, or the attic. That is, if you don't mind being responsible for it. If we do that, you won't have to worry about coming over here every Friday. That way, you can leave straight from the store to go visit your daddy."

"Me and Joyce wouldn't mind storing the money at all." I never expected to hear something so sweet. I was so relieved.

"That's good, son. The time you save would be more time you could spend with your daddy; bless your soul," Mac tossed in.

My heart felt like it was doing somersaults.

"Just let us know when you want me to start taking the money home. Now if y'all don't mind, I'll put this away and be on my way. I don't want Daddy to worry or think I ain't coming."

"All right then." Mac grinned. "Just don't step on my fishing poles when you go in the pantry."

I chuckled to myself when I got inside the pantry. It was hard to believe that such a ordinary-looking room had a small fortune in it and had become my own personal piggy-bank. After I deposited the money and conversated a few minutes more with my in-laws, I hugged them and skittered back out the door. I had to go by my house to drop off the money I told Joyce I'd give her to give them devils this evening.

When I let myself in the front door, she shot out of the kitchen and into the living room like a bullet. She didn't stop until she got up to me and gave me a quick kiss. "Hello, sweetie. Did you bring the money for me to take next door?" she panted. "I expected you before now. I was beginning to think you'd forgot and had headed to your daddy's house."

"I didn't forget, baby." I sucked in my breath and folded my arms. "You ain't got to be so anxious about this thing."

"Well, it's just that Yvonne and Milton are really looking forward to the money. Since you said you'd give me the whole hundred, I didn't go to the bank to cash my check. I don't have that much on me, so I hope you have the full amount. I don't want to disappoint them."

I wanted to scream! Disappoint them crooks? They'd been disappointing me for weeks. "Yeah, I brung it all." I rolled my eyes and took out my wallet.

"I wish we could give them even more," Joyce said as I handed the bills to her.

"A hundred dollars is more than enough to be giving away with no strings attached. I'm glad that's all you told them we'd give," I said in a gruff tone.

"The next time I won't offer to give them money unless I discuss it with you first."

I gasped. "*Next time?* Joyce, I pray to God there won't be no next time. We ain't rich. I don't want you to make them get the notion that they can fall back on us whenever they get in a pickle."

"All right," she said, barely above a whisper. I didn't like the pout on her face, so I pulled her into my arms and kissed her. We was still standing in front of the door. But I wasn't going to stick around much longer. She had other ideas in her head, though.

"Sugar, can you wait a little while before you leave?" she cooed, nodding toward our bedroom. "My period is probably going to start tomorrow, and I'll be out of commission by the time you get back home on Sunday . . ."

Now that she was back in a good mood, I had to take advantage of it even though it was going to delay me. "I can't think of nothing I'd rather do more. A little loving would be a good way to start off my weekend in them boondocks with Daddy and that crazy wife of his."

After I'd pleasured Joyce and myself for about twenty minutes, I got back in my clothes and took off. I didn't want to waste no more time washing up, and I would be sorry I hadn't.

When I got to Betty Jean's house, she met me at the door with her arms wide-open and her lips puckered. We embraced and kissed so passionately my whole body tingled. After having three babies, her body was still amazing. Her breasts and butt were as firm as they'd been when I met her. She was only eighteen then. The rest of her was soft where she was supposed to be soft. I loved the way she felt, and I thought she was enjoying being close to me, too, until her body got stiff. Now it felt like I was hugging a tree. She reared back and looked up at me with her eyebrows furrowed. "Odell, you could have at least cleaned yourself off before you came over here."

"What do you mean? I ain't dirty."

"I smell Joyce all over you. Even on your lips . . ."

I felt picked on and abused, and I let Betty Jean know that right away. "What do you expect? Joyce is my wife. I have to give her some pleasure, too."

I could tell from her long, loud sigh that she felt frustrated and slighted by what I'd just said. "And you ain't never going to let me forget that." She frowned, pried my arms from around her, and stormed into the kitchen.

"Don't you start," I advised, stumbling along behind her. When we stopped in front of the stove, she snatched a long-handled spoon off the counter and started stirring the pot of turnip greens she was cooking. My marriage wasn't what I wanted to conversate about, so I abruptly changed the subject. "Where the boys at?"

She didn't turn around to face me. "They went down the road to play with them Martin kids. I told them to come home before dark."

"Good. We got the house to ourselves so

we can get as loud and frisky as we want to." I wrapped my arms around her again. She pushed me back so hard with her elbow, I fell against the kitchen table. "What's wrong with you? How do you expect us to make that baby girl we want so bad?"

"You ain't putting your hands on me until you wash your nasty self!"

I didn't say nothing else. I wanted to get back to her as quick as I could, so I spun around and zoomed into the bathroom. I gargled with some baking soda and hot water and scrubbed myself until I was squeaky clean.

CHAPTER 22
JOYCE

Odell had been gone about an hour before I decided to go next door. When I walked into the living room, Milton was in a corner chatting with Sweet Sue. His hand was on her arm and he was looking at her like she was a beauty queen. How Yvonne could stand to let that happen in her own house was a mystery to me. I had to keep reminding myself that they didn't have the high morals Odell and I had.

While I stood there scanning the room and taking off my coat, Willie Frank strutted over to me. The next thing I knew, he snatched my coat out of my hand and draped it across the back of the couch. Then he grabbed my arm and guided me to a corner. Other than drinking and having a good time, he and I had nothing in common. But I liked him because he was so amusing and fun to talk to. "Joyce, let's me and you chitchat for a spell. I need a little downtime before I go bust up that glee going on between Milton and Sweet Sue," he said with a mighty belch.

Before I realized what I was saying, words I hadn't given much thought slid out of my mouth before I could stop them. "Well, she is a busy lady when it comes to men. Everybody knows that's how she makes her money."

Willie Frank laughed. "And everybody knows she's my old gal. But she still has to beat men off with a stick — even when I'm around!"

"I guess she can't help it because she gets a lot of attention for a . . . uh . . . ordinary-looking woman." I couldn't believe that an "ordinary-looking woman" like me could let such a statement slip out! But because Odell told me how beautiful I was so often, sometimes I forgot how I really look.

I was glad Willie Frank brushed off my comment. He even laughed again, but I noticed a tinge of sadness in his tone. "Well, I'll tell you. Me, and a heap of other men, are more interested in what a woman's got from her mouth on down, and what she can do with it."

I laughed, even though my face got so hot I had to fan it. "Willie Frank, you stop that! We'll chat some more later." I moved away before he could say anything else.

Yvonne was standing alone by the wall, sipping from a large jar. Her face lit up when she saw me, so I started walking in her direction.

When I stopped in front of her, she waved the jar in my face. "Hi, Joyce. I'm glad you made it. This is the third and last drink I'm having tonight. I need to keep my wits about me," she slurred.

"Hi, Yvonne. You sober enough for us to talk?"

"Hell yeah! What about?"

I looked around to make sure nobody was close enough to hear what I was about to say. "Um . . . you can let Milton know I brought the money," I whispered.

Her lips formed a smile that was so extreme, she looked like a clown. "You brung the whole hundred?"

"Yup, I did. Don't talk so loud. I don't want folks to know my business."

"Okay. I'm so pleased you came through for us," she said in a low tone with a wistful look on her face. "You and Odell been so good to us. I just wish that we was half as sophisticated and classy as y'all. That way we could relate to one another better and our relationship might be even closer than it is now."

209

I rarely saw Yvonne's sensitive side. When I did, I wished that Odell and I had not started feeling resentment toward them so soon in our relationship. I hoped that in the future we'd move past our petty differences and be more tolerant and actually become *real* friends. "I appreciate hearing that. I feel the same way," I replied, hoping she'd change the subject before one, or both of us, became too emotional.

Yvonne gave me a curious look and then she whispered, "By the way, did you ever try that headstand trick I told you about that could help you get pregnant?"

"Pffft! Girl, please." I giggled and gave her a dismissive wave. "I tried it one time and almost fell over and broke my neck. With my gangly long legs and arms, I am not graceful enough to stand on my head for one minute, let alone ten."

"I know what you mean. I don't know what made me suggest something like that to a woman your size in the first place."

I wished she hadn't added that last comment, but I was determined to overlook as many of her put-downs as possible. So I just giggled again.

"Listen," she went on, still whispering. She paused and leaned closer to me. "You ever thought about going to visit a hoodoo?

Maybe one of them could give you something that would do the trick. Like Aunt Mattie. She done cured a lot of sick people, changed folks' luck, and done a bunch of other things, good and bad. Or so folks claim. Helping you get pregnant ought to be a piece of cake for her."

My mouth dropped open and I stared at Yvonne like she was crazy. "Hoodoo? Do you believe in that stuff?" My heart started beating so hard and fast, I got scared.

She gave me a pensive look before she replied. "To tell you the truth, I'm too scientific to believe everything I hear about that. But . . ."

"But what?"

"Well, for all I know, it could work. I done heard a lot of stories about folks getting what they want by going to a hoodoo."

"If you think there's something to it, how come you haven't tried it? If anybody could use some help getting their lives in order, it's you and Milton."

Yvonne narrowed her eyes. "We doing all right without it. You see they didn't keep us in jail!" she snapped. "I'm just trying to help you out," she added in a softer tone.

"And I appreciate it," I said. "Uh . . . I'm scientific, too, so I hadn't thought about anything as extreme as a hoodoo," I lied.

"Besides, Aunt Mattie has such a long tongue, she'd blab to the wrong person and I don't want folks to know how desperate I am to have a baby." Yvonne was the last person I'd tell about the neipee I'd tried. I didn't think she'd blab my business to somebody else, but information as juicy as me turning to hoodoo would probably be something else for her to rub in my face that would make me feel like a freak. "I'm just going to keep praying and hope God will bless me before I get too old."

"Well, I'll keep praying for you, too." She let out a loud sigh and turned her attention toward Milton. When she motioned for him to join us, he scurried across the floor like a squirrel. I followed them into the kitchen to a spot in front of the broom closet.

"What's up?" he asked, glancing from me to Yvonne. He looked as excited as a kid on Christmas morning.

"Baby, Joyce brung that hundred dollars we been expecting."

"God is good! Give it here!" Milton hollered, already holding out his hand.

I pulled the wad of bills out of my purse. "It's mostly fives and tens. You want to count it?"

"Naw, that ain't necessary. We trust you." Milton snatched the money, folded it, and slid it into his pocket. Then he turned to Yvonne. "Baby, you go back out there with Joyce and I'll go put the money away." Before she could respond, he whirled around and darted across the floor so fast, he almost ran into the wall.

After two drinks, a few deviled eggs, and some fried green tomatoes, my stomach started feeling queasy. I went home and took a pill, but it didn't make me feel any better. I read for an hour, took another pill, and went to bed.

I was on the couch drinking my first cup of coffee when Yvonne knocked on the door Saturday morning at seven thirty. I had drunk a neipee drink a few minutes ago. This time I'd used a whole teaspoon of the powder and it had left a foul taste in my mouth. The coffee was helping get rid of that nasty taste. I was getting impatient with the neipee mixture, and I felt much better than I had last night, but not well enough to entertain company. I smiled anyway. "Good morning, Yvonne."

"Morning, Joyce. Brrrr. It's getting so cold outside," she complained, blowing on her hands. She wore a man's black, double-breasted peacoat over a bright red dress with black buttons from the neck down to

213

the hem. She looked like the inside of a watermelon. I had never seen her in these homely pieces before.

I winced as I looked her over. I had never seen her looking so dowdy. She was more into cute skimpy dresses, skintight britches, and low-cut blouses. I had to comment on her outfit. "I'm not used to seeing you dressed like that."

She slapped the side of her thigh and guffawed like a hyena. "I ain't used to dressing in nothing this plain. Somebody left this coat at the house one night and never asked for it back. And I don't remember where I picked up this dress. I put it on because I ain't done laundry this week. But there wasn't no reason for me to put on no makeup and one of my good frocks just to come next door, right?" I wondered how she could rattle off so many words all in the same breath.

"Right. Well, since you're here, make yourself at home." I sighed as I slowly beckoned her in.

"How you feeling now?" She rushed in and immediately started walking toward the couch with me dragging my feet behind her.

I decided that if she stayed more than ten minutes, I would claim to be sick again, and needed to be in bed. "Much better. Thank you for asking."

"Good. I'd hate for you to be sick over here by yourself."

"I'm used to being by myself." We dropped down on opposite ends of the couch. "You want some coffee?"

"Uh-uh. I already had two cups." Yvonne paused and scratched the side of her head. "Thank you again for that money you gave us last night."

"You're welcome. Um . . . you're out and about mighty early today. You could have waited until later to check up on me."

"I know. But I was at such loose ends, sitting around the house twiddling my thumbs. You know me, I always like to be doing something. I seen you go out and empty the trash a few minutes ago, and I decided to come over and check on you. And to see if I could borrow some nutmeg. I want to make candied yams for the Thanksgiving supper at Dr. Patterson's house."

"I don't have any right now. I'm making yams, too, so I'll tell Odell to bring some from the store on Monday."

"You think he'd mind bringing enough for me?"

I waved my hand and chuckled. "Girl, please. You know Odell would be happy to bring enough for you. He's so considerate

215

and thoughtful." I didn't know if anybody noticed how often I praised my husband. But I couldn't help myself. He was one of a kind. "He'd give anybody his last dollar if they needed it. And he's got a few other qualities that set him apart from every other man I know. I feel sorry for women who are stuck with dull, weak, cheesy men. By the way, where is Milton?"

"At the house. Unless him and Willie Frank is going fishing, he don't like to go out too early in the day on a weekend. He says when he do, bad luck always seem to come his way."

"Oh? It seems like bad luck finds him any day, any time. I'm sure he's still trying to get over that beating he got last month."

"Pffft. He done almost got over that," Yvonne chirped.

"I guess it was nothing compared to y'all getting arrested and roughed up this month, huh?"

"That's for sure." She exhaled and stood up. "I guess I'll be getting back to the house. We still have a little cleaning up to do. You wouldn't believe all the ashes and crumbs folks dropped on my floor last night. Our place is a pigsty."

"Tell me about it," I said with a groan. "Every time I'm over there, I step in enough ashes to build an ant hill. I know y'all do a little cleaning up every night after your guests leave. But y'all need to do a lot more." I immediately wished I hadn't made those comments. The woeful look on Yvonne's face now was so extreme, it made me feel bad. I had to backpedal. "Oops." I chuckled. "I need to watch what I say. I'm sure some folks say the same thing about my house."

"Your house look like a showroom every time I come over here." Yvonne sighed and started inching toward the door. I stood up and followed her. The way she was taking her time, I was afraid she'd change her mind and stay longer.

When we reached the door, I opened it immediately. "I think I'd better get back in bed. My stomach is starting to feel queasy again." It really was feeling queasy again, but not enough for me to go back to bed. I just didn't feel like entertaining an uninvited guest. She looked a little hurt and I felt bad about that. I had to keep reminding myself that Odell and I were supposed to be helping them get over their arrest ordeal. I decided I'd wait about an hour or so and then I'd go to her house. "I sure don't want to be sick on Thanksgiving."

"Get plenty of rest, eat right, and you'll

be just fine," she advised, patting my arm. "By the way, do you and Odell have big plans for Thanksgiving?"

I took a deep breath and puffed out my chest. "Do we? It's going to be such a blessed event. I'm going to cook a nice turkey supper with all the trimmings for just the two of us. I'm even going to put candles on the table. Oh! It's going to be so romantic. I swear to God, if folks didn't know any better, they'd think Odell and I were still newlyweds." There I was praising him again, but it was hard not to. "That's how we've celebrated the day for the past three years. We used to spend it with Mama and Daddy, but they always invite so many folks from church and the neighborhood, it gets to be too hectic. That's why we stopped going. They do the same thing for Christmas every year. It's the most important holiday to them, and us. If we stopped eating with them on the Lord's birthday, we'd never hear the end of it."

"Me and Milton talked about having a Christmas party, but we ain't made no definite plans yet. With the extra money from y'all, I can buy a bunch of gifts for my kids."

"Oh? Do you think your aunt and uncle will be bringing them over to celebrate

Christmas with y'all?"

"I wrote a letter to Aunt Nadine last week and asked her. She wrote back right away and said no because they'd already brung them over here a few weeks ago. Besides, my uncle's arthritis is so bad he hates to drive all the way from Mobile. Aunt Nadine never learned how to drive, so they only get in that old truck when they have to these days."

"That's too bad." I gave Yvonne a sympathetic look and shook my head. "It's a shame your folks still don't want your kids to know you're their real mama until they get grown."

"Well, I agreed to that arrangement when they was babies because I was living from pillar to post with all the wrong men. There ain't nothing I can do about that now. Them two years I spent in jail, then marrying Milton and starting a bootlegging business, clinched the deal. My folks is so holy, they would never overlook my lifestyle and bring my kids to visit me more often." A sad look crossed Yvonne's face. She sniffled and cleared her throat before she spoke again. "We might also use some of the money from you and Odell to ride the bus to Mobile. That way we can spend Christmas and a few days with my kids."

I folded my arms and gave her a stern look. "I don't think that's such a good idea."

"Huh?" Yvonne looked so confused you would have thought I was speaking Spanish. She blinked and hunched her shoulders. "You don't?" She didn't sound so chirpy now.

"The thing is, if you and Milton miss more work too soon, y'all will have more money problems. And I don't think Odell would be willing for us to give y'all another cash gift anytime soon."

"Well, we'll cross that bridge when and if we get to it. Thinking about money all the time is so stressful." Yvonne didn't look like she was worried at all. But I was. I had a feeling I'd regret getting involved in their business when money was the issue. And I was sure Odell would feel the same way.

CHAPTER 23
YVONNE

When I got back home, Milton was standing at the kitchen sink cleaning the chicken feet I was going to cook and serve to our guests tonight. "How come you back so soon? Queen of Sheba must have said something you didn't like again." He chuckled.

"You got that right. But that didn't bother me much. I didn't bother saying nothing mean about her this time. It ain't never done no good. Anyway, I told her we might use some of the money they gave us to buy gifts and take the bus to Mobile to see my kids next month." I got up close to Milton and nuzzled the back of his neck. He whirled around and gave me a peck on my cheek. "Baby, you wouldn't believe what she had the nerve to say when she heard that."

"I'd believe you. That Joyce got such a reckless tongue, she is liable to say anything." Milton wiped his hands on the dishrag. He winced when I told him what Joyce had said about our future money problems. "Humph. She might not think Odell will give us no more money. But we ain't worried, is we?"

"Nope. Them words came from her, not him. He is the cash cow in that house, and we will milk him as much as we can. Did you ever get around to asking him to give us Lamar's money in installments?"

"Yeah, I asked him. But he didn't go for that. He claims he'll give it all to me at the same time."

"Is that the day we tell Joyce about him and Betty Jean?"

"No, Yvonne. I think we should hold off on that a little longer."

"Why? So we can get a little more money from him?"

"Uh, I doubt if he'll give us any more after giving us the four hundred."

"*Four* hundred?" I had to act surprised, but I really wanted to laugh and get in Milton's face about lying to me about the amount. But it was not that big of a deal to me anymore. Besides, I'd never tell him when I got extra money from Odell to spend on myself.

"Oops. Did I say four hundred? I meant three hundred. I got confused. Um . . . . I guess I was counting the hundred Joyce gave us last night. That'd make it four hundred. I declare, I need to stop drinking so much. It's throwing my brain off-kilter." Milton grinned and started rocking from side to side.

"Yeah. The same goes for me." I gawked at him from the corner of my eye. He stopped grinning and rocking and I went on. "Guess what else she said?" He didn't answer. He just dipped his head and stared at me with a amused look on his face. "She had the nerve to say she can't tell the difference when I do my housecleaning."

"That uppity bitch. She got some nerve insinuating you ain't a good housekeeper."

"I'm sick of her being so high-and-mighty. When we tell her about Odell and Betty Jean, let me do most of the talking. And before we do that, I'm going to practice everything I want to say. That way I won't forget nothing."

Milton blinked and scratched his chin. "Where do you think we should tell her at?"

"It don't make no difference where."

"Yes, it do. We can't tell her over here. She might go berserk and scream her head off. If guests show up before we can hush her up, we'd have some explaining to do. A outburst like that could spook folks."

One reason Milton made a better criminal than me was because he always thought things through more than I did. "I hadn't thought about that. What if we go to her job and tell her there?"

Milton rolled his eyes. "What's wrong with you? With all them teachers and uppity school folks in the mix, that would be even worse. I think we should just go over to her house one day. It'd have to be a weekend when Odell ain't there. If she gets hysterical and her body shuts down, she'll be in the comfort of her own home."

I blew out some air and shook my head. "What if she don't believe us? We ain't got no proof."

A concerned look crossed Milton's face. "Hmmm. That's a good point. Odell got her so dick-lashed, all he'd have to do is deny everything. She'd probably believe him over us."

"No matter what she believes, our relationship with them would be over."

"Humph. Our relationship with them was over the day Odell made that call to Sheriff Potts. We'll just continue to act normal, and keep everything on the back burner until we get paid." Milton sighed and picked up another chicken foot. I was surprised to see such a miserable look on his face now. "I

224

had such high hopes. I thought that by associating with them, we'd learn how to be more polished and mellow. I never thought we would end this way."

"Well, one good thing that came out of this mess is that we'll get the money we need to pay off Lamar," I reminded him.

Milton narrowed his eyes and wagged the chicken foot he was about to clean in my face. "That's so true."

"What happens after we get it?"

"We'll give it to Willie Frank, and he can give it to his uncle Lamar."

"What I meant was, what'll happen after we pay that off?"

"Yvonne, I ain't following you. The important thing is, we'll be in the clear."

"With Lamar, yes. But we'll still be in a hole."

Milton gave me a curious look. "What about that hundred-dollar cash gift Joyce brung us? That'll cover them days we had to miss work last week, and then some."

"We'll be halfway in a hole, then. Maybe we should still try to get some money from Aunt Mattie, Mr. Cunningham, and Dr. Patterson. That way we'll have a cushion to get us through the rest of this year."

"Yvonne, whatever we get from them, we'd have to pay back. If we don't borrow no money, we won't owe nobody. What's the point of getting out of one black hole and diving into another?"

"Then we should ask Odell to add another three hundred to that three we already getting from him, huh? A jackpot that big would suit me just fine. We'll have the kind of Christmas we deserve."

"Hold on now. We don't need to be greedy."

"Milton, if he already agreed to give us three hundred dollars, it shouldn't be that hard to get him to give us a extra three. Besides, this will probably be the only time in our lives we'll have a chance to get so much money free and clear."

"That's a good point."

"You damn right. If you don't want to ask him to give us six hundred this month, we'll settle for the three he already promised. We'll wait a little while and ask for the other three. Maybe a week or two later." I folded my arms and gave Milton a hopeful look. "Well?"

"I'll have to think about it."

"Don't 'think about it' too long. We need to get paid before we tell Joyce about him and Betty Jean. Whatever day we get the last lump sum, we'll tell her."

"I guess that makes a lot of sense." Milton

paused and gave me a thoughtful look. "I'm having second thoughts about us telling her at her house, though. If she was to flip out and start throwing and breaking things, we could get clobbered."

"I ain't scared of Joyce. I don't care how much bigger she is than me, I'll fight her if I have to."

Milton cussed under his breath and gave me a sorry look. "Shut your mouth! The last thing we need to do is get in a violent situation with a woman who is already going to be hurting like a broke leg when we tell her what kind of snake she married. If we tell her when she ain't close enough to grab something, we'll be fine. Let's come up with a better place than her house."

After hearing what Milton just said, a thought jumped into my head so fast, it almost gave me a buzz. "I got it. I know where we should tell Joyce about Odell and Betty Jean in a way she'll have to believe us." I didn't wait for him to say nothing. "We'll tell her we want to treat her to a nice supper for being so generous to us. We can let the cat out the bag in a restaurant."

"Didn't I just say we don't need to tell her in a place where she can grab something to hit us with?"

I nodded. "Yup. The only weapon she

227

could get her hands on in a restaurant would be something like a chair. With waiters and waitresses milling about, I don't think they'd let her go too far. As soon as she gets hysterical, they'd just make us leave." I was talking so fast I had to stop and catch my breath.

"Yvonne, why do you want to do it in a restaurant?"

"Hush up and hear me out. I ain't talking about just any restaurant. We'll borrow Willie Frank's truck and take her to the same one in Hartville where Odell hangs out with that woman and them kids. When we get up in there, we'll ask around until we hook up with the waitresses that know him, and we'll get them to back up our story."

Milton's eyes lit up like lightbulbs. "Baby, that's brilliant. Ooowee. I can't wait." His excitement didn't last long. A few seconds later, his eyebrows furrowed and he shook his head.

I put my hands on my hips and glared at him. "What's wrong now?" I asked.

He hesitated before he answered. "Baby, we still got to worry about Joyce getting hysterical. She'd draw all kinds of attention that'll make us look bad, too. People might think we as crazy as she is just because we with her."

"So what?" I snickered and shook my finger in Milton's face. "The important thing is, with them waitresses backing us up, Joyce will have to believe what we tell her."

"But how would we keep her calm during the ride back to Branson? You know what a fool she is for Odell. She might forgive him and get mad at us for busting her bubble."

"Milton, we ain't responsible for Odell fooling around on her."

"She might pull a kill-the-messenger stunt on us."

"You mean blame us for delivering bad news?"

"Exactly. Please keep that in mind."

"I will, sugar. But I don't think we should let that stop us."

"Look, Yvonne. The bottom line is, we'll tell her and deal with the consequences the best way we can. Now go in the tool drawer and get me them pliers so I can pull the toenails off these damn chicken feet."

229

CHAPTER 24
MILTON

I was glad I had come clean and told Yvonne I'd been blackmailing Odell, but I didn't see no reason to keep coming clean. It was too late in the game for me to do something that extreme — and stupid. I thought I'd bust a gasket a few minutes ago when she brung up the subject of us asking Odell for a extra three hundred, and I'd let "four hundred dollars" slip out. I'd played it off real good. The last thing I wanted her to know was that I was up to no good. That wasn't likely to happen no time soon, though. My woman trusted me and believed everything I told her. She was almost as easy to manipulate as Odell.

The way things was going with him, and since he was going to be out of the picture soon, I didn't see no reason not to get additional money from him. Before Yvonne brung it up, I had already decided that I really was going to put the bite on him for another *five* hundred. With the extra one hundred I was already going to get from him on top of the first three hundred we had coming, two hundred more on top of the *other* three she suggested would suit me just fine.

After Yvonne left the kitchen, I put the chicken feet in a vinegar marinade and set the pan in the ice box. I was relaxing on the living-room couch with a stiff drink when somebody stomped up on the porch. I got up right away and opened the door, surprised to see Joyce. It had been a hour and a half since Yvonne had left Joyce's house. "Come on in. We was just talking about you."

"Something good, I hope." She grinned. "Is Yvonne here? I went over to see my mama after she left my house and Mama had some nutmeg. I borrowed some for Yvonne to use." I gave Joyce a confused look. "She told me she wanted to make some candied yams to take to Dr. Patterson's house when y'all go over there for Thanksgiving," she explained.

"Oh. That's right. Hold on, I'll go get her. Have a seat."

Joyce handed me a little glass container with a lid on it. "I couldn't take the whole can so I put some in this jar. I hope it's enough," she said, dropping down onto the couch. "I hope Yvonne keeps improving her cooking skills. I'm going to put together some recipes for her."

I knew that sow had to throw in a dig at one of us. "Yvonne appreciates all your help, Joyce," I said with a smirk, which I'm sure she didn't even notice. That was the way it was with people wrapped up in themselves like her and Odell. I set the jar on the coffee table and scurried into the bedroom. Yvonne was making the bed. "Baby, Joyce just brung you some nutmeg."

"That's nice to hear. Tell her I said thanks."

"Come tell her yourself. If I got to listen to another one of her digs, I don't want to be by myself."

Yvonne let out a disgusted sigh and scrunched up her lips. "Whatever she said this time, I don't want to hear it. They low-rate us enough."

"Don't worry, sugar. We still got the upper hand. They just don't know it yet. Do you think we should go in there and invite her to go out for supper now?"

"Now? Uh-uh. We still got almost two weeks before we get our first big payout from Odell. If we ask her too soon, something could happen that'd make her change her mind. She could tell Prince Charming and he might insist on going with us."

"Yvonne, you know me. I already thought of that. We'll tell her we asked Mr. Cunningham if we could borrow his truck to go out in, but he can't let us use it until sometime next month. We'll pick a Friday, so Odell won't be able to go when she tells him about it. He wouldn't cancel a visit to Betty Jean's house to go to heaven, let alone to go have supper with us."

"That's for sure. But if we tell Joyce we want to eat at that place in Hartville, you know she'll mention that to Odell. And what do you think will go through his mind?"

"I got that covered, too. Girl, I'm always on the ball," I said with my chest puffed out. "We'll make her think we're going to supper at a restaurant in Branson or Mobile. At the last minute, we'll tell her we want the supper to be even more special; so, we decided to go to one in Hartville that's real popular with our guests. Now come on and let's talk to her together."

When we got to the living room, Joyce was dusting the coffee table with a handkerchief. That heifer! "I can't stand to be around a lot of dust. It makes me sneeze and it looks so nasty," she complained with a grimace on her face. "Yvonne, if you don't have any furniture cleaner, you can use vinegar and water, or just plain water."

Yvonne sucked in her breath. From the corner of my eye, I seen her jaws twitching. "Thanks for the housekeeping advice, Joyce. And thanks for the nutmeg," she mumbled, looking at the little jar like it was a rotten apple. "I thought you was sick and in the bed?"

"Yeah, but . . . uh . . . I felt better quicker than I thought I would. So, I got back up and went to visit my mama."

"Well, you look fit as a fiddle, Joyce. Now look-a-here; we want to show our appreciation to you for being so nice and generous to us lately. We got a itching to treat you to supper at a nice restaurant. There is a place in Mobile that sells some scrumptious crab cakes and mustard greens. Mr. Cunningham said we can borrow his truck. We'll all get gussied up like film stars. Marcel your hair, dress up in something fancy, and splash on a heap of one of them smell-goods you own. We want it to be a evening you will remember for years to come," I said.

From the stupefied look on Joyce's face, you would have thought I'd just handed her a pot of gold. "Y'all want to take me all the way to Mobile just to eat? It's been two years since I went to a restaurant over

234

there!" she exclaimed. "That would be so nice. The last time I dressed up was to attend a funeral. But first let me check with Odell to see if he'll be available. I'll have to make sure his blue suit is clean. Not that he doesn't look dapper in any of his other suits."

"See . . . uh . . . the only thing is, me and Yvonne want to go on a Friday or Saturday. We know how much you like peach cobbler and them is the only days they serve it. Odell is with his daddy on them days every week."

"I already eat too much peach cobbler, so y'all don't have to accommodate me for that reason. In that case, why don't we go on a weekday? I'm sure he'd love to join us," Joyce chirped.

"The only thing is, we can't not do business at home on no weekday nights for a while. We need the money. I thought about your suggestion that we don't take no time off work again too soon," Yvonne piped in.

Joyce raised her eyebrows and looked from Yvonne to me and back. "If we go out on a weekend, y'all wouldn't make any money that night, so what's the difference?" I had no idea she would be this difficult. But we wasn't about to give up. We was going to get her to that restaurant in Hartville even if we had to knock her out and hog-tie her.

Yvonne came up with a answer real quick. "I got it!" she yelled, snapping her fingers. "We'll do some overtime to make up for that evening. For the next couple of weekends, we'll let our guests know they can come to our house and start drinking around noon instead of them waiting until evening."

I held my breath. I was scared Joyce would ask how come we hadn't already done that before. She didn't, so I went on. "Another reason we have to go on a Friday or Saturday is because Mr. Cunningham said we could only borrow his truck on a weekend. His nephew uses it to get to work every evening during the week."

"Oh. Well, I'd sure hate for Odell to miss out on a nice supper. What about borrowing Willie Frank's truck? Then we wouldn't have to go out on a weekend," Joyce said.

"His motor is on the blink and he ain't sure when he can get that took care of," I said. "He don't think it's a good idea to be driving on the open highway in a truck that might break down." It was a good thing I was such a good liar. I could make up believable fibs at the drop of a hat. When Joyce found out we was going in Willie Frank's truck after all, which she wouldn't know until we got ready to go, I'd tell her he got the motor fixed. And that's when we'd tell her we decided to take her to a restaurant in Hartville that was even better than the one in Mobile.

"Okay. When do y'all want to go?"

"Well, one of the dishwashers at the grill owes me a few dollars and can't pay me until next month. I don't want to dip into our money, so we can't go until I get my money from him," I told her.

"All right. Ooh, I can't wait. I'm going to buy a new outfit just for the occasion. Odell says I look good in pink. I'm going to start looking for the right outfit as soon as I can," she squealed. "Thanks for being so thoughtful. But y'all don't have to do this."

"No, we really want to," Yvonne said.

Joyce stood up. "Oh, I need to say something." She paused and looked like she was about to laugh. Then she said in a serious tone, "I sure hope y'all don't wear anything too outlandish."

My blood was getting hotter by the second. I prayed in my head that she'd leave before it reached the boiling point. "Joyce, believe me, we won't wear nothing that'll embarrass you. All the dressing and grooming advice you and Odell done gave us is really helping."

A skeptical look crossed her face. "Well, I hope it becomes more noticeable soon." Her smile didn't help me feel no better about her latest digs. I still managed to smile, and so did Yvonne. Joyce exhaled, squinted, and scanned the room. There was a mild frown on her face the whole time. "If I didn't have so many chores to do at home, I'd stay longer." She gave Yvonne a pitiful look and shook her head. "I could help you do some of the dusting and all that other housekeeping you haven't been able to get to."

"Joyce, that's so neighborly of you. If you can come back before our guests start coming, I'll have a broom and dust rag ready for you," Yvonne said in a snippy tone. I could tell from the way she narrowed her eyes that she was offended by Joyce's remarks. I wondered if this snooty ox would ever stop saying things that insulted us in some way.

"I won't be back tonight. I don't think I'll be coming over to drink for the next couple of days," Joyce said, trying to act apologetic.

"You going out with one of your friend-girls from work?" Yvonne asked.

"Uh-uh. My stomach has been acting up quite a bit lately. It started right after I ate some of those snacks you served last Friday. I gobbled up quite a few deviled duck eggs.

Yvonne, I keep telling you not to be so heavy-handed with the salt. But the tea cakes you served the same night was pretty good. I'm glad you used my recipe."

"I'll remember to use less salt next time," Yvonne said with a tight smile, but I could tell she was still feeling insulted.

When Joyce left, Yvonne waved her hands in the air in anger. "Ooh. When we knock her off that high horse she been riding way too long, her butt will hit the ground so hard, it'll leave a foot-deep dent in it."

Milton laughed. "I thought you was concerned about how hurt she'll be when we spill the beans on Odell."

"I was concerned about her . . . a little. But now I'm more concerned about how much more hurt we'll suffer if we keep taking her verbal abuse. I can only hope she don't say something that'll make me snap before we get her to that restaurant."

Me and Betty Jean was on the couch, hugging and smooching like we did so often. Even after all these years, we still couldn't keep our hands off each other. We had just come home from the afternoon church service a few minutes ago. The boys was in their room playing with some of the games and toys I had brung them this weekend.

As usual, we had ate supper at Po' Sister's Kitchen on Friday, and again yesterday. We loved that restaurant because the food was so good, and all the employees treated us like family. Betty Jean's older sister, Alline, worked in the kitchen. That's why we never had to wait in line like everybody else. I also loved the place because it was where me and Betty Jean met for the first time.

I often wondered what I would be doing now if she hadn't come up to me while I was standing in that long line waiting to get in that day. Me and Joyce had been married only a few weeks. From the minute Betty Jean noticed me, she came at me like a gangbuster, and didn't let up until she'd got me where she wanted me: in her bed. After our first rendezvous, I was no longer responsible for my actions. I got hooked on her like a addict got hooked on dope.

Another thing I wondered about from time to time was, if Betty Jean hadn't made me disregard my wedding vows, would it have been another woman? Would she have made me as happy as Betty Jean had? I didn't like to spend too much time dwelling on them questions. I pushed them to the back of my mind. Despite the new mess I was in with Yvonne and Milton, I was still enjoying what was left of my visit.

Me and Betty Jean and the boys usually spent Sunday afternoon fishing and visiting some of her kinfolks or members of our church family. But it was too chilly to take the boys to a fishing hole today, and it was threatening to rain.

I usually stayed long enough to eat supper every Sunday. I couldn't do it today, even though Betty Jean had smothered a chicken just for me. "Sugar, I would love to stay long enough to eat with y'all, but it looks like a serious storm is in the making. I don't like to drive in the rain," I explained as I adjusted her head on my shoulder. "And I have to leave before dark on account of my headlights ain't as bright as they used to be."

"I sure wish I could go with you," Betty Jean mumbled with a pouty look on her face.

I gasped. "Go with me to Branson? What's wrong with you?" My face got hot and my stomach churned. "How many times do I have to tell you that ain't *never* going to happen? What's wrong with you?" I got so agitated, my hands started shaking.

"I get gloomy every time you leave. I'd like to see where you live and work at least once before I die," she griped. "Sometimes it seems like I'm married to a stranger."

"Betty Jean, I'm *married* to Joyce." Now I was sweating, too.

She rolled her eyes and snickered. "Odell, you ain't got to get so skittish. You shaking and sweating like you just seen a ghost. It ain't no big deal. Let me pour you a glass of elderberry wine before you go. It'll help calm your nerves before you start that long drive."

"All right then," I said, pinching the tip of her nose.

Then she said something else to rile me. "Can you come back one day next week and bring me the turkey and all that other holiday food you promised?"

"I told you I'd bring everything when I come next Friday." I was getting so exasperated I was about to bust. One reason I loved Joyce so much was because she rarely agitated me. Betty Jean made a sport of nagging me. But I really didn't mind that much because the positive things about her outweighed the negative ones ten to one.

"I know you did. I was hoping you could sneak away from Joyce and bring it before then. Like on Tuesday or Wednesday. This year I'd like to cook Thanksgiving supper *on* Thanksgiving Day like everybody else, not the day after."

My mouth dropped open. "Me and you and the boys have always celebrated the day after. That ain't never going to change. I wish you would stop whining about it every year."

"I'm sorry. I was hoping that just this one time —"

I cut her off so fast she flinched. "Look, you and the boys always eat supper with one of your folks on Thanksgiving Day anyway. Ain't that good enough for you?"

Betty Jean laughed. "Well, I knew what you was going to say before I asked. I had to ask anyway. I didn't mean to get you more upset."

Before I could say another word, all three of my boys came galloping into the room. Leon jumped into my lap and Jesse jumped into Betty Jean's. Daniel stood in front of me holding a whistle I had brung to help him stop sucking his thumb. "Daddy, Leon chewed a hole in my whistle," he complained. Then he stuck his thumb in his mouth and started sucking it so fast it made my head swim. I made a mental note to bring some hot sauce to put on his thumb. That was how my mama got me to stop sucking mine when I was his age.

"I didn't do nothing. That whistle already had a hole in it," Leon claimed as he tugged my sleeve.

"Daddy, when you come back, bring us some more moon pies," Jesse said in his tiny voice. He had just started talking like a real person a few weeks ago. The boy was smart and learned so fast, he could conversate almost as good as kids twice his age.

"Bring that chewing gum you said you'd bring," Daniel reminded me.

"And some marbles," Leon added.

I held up my hand. "Y'all hush up. I already got a headache. I got to leave in a few minutes, and I don't want to spend the rest of my visit listening to a bunch of bickering and begging." I rubbed my forehead and let out a loud sigh.

"Boys, y'all go out and play," Betty Jean ordered, already sliding Jesse off her lap.

"It's cold out there," Daniel protested.

"Then go back to your room. I need to talk to Daddy."

The boys left, grumbling and stomping all the way to their room. When we heard them slam the door, Betty Jean touched my arm. "Baby, what gave you a headache?"

I couldn't even face her. "Don't worry about it. It don't concern you."

"Yes, it do. You might as well tell me because I'll badger you until you do." She chuckled.

As much as I shared with Betty Jean, there was no way I could tell her that I was planning to kill two people. "Baby, it ain't nothing important."

I left five minutes later.

When I got home, I could hear Joyce in the kitchen humming one of the silly ditties she had taught them schoolkids. She done a double take when she came in the living room and seen me sitting on the couch. "Odell, don't scare me like that. I didn't expect to see you until later."

"I wanted to get home before it started

raining too hard," I explained in a bone-weary tone. I had already kicked off my shoes, propped my feet up on the coffee table, and put two throw pillows up under my head. I still didn't feel comfortable, though. Leading two lives was so tiresome. But the rewards was worth it.

"I'm glad I decided to cook supper early. I just have to make some hush puppies." Joyce sat down next to me. "I hope you're not too tired. I was thinking about going next door for a drink or two after we eat."

"Um, I don't feel like going over there tonight, baby. I got a headache." I snorted and rubbed the back of my head. "I'm going to swallow some pills and take it easy."

"All right, sugar. Do you want me to stay home with you?"

"No, you go on. Tell Milton and Yvonne I'll see them again in the next few days." I still had to decide when and how I was going to kill them low-down dogs. I had no idea that Joyce would be the one to come up with the perfect solution. Bless her soul, what she said next made me so dizzy with excitement, I could hardly sit still.

"Odell, before I forget, the lamp in the bathroom is almost out of kerosene. If you plan on taking a bath later, you might want to refill it first. And be careful with that stuff. It's highly flammable. Don't forget how you caught your shirtsleeve on fire the last time you refilled the lamp in the pantry."

Kerosene! If I used enough, I could burn down the house next door while them two devils was sleeping. They was going to burn in hell anyway, so dying in a fire would be a good send-off. So many folks used kerosene, I always kept a huge supply in stock at the store. Praise the Lord.

Joyce interrupted my thoughts. "Did you hear what I said about that kerosene?"

"Huh? Oh yeah. I'll put some in the bathroom lamp. And don't worry, I'll be careful. Now you go on next door and have a good time."

CHAPTER 26
ODELL

Right after Joyce left the room, I rushed to the kitchen and looked in the pantry to see how much kerosene we had on hand. There was only enough to put in one lamp, so I would have to get some from the store. It would take several gallon-size cans to get the job done.

Now that I had decided how I was going to do the deed, all I had to do was figure out when. It would be good to wrap things up before I gave Milton the four hundred bucks. If I didn't get it done by then, maybe I could before they gave the money to Lamar.

The Friday after I was supposed to give Milton the money, would be the first day in December. I'd go to visit Betty Jean like always, and double back to Branson in the middle of the night with the kerosene. Getting in the house next door wouldn't be no problem. Yvonne left a side window in the

248

kitchen cracked open every night to let in some fresh air. If she forgot to do it that night, I knew it would be unlocked. I couldn't hoist myself up and crawl in with the kerosene, so I'd set it on the ground until I got in and unlocked the kitchen door. I'd sprinkle every drop of it throughout the house. Before I started the fire, I would wake Yvonne and Milton up and give them a big piece of my mind. Then I'd demand my money back, if they still had it. I planned to carry a hammer or some other weapon with me for protection. I wanted the last thing they heard and seen on this planet to be me.

After my speech, I'd knock them both unconscious, and strike matches to toss on the kerosene. If the smoke didn't kill them, the flames sure would.

Afterwards, I'd hightail it back to Hartville before anybody noticed the blaze. If Betty Jean woke up while I was gone, I'd tell her that I had went for a drive to clear my head. I done that every now and then, and I always blamed it on insomnia. So far, she'd never made a big deal out of it.

Joyce stayed next door only a little over a hour. When she came home, I was in bed. "Odell, I'm back," she yelled from the living room.

"I'm in here, sugar," I replied in a weak tone. "I . . . I'm in bed." I needed to sound as sick and pitiful as possible. Then she wouldn't expect me to get affectionate with her. With all that was going through my head, sex was the last thing on my mind.

Joyce rushed into the bedroom with a concerned look on her face. "That must be some headache." She leaned over and felt my forehead. "You look flushed, but you don't have a temperature." She sat down on my side of the bed. "If you keep getting sick, I'm going to make an appointment for you with Dr. Patterson."

"I ain't that sick," I insisted. "I just been working too hard."

"Well, you better slow down."

I knew I couldn't play sick too many more times without Joyce or somebody else making a fuss.

She went on. "When I told Milton you had a bad headache, he wanted to come over here and check on you."

My chest tightened. Just hearing that gave me chills. I didn't want a man I was going to murder, spending any more time in my house than necessary. It was a bad omen. "I'm glad he didn't. I didn't feel like having no company," I mumbled. "I took some pills and I feel a little better, though."

"I would have stayed over there a little longer because I was having a good time. I swear, that Willie Frank is so funny. I bet if he joined a circus, people would pay big money to watch him dance." Joyce chuckled. She stood up and started taking off her dress. "But the more I thought about you over here by yourself, sick as a dog, the guiltier I felt. When I brought that up to Yvonne, she made a comment about you never feeling guilty about leaving me by myself so often."

"Our personal life ain't none of her business!" I snapped.

"I know, but I didn't say anything. I just let her ramble on like always." Joyce grabbed her nightgown off the foot of the bed and put it on. "Oh! I forgot to tell you that she and Milton invited me to have supper with them one evening next month."

I sat up and blinked. "Did their invitation include me?"

"No. But it wasn't meant to slight you. You know better. They explained that they were only asking me because you'd be at your daddy's house."

"Why do they have to take you out on a weekend? And why can't they do it before next month?"

"Something about that being the only

251

time they can borrow transportation, and somebody owing Milton some money." Joyce fluffed up her pillows and got into bed. "I can tell them I'd rather wait and go when you can come."

"No, you go ahead. What brung this on in the first place? All these months they been living next door, they ain't never invited me or you to go out for supper."

"They just want to show how much they appreciate us giving them that cash gift. But don't feel left out. They did say they'd take us out together some other time." Joyce gave me a pensive look. "Hmmm. I think I'll ask them to wait until after Christmas when the restaurants won't be so crowded, and you won't be so busy. That way you can drive."

"We'll see. If they having money problems, how can they afford to be taking anybody out to a restaurant?"

"Odell, I'm sure they've figured out a way to cover that. Otherwise, they wouldn't have asked." Joyce slid closer to me. She went to sleep right away, but it took me more than a hour to doze off.

When I opened the store Monday morning, the first thing I done was check to see how much kerosene we had in stock. There was six gallon-size cans on the shelf. I wondered if it would really do the trick. Catching my shirtsleeve on fire was one thing. Burning down a whole house was another. Gas would have been better because it burned faster and hotter. But I'd have to get it from a filling station. That was too risky. Every station I knew of was owned by white folks. They would get nosy and suspicious if a colored man came in and filled up some cans with gasoline. I had no choice but to use kerosene. I didn't know how much I'd need to burn down a house, so I decided to take all we had.

Buddy went to lunch at noon and I worked his cash register until he got back a hour later. Sadie took her break a few minutes after he got back, and I done the same thing for her. When she returned, I made myself a Spam sandwich, grabbed a bottle of Nehi grape soda pop, and went back to my office. I stayed there until four thirty.

When I returned to the main floor, the last customer was walking out the door with three big shopping bags. "Boy, what a day," Buddy said as he wiped sweat off his face with both hands. "I don't remember the last time we was this busy. Every time I tried to get to the toilet, somebody came up to my counter with a cart overflowing with items for me to ring up. It's a wonder my bladder ain't busted wide open."

"Well, this is the holiday season. We need to be thankful we got so much business, and not be complaining," Sadie scolded. "There is hundreds of thousands of folks still out of work. Being busy at any job is a blessing."

"I ain't complaining!" Buddy snapped. "I was just making a comment. You been moaning and groaning all day. If anybody is complaining, it's you."

Sadie gave him a sheepish grin. "Oh well. Anyway, I can't wait to get home. I need to soak my feet. My bunions feel like somebody dropped a brick on them. But I ain't complaining."

"I really appreciate how hard y'all worked today," I said, giving them my warmest smile. "Y'all can get your things and go on home now. I can handle the next half hour by myself."

"Will we still get paid for the whole day?" Buddy asked with a anxious look on his face.

"I'll pay y'all for the whole day," I assured them.

They didn't waste no time gathering up their things and leaving. I waited by the cash registers after they'd left in case another customer wandered in. When nobody had come by five minutes to five, I dogtrotted to

254

the aisle where we stocked the kerosene.

I was about to walk out the rear exit door holding a box with all six cans of the kerosene when I heard Buddy's voice. "Odell, what you doing?"

I whirled around so fast, I almost dropped the box. "W-what? I thought you left."

Buddy strutted up to me with his hands on his hips. "I did leave. I forgot my spittoon under the counter." He squinted at my burning face, then at the box. I hadn't put a lid on it, so he seen what was inside. "What you going to do with all that kerosene?" He took his hands off his hips and made a sweeping motion toward the kerosene and peered at me from the corner of his beady eye.

"Oh, didn't I tell you? My daddy asked me to bring it to his house and torch them tall weeds in his back yard."

"You need that much?"

"He got a big yard."

"Oh. I'll help you tote it to your car, if you want me to. Them cans is heavy, so I hope my back don't go out again . . ."

"No, I don't need no help." I waved him away. "You . . . you get your spittoon and go on home. I can take care of this. Besides, we too busy for you to miss work because of your bad back."

Buddy looked relieved. "That's for sure. Lord knows I can't afford to take off time with no pay. Anyway, I've had to torch my yard a few times to get rid of them weevils and other creatures. I can go to your daddy's house with you to help. If we both use sprinkling cans, we could get the job done in half the time it would take you to do it by yourself. I ain't seen Lonnie in a while, and it'd be nice to see him."

"Buddy, don't worry about it. You know how crazy my stepmama is. I don't want to show up with company she ain't expecting."

"You got a good point. Lord knows I ain't in the mood to lock horns with that she-devil." Buddy grinned. "I'll see you in the morning. Now you be careful with that stuff. Once you strike a match, it'll burn fast."

"I know."

When Buddy left, I took the box to my car anyway. I couldn't burn down Milton and Yvonne's house now. Then something else jumped into my mind. A burned-down house next door to mine would be a real eyesore on our deluxe street. Dagnabbit. I had to come up with another plan.

CHAPTER 27
YVONNE

A lot of our regulars visited us on Monday and Tuesday night. I was surprised Joyce and Odell didn't come. Several folks asked about them. "You reckon Odell done got even sicker? He sure is having a lot of problems with his health these days. He was sick the night y'all got arrested," Aunt Mattie said Tuesday night, giving me a curious look. Me, her, Sweet Sue, and Milton stood across the room facing the couch where Dr. Patterson, two unmarried young nurses who worked at the colored clinic, and Mr. Cunningham sat jabbering away. I didn't know where Willie Frank was in the house, but I could hear him guffawing like a hyena.

"Joyce ain't been feeling too good lately neither," Sweet Sue tossed in.

"Sounds like they could use one of my potions," Aunt Mattie said, pursing her mouth in a self-satisfied smirk. "That's what's been keeping me and my gals fit as

257

fiddles. One of our tricks brung me some fish heads the other day. With a pinch of one of my special spices, they make a stew that go right to the source of whatever ails a person. We can drink booze all night and don't have no hangovers."

"When Aunt Mattie cooks something, she put her foot in it," Sweet Sue said, snapping her fingers. "Nary one of us have to worry about the clap slowing down business. A bowl of that stew will dry it up in less than a day."

"Aunt Mattie, we all know about your powerful God-given talent in the conjuring business, and we appreciate your offer. But like me and Milton, Joyce and Odell is too scientific to dabble in hoodoo," I blurted out. I would never tell Aunt Mattie, or anybody else, that I'd tried to encourage Joyce to get help from her so she could get pregnant. After I'd had time to really think about it, I was glad Joyce hadn't took my advice. I didn't want a innocent baby to get caught up in the mess that was going to happen when me and Milton told Joyce about Odell and Betty Jean. I would have felt bad about that.

"That's the truth. Anyway, I'm sure we'll see Joyce and Odell tomorrow," Milton said, giving me a self-satisfied look. "If they don't come over here, we'll pay them a visit to make sure they doing all right. I believe in being neighborly at all times."

We had over two dozen guests when Odell came by hisself to the house Wednesday night a couple of hours after we got home from the grill. He greeted a few folks before he motioned for Milton to go in the kitchen with him. Five minutes later, Odell came back into the living room with a poker face like I had never seen before. He bolted out the front door like he had ants in his pants. I prayed Milton hadn't said nothing too mean to him. I excused myself and skittered into the kitchen. Milton was using his hand to fan the chicken wings I had took out of the oven and set on top of the stove to cool off a little while ago. "Prince Charming didn't look too happy just now," I commented.

Milton held up the same hand he'd been fanning with in my face so fast, it made a whooshing sound and I felt a mild breeze. "So what? If I was in his shoes, I wouldn't be looking too happy neither. He'll be all right after a few drinks. Make sure you give him some of the recycled stuff."

"I always do. I wish you would stop telling me that. Anyway, he didn't stay."

"Oh? Hmmm. I guess I did say something he didn't like." Milton scratched his chin and gave me a preoccupied look that was so serious, I got the heebie-jeebies.

I was scared to hear what he was going to say next. But I asked anyway. "And what was that?"

"After he paid me my hush money for this week, I just suggested that I would like to have them three hundred dollars no later than Wednesday next week. He made a big stink about it, so I ain't counting on it."

"Is that all?"

"What do you mean?"

"Milton, the way you was looking a second ago, I thought you was going to tell me something bad." I was so relieved; a wide smile crossed my face. "Well, it would be nice to get the money early. But we don't have to pay Willie Frank's uncle back until the end of the month, which would be next Thursday," I reminded him.

"If we get it a day before it's due, we'll be able to breathe easy and sleep good the night before. What if something was to happen to Odell before Thursday, and he can't give it all to us in time? He could have a car wreck and be laid up in a coma for weeks. Then we'd have a mess on our hands."

"I hadn't thought about nothing like that.

And since you brung it up, we need to be real concerned." I was tempted to tell Milton that Odell could get laid up tomorrow, too. I didn't because I didn't want to make the situation no more worrisome than it already was. I decided to soothe him. That always made him feel good. I sniffed and brushed off the sleeve of his plaid shirt and smoothed back his greasy hair. "Honey, you look so good right now. I'm glad you decided to wear your new suspenders tonight. I bet every man here is jealous of you for being so sporty. Wear one of your pin-striped suits when we go to the Patterson's house for Thanksgiving supper tomorrow. They make you look so . . . um . . . dapper. Almost as much as —"

Milton didn't waste no time cutting me off. His eyebrows furrowed and his lips quivered. "Don't you dare mention Odell's name! I thought we had got beyond you comparing me to Prince Charming!"

I wanted to bite my tongue off. The reason Milton had lost his cool and told me about Odell and Betty Jean in the first place a few weeks ago, was because he'd got sick and tired of me telling him he should be more like Odell.

I smiled and caressed the side of his face. That calmed him down a little. "Baby, I'm sorry. Now that I know what a fraud he is, I won't never compare you to him again."

"You told me that before."

"I'm telling you again."

"Good. I'd rather you liken me to a mud-puppy."

"Hush up and stop overreacting. You know I didn't mean no harm." I stopped him from speaking again by covering his lips with mine. The next thing I knew, his arms was around me. He started grinding against me so hard, I was tempted to wrestle him to the floor and have my way with him. I decided to wait until our guests left to do that. I gazed deep into his eyes. I loved how he looked at me when he got hot. "Baby, don't get too carried away. We got guests to tend to," I panted.

"Then stop egging me on, *Jezebel,*" he teased, making a slurping noise with his tongue. "You know what a passionate man you married." He laughed and that made me feel better.

"Tell me about it." I laughed, too, and pried his arms from around me. "I wonder why Joyce didn't come with Odell tonight."

"He said something about her having a bellyache." Milton paused and snickered. "He ailing one day, she ailing on another day. I ain't never seen two people take turns getting sick so regular. We better pray that they don't get too sick to function until after we get our money."

Milton's last comment really shook me up. That was something I didn't want to hear. "Hmmm. Maybe we shouldn't wait too close to the deadline then. You ought to tell Odell he has to get that money to us by next Tuesday. Next Monday would be even better," I suggested.

"I agree."

"The store will be closed for Thanksgiving and the day after. He won't be available again until Monday, or Sunday when he get home from . . . visiting his sick daddy." We laughed, but got serious again real quick. "If you don't let him know until Monday when he is back at the store, he might not have enough time to get it to us on the same day. After we leave Dr. Patterson's house tomorrow, let's go tell Odell we definitely need that money earlier than we said."

"What about Joyce? We can't ask him for no more money with her too close by. She won't let him out of her sight as long as we over there."

"Milton, you let me worry about her. I'll make up something that'll get her out of the room."

"Oh, okay. And don't forget, this particular business transaction is between me and Odell. In case you get stuck with him alone before we can get out of there, don't you say nothing to him about it."

"I won't."

CHAPTER 28
YVONNE

I was glad Thanksgiving had finally arrived.
I was thankful and happy I had so many
blessings. But it was always a hard day for
me to get through without feeling some sadness. I got in a mild funk on every holiday
— except Halloween — because I didn't
have enough family members in my life to
celebrate with. My two older sisters lived
with their husbands and kids up North. I
had a bunch of other kinfolk in Alabama,
but I rarely seen them. They was so into
church and the Bible, they didn't feel
comfortable around people like me and
Milton. I was glad we had close friends who
treated us like family. Especially well-
respected professionals like Dr. Patterson.
His invitation for us to eat Thanksgiving
supper with him and his family meant a lot
to me and Milton.

We left home a few minutes before three
p.m. to go to the Pattersons' house, which

was only four houses from ours on the same side of the street. More than a dozen of their relatives, friends, and several other neighbors had also been invited. Mrs. Patterson had bought a lot of food to make sure there'd be enough to feed everybody. But she was still glad I'd brung a big pan of candied yams.

Since there was so many guests, we ate buffet-style. That made it more fun because we could eat standing up and mingle at the same time. They didn't serve no alcohol, but everybody was almost as rowdy as the folks who came to drink at our house. The reason there was no drinking was because Dr. Patterson's elderly mama lived with them. She didn't tolerate booze in the house because there was always a bunch of grandkids and other young relatives on the premises. I couldn't tolerate such a strict rule in my house, even if we wasn't bootlegging. It was no wonder Dr. Patterson and his wife spent so much time visiting us.

We was having a good time and ate way more than we should have. After three helpings each, Milton had to loosen his belt. I was so full, my stomach felt like it was going to explode at any minute. People we had never met before was hugging and chatting it up with us like they'd known us our whole lives. "Yvonne, I ain't never met no bootleg-ger like you," Dr. Patterson's handsome young nephew commented. We had finished eating and everybody was standing around drinking cider in the huge living room.

"And one so pretty and ripe," his brother added, ogling me like he wanted to rip off my bloomers right then and there. There was a smirk on his face when he turned to look at Milton. "Milton, no matter how hard I try, I ain't been able to get me a woman as good-looking as this pretty little Red Bone you got. Why do you think that is? I know how to make a woman happy."

"Maybe you ain't got enough equipment to make one as happy as I can," Milton shot back. Everybody gasped and laughed. The banter went on like that for so long, I got tired of laughing and started getting bored. I couldn't wait to leave. From the blasé expression on Milton's face now, I knew he was anxious to haul ass, too. But we was gracious enough to spend a little more time socializing.

All the folks from out of town got angry when we told them about our arrest. One hefty, mean-looking cousin from Huntsville even offered to help us chastise the culprit that had made the bogus call to the sheriff, if and when we found out who he was. "We can take care of our own business. What he done to us will seem like a blessing compared to what we going to do to him," Milton growled.

Discussing this subject with folks we had just met today was making me uncomfortable. When I looked at Milton and nodded toward the door, he knew what that meant. He didn't waste no time rushing into one of the bedrooms, where they had put all the coats and jackets, to get ours. Dr. Patterson and his wife was so busy tending to their guests, they didn't even notice when we slunk out the front door a few minutes later.

"Let's make tracks before somebody else come up and start yakking away again," Milton said as we stumbled out to the sidewalk, burping and rubbing our stomachs. We sprinted toward home until he abruptly stopped in front of our fence gate. It wasn't that dark yet, but I was glad we had left the light on in our living room. The only light on in Joyce and Odell's house was the one in their bedroom. Odell's car was parked out front, so we knew they was at home. "We better get a move on before they go to bed."

"Baby, you go talk to Odell. I want to get in the house and start preparing for our guests. We already getting a late start," I said, dismissing him with a wave.

Milton shook his head. "Uh-uh. We got business to tend to. I know damn well you ain't forgot what we planned. I need you there to distract Joyce so I can talk to Odell."

"Okay then. Let's go and get it over with."

Nobody answered when Milton knocked on the front door. We crept around to the kitchen entrance, and he knocked even louder. Just as we was about to give up and leave, Joyce finally opened that door. She looked surprised to see us. I was surprised to see her in such a skimpy see-through nightgown with her husky self. She didn't look the least bit happy to see us. "I figured it was y'all at the door," she mumbled. "We thought y'all were having supper at Dr. Patterson's house."

"We did. But we had to leave in time to be home for our guests tonight," I explained. "Can we come in?"

Joyce shifted her weight from one foot to the other and glanced over her shoulder. "Odell and I really would like to be alone tonight . . ." Her tone was so stiff, you would have thought she'd been eating starch.

"We won't stay long," Milton said before

269

she could throw out another hint for us to leave.

"Well, Odell is resting. I guess I can talk for a minute or two. But do y'all really need to come in? This is not a convenient time."

I wasn't going to give up too easy. "We just wanted to drop in and say hello and wish y'all a happy Thanksgiving." I looked Joyce up and down. She smelled like she had doused herself with two or three different smell-goods. "I can see you already dressed for bed, so I guess y'all won't be coming to the house for a drink tonight, huh?"

I could tell by the expression on Milton's face and the way he was fidgeting, that he was getting aggravated. So was I. But when it came to Joyce and Odell, aggravation came with the territory. "Joyce, we'll let you get back to whatever you was doing," he muttered. "Tell Odell we stopped by, and that we'll come back tomorrow."

"We won't be home tomorrow. I'm going to spend the day with Mama and Daddy visiting relatives in Lexington. The store will be closed tomorrow, so Odell is going to head out to his daddy's house early in the morning."

"Oh. All right then." Milton snorted. "Do me a favor and tell Odell I'll be coming to the store on Monday when I take my lunch break."

Joyce cocked her head to the side and gave us a curious look. "Is there something you need from the store? Let me know what it is so I can tell him to set it aside and not sell it to anybody else. I'd hate for you to make a trip to the store for nothing," she said with a weak smile.

"Yeah. Tell him to set aside that . . . item . . . me and him talked about recently." Milton chuckled and leaned toward Joyce and whispered, "It's for a manly issue. And I . . . I'm a little too embarrassed to talk about it in front of women . . ."

"I see. Well, I hope it's nothing catchy." She shuddered and closed the door a few inches. "I'd hate for Odell to come down with something while he is so busy at the store these days and has to spend so much time taking care of his daddy. He's been sick enough lately."

"Don't worry. Milton ain't got nothing serious, and it ain't catchy," I said, rolling my eyes. We all laughed.

"Is there anything else?" Joyce asked, shutting the door a little more.

"Naw, I guess not," I told her. "I hope you and Odell enjoyed your holiday today."

A dreamy-eyed look suddenly crossed

Joyce's face. "I declare, we sure did. Spending the holiday with just each other this year was even more romantic and fulfilling than last year, and the year before. Since Odell is gone so much, it's important for us to spend time alone whenever we can. Did y'all enjoy yourselves at Dr. Patterson's house?"

"We sure did. We met a lot of his out-of-town relatives. They made us feel right welcome," I gushed.

"That's nice. Well, I'll let y'all go on home to get ready for whoever shows up tonight. Bye now." With a smug look on her face, Joyce shut the door before we could say anything else.

Me and Milton looked at each other and shook our heads. "Humph. I hope that uppity heifer enjoys the rest of her 'romantic and fulfilling' holiday night with Odell. This might be their last one," Milton snarled. He wrapped his arm around me and led me home.

CHAPTER 29
JOYCE

I couldn't lock the door fast enough. When I heard Yvonne and Milton stomp down the porch steps, I breathed a sigh of relief.

I checked to make sure I'd put the leftover Thanksgiving food away before I went to the bathroom to pee. I had already done my nightly face cream ritual and taken a quick bath so I could get cozy with Odell sooner. I didn't want him to wait too much longer. That was why I didn't roll my hair with the leather curlers I used sometime. The way he had repeatedly squeezed my knee, tickled my chin, and ogled my bosom during supper, I knew he'd get right frisky when we got in bed. And my curlers would end up on my pillow.

"Who was that, sugar?" Odell asked when I got back to our bedroom. He was in his pajamas, sitting at the foot of the bed, fiddling with the radio we kept on top of the dresser. If he could find a station that didn't have a lot of static, we planned to nestle in each other's arms and listen to some gospel programs before things got more intimate.

"Guess," I snickered and flopped down on my side of the bed.

"Yvonne and Milton?"

I nodded. "Milton said to let you know he'd be coming by the store Monday to pick up some item he discussed with you."

"He came over here for that? I thought you had told Yvonne we'd planned to spend today alone."

"I did. I made it clear to her that we didn't want any company."

"And they showed up anyway. Them people ain't got no kind of manners, and it's beginning to get on my nerves," Odell snarled. His mood was so gloomy now, I wished I had not answered the door. I didn't think them coming over unannounced was that big of a deal, but I guess he did. That was the problem with us being more sophisticated than they were. They didn't have a clue when it came to acceptable etiquette. And with all the things Odell had to deal with, I could understand why it bothered him so much on a day we'd planned not to see anybody. "Oh. Yeah, me and him talked about that 'item' when I was over there last night. It's kind of embarrassing."

"Speaking of last night, how come you didn't stay over there longer?"

"I wanted to. But when I mentioned that you wasn't feeling good to a few women, they said their husbands would never leave them alone if they was sick. That made me feel bad. That's why I came home so soon." Odell set the radio on his nightstand. Then he got in bed and pulled the covers all the way up to his neck.

"Well, Milton admitted that he needs something from the store to deal with a manly issue. Yuck. That's all I want to know." I snickered again. "I'll bet it's a glitch *down there* that's interfering with his performance."

"Um . . . something like that."

"Whatever it is, I'm glad you don't have the same problem. I'd be climbing the walls in no time."

Odell had been in a more romantic mood before Yvonne and Milton interrupted us. Now his level of physical interest in me was so low, he didn't even touch me when I slid under the covers and pressed myself against him. I poked his backside with my knee. When that didn't arouse him, I gave up. We didn't listen to the radio or do anything else.

I had told Mama and Daddy that I'd be

275

coming to their house at seven a.m. and eat breakfast with them before we left to go to Lexington. I assumed Odell would eat breakfast with us before he left to go to his daddy's house, even though we hadn't discussed it. I was surprised when I opened my eyes Friday morning at six thirty and saw that his side of the bed was empty. He'd left a note on the kitchen counter telling me he'd already left to go to his daddy's house. I couldn't hide my disappointment. The minute I walked through my parents' front door, Mama could tell that something was bothering me.

"Why is your face so long this early in the morning?" she asked as she steered me into the kitchen. Daddy was already at the table wolfing down grits and eggs and belching like a bull.

"Odell left before I woke up. I thought he'd at least come over here and eat breakfast with us," I explained as I plucked a biscuit off a platter next to a mountain of grits on the table. I gobbled it up right away, but I wasn't in the mood to eat anything else. Odell's abrupt departure had made me lose my appetite.

"Maybe he didn't want to," Daddy grunted. "You can't expect that man to do everything you think he should."

I was too antsy to sit down, so I leaned against the counter. "Daddy, please. He could have at least woken me up and kissed me good-bye," I complained as I glanced at the clock on the wall. "What time are we leaving to go to Lexington?"

"We ain't," Mama said, sounding disappointed. Before I could ask why, she went on. "Cousin Mervis called last night. She said she had just got a call from her and Jubal's son in Mobile. After birthing six girls, his wife done finally had a boy."

"That's nice," I muttered. I didn't waste any time steering the conversation in another direction. I was not in the mood to hear them remind me again that I hadn't given them a grandchild. "Um, too bad we won't be going to Lexington. We could have stopped at Odell's daddy's house for a few minutes since it's along the way."

"Mac, we ain't got nothing else planned for today, so why don't we drop in on Lonnie anyway. I'm sure him and Odell would be glad to see us," Mama piped in. "Can't say the same about that she-devil Ellamae, though," she added with a snicker as she poured coffee into Daddy's cup. She eased down into the chair across from him and started piling food onto her plate.

"That's a good idea. I wouldn't mind

stopping to holler at Lonnie," Daddy replied. "We ain't seen him and that shrew he married since her cousin's funeral three years ago."

"I hope him and Ellamae is up to having company today. The only thing is, I was raised to believe it's rude to drop in unannounced on folks," Mama said with her eyebrows furrowed.

"It sure is rude," I agreed. "Last night Milton and Yvonne did just that. And we sure didn't feel like having any company."

"You shouldn't have answered the door and let them jailbirds in," Mama snarled. "I declare, this neighborhood ain't been the same since they moved over here."

"Ain't it the truth. All them loud cars and trucks whizzing past our house to get to theirs seven days a week every evening is getting on my nerves," Daddy grumbled as he snatched a biscuit off the platter in front of him. "I don't remember the last time I got a good night's sleep. I don't know how you and Odell can tolerate them heathens, especially with them living just one house over."

"I was annoyed with them when they showed up last night. I let them know right away that we didn't want any company. They were gracious enough to leave after a few minutes," I said.

"Humph. You mean to tell me they got some manners after all?" Mama sneered.

"Yeah, and they can be a lot of fun sometime. That's why Odell and I visit them so often," I admitted. "By the way, they want to treat me to supper one evening next month. They're going to borrow somebody's truck and take me to a real nice place in Mobile."

"Oh? Well, butter my butt and call me a biscuit. I reckon it's true that there ain't a pot too crooked that a lid won't fit. Even so, before you go gallivanting with folks that got such unsavory reputations, you better make sure you got enough money on you to pay for your supper, and enough bus fare to get back home in case their money comes up shy," Daddy warned, shaking his fork in my face.

"Daddy, if they're taking me to a restaurant, I'm sure they'll bring enough money to cover the bill, and they'll drive me back home. You sure are getting suspicious in your old age. I'm disappointed in you," I teased.

"I ain't done nothing for you to be disappointed about. Being suspicious is what helped me live this long. You remember that!" he fired back. He and Mama laughed.

"Joyce, what do you want to do? You want us to drive you out to Lonnie's house or not?" Mama asked.

"I don't think that's such a good idea after all. Lonnie might have Odell involved in all kinds of things and us showing up might derail his plans," I answered. "Going out there every weekend is hard enough on Odell."

CHAPTER 30
MILTON

Me and Yvonne had a busy Saturday and Sunday night at our house. Some of the regulars we thought we'd lost had came back. When we got to the grill Monday morning, we got busy right away. It was going to get even busier with Christmas just a few weeks away. Every year, some folks had so much cooking to do, they came to the grill the month before and ordered extra stuff to go with everything else they planned to serve on Christmas Day. They met with Mr. Cunningham for hours on end discussing menus, prices, and how they wanted everything cooked. We took so many advance requests for various items today, Mr. Cunningham was threatening to stop taking orders by the middle of December. He said that every year and never followed through.

All them orders meant a lot of extra work for me and the other cook, but I never complained. I loved working at such a popular place because it meant job security. Mr. Cunningham often told folks that he was in no hurry to retire — even though he was old enough — because he enjoyed what he did. He'd also told us that if he got disabled or died, he had already lined up relatives to take over the grill. But he couldn't promise that they'd keep us on. Because of that and the Odell thing, me and Yvonne didn't know what was going to happen in our future. For now, we would take life one day at a time.

Even though Mr. Cunningham was griping about all the rush orders, he was as happy as me and Yvonne was that we had such good business. This morning a lady representing a church group came in and ordered enough food to feed more than a dozen members of her congregation at her Christmas Eve supper. She wanted everything cooked and ready to go the day before Christmas Eve. To make sure she got special attention, she paid in advance and left a huge tip. Mr. Cunningham got so slaphappy, he didn't even bat a eye when I told him I might be late coming back from lunch.

Willie Frank came to the grill a few minutes before noon. He had promised to let me use his truck again so I could pay Odell another visit. He had brung Sweet

Sue with him so they could eat lunch while I was gone. White men could enjoy romantic escapades with colored women behind closed doors. But when they was in public, they couldn't hold hands, or do nothing else to show that they was more than just friends.

Sweet Sue had to walk into the grill behind Willie Frank and keep her head bowed, the way a servant would. With her ordinary looks and a head that looked like a brown peach, I suspected that the white folks present today thought she was his family's mammy. The colored folks on the premises who knew better, knew better than to do or say anything that would blow their cover.

Yvonne seated Sweet Sue in a booth right away and Willie Frank walked me to where he'd parked his truck on the side of the road. "Thank you again, buddy. I hate to keep pestering you for your truck," I told him, giving him a playful punch on his arm.

"Aw shucks, Milton. You know you can borrow my wheels any time you want to. Besides, Sweet Sue had a itching to eat lunch here today. She likes to take her time, so we'll be here at least a hour and a half. Pleasing her is important to me," he said with a dreamy-eyed look on his face. "You know, someday I would like to let the world know how I feel about that gal. It's a shame people in love have to go around hiding it just because their skin colors don't match."

I couldn't relate to Willie Frank's situation, but I could see how important it was to him. Today was the very first time I seen him get emotional over a woman, and I felt sorry for him. I wanted him to be as happy in love as I was. "Well, things change all the time. I hope we live long enough to see new laws that will allow colored and white to be in love without worrying about going to jail or getting lynched."

"That would be a dream come true."

"In the meantime, you show your love to Sweet Sue any which way you can."

"Oh, I will. She feels the same way about me."

"And all the rest of her tricks." I laughed, but Willie Frank didn't. I held up my hand and tried to look apologetic. "Look, I didn't mean nothing by that. You know I don't know when to shut up. I didn't mean to ruffle your feathers."

"Pffft. I know that. I know what Sweet Sue is, but it don't matter none."

I glanced toward the front door. When I looked back at Willie Frank, he was grinning from ear to ear. I was glad to see he had perked back up. "By the way, I been meaning to ask you — what do you see in her to be so lovestruck? Her face ain't too bad, but she is damn near bald-headed and she skinny as hell. You ain't been with no other woman but her lately. There is better-looking, thick-bodied women working at Aunt Mattie's place to fall in love with."

Willie Frank winked. "I'll tell you what all we men know. When it comes to good loving, it ain't the beauty, it's the booty." We guffawed long and loud. Willie Frank snorted and went on. "I took a shine to her the first time I pestered her. I fell even deeper for her when I got to know her." Willie Frank abruptly stopped talking and gave me a guarded look. "By the way, ain't you one of her steady tricks?"

"Yup," I admitted with a sheepish grin. "But she ain't nothing but a piece of tail to me. Yvonne is the only woman I love."

Willie Frank's tone got more serious. "Um . . . I don't want you to think that Sweet Sue is just another piece of tail to me. I really do love her."

"Oh? More than that woman responsible for you going to prison for cutting her husband when he caught y'all frolicking in bed together?"

"Milton, I was young and foolish back then. Of all the women I've ever known, colored and white, Sweet Sue is the only one who really listens to me when I talk. She asks me all kinds of things about my feelings and whatnot. I feel comfortable talking to her about anything. I bet if I gave her enough attention — and money — I could turn her around and she'd quit turning tricks. But her world-beating bedroom skills is icing on the cake. I love to have my cake and eat it, too." We laughed some more. Willie Frank suddenly got serious again. "I hate to bring up this next subject, but I think I should let you know that I don't feel comfortable at your house no more when Odell is there."

"Me and Yvonne don't neither. Don't worry. He won't be in the picture too much longer."

"Did you and Yvonne decide if you want me to get the Klan involved?"

"I'll know in a week or so exactly what we should do to that scoundrel," I said as I climbed into the truck.

"All right. You drive careful now."

I sped off like the police was chasing me. About half a mile from the grill on the same road, there was a bunch of convicts doing repair work on the road. Mean-looking guards stood off to the side holding shot-guns. Vicious coon dogs on leashes was

286

barking nonstop. Boy, did them things bring back some bad memories. It seemed like just yesterday that I was in a striped suit and working on the same kind of chain gang. I slowed down because I didn't want to rile up them guards to make them suspect me of something. There was a heap of colored men rotting in prison now that hadn't done nothing except be in the wrong place at the wrong time. When I got another half mile, I speeded back up.

The city never done much for roads this far away from downtown. I had to swerve numerous times to avoid hitting all kinds of odds and ends that other drivers had littered the road with, including a old rocking chair that must have fell off the back of a wagon or a truck. I drove over a dozen potholes and half as many lollygagging squirrels.

I didn't breathe easy until I parked in front of MacPherson's. There was long lines of customers checking out. They kept Buddy and Sadie from accosting me as I hurried past them. I didn't see Odell on the main floor, so I rushed on to this office. The door was open and I strolled in. He was sitting behind his desk reading a magazine. When he looked up and seen me, he dropped the magazine and started grumbling under his breath.

"Hello, Odell."

"I was hoping I wouldn't see you today," he growled. The frightful scowl on his face made my flesh crawl.

"I wish me and Yvonne could have talked to you when we stopped by your house Thanksgiving evening. We was in a holiday mood and really wanted to share our joy." I closed the door and plonked down in the chair facing him.

"Me and Joyce was busy, and I didn't feel like entertaining no company nohow," he snarled.

"Oh, we didn't come over to be entertained. We had just been entertained enough at Dr. Patterson's lovely house. They served up a world-beating feast. And his family and friends treated us real special."

"Was that what y'all came over to tell me and Joyce that night?" He smirked.

"Nope. We had came to talk business."

Odell sat up straighter, and the look on his face got even meaner. "I know I promised to give you that four hundred dollars by the end of the month. You can come back and get it this coming Thursday."

I shook my head. "It'd be more convenient if you could give it to me sooner."

"Sooner? Milton, Thursday is only three days away, and you said I had until the end of the month."

"Well, I decided I'd like to have it by tomorrow or Wednesday. Today would be even better. Lamar Perdue is a busy man. I don't want him to be unavailable for us to get his money back to him by the deadline he set up. What if he goes out of town?"

"So what? If he ain't around when you take him the money, that ain't my problem," he whined.

"Odell, I ain't going to let it turn into my problem." I couldn't stand to listen to this crybaby no longer. I stood up, anxious to get away from all the negative energy he was putting out. "If I don't come back tomorrow, I'll see you on *Wednesday*. You better have my money then, including my weekly payment."

I didn't wait around to hear nothing else he had to say.

CHAPTER 31
ODELL

After Milton left, I stayed in my office with the door shut so I could organize my thoughts and come up with a better plan to get rid of him and Yvonne. I never knew that planning to murder somebody could be so much trouble. I went to school with a guy who shot and killed three people — in separate unrelated incidents — while he was still in his teens. He would have got away with all three murders if he hadn't got drunk at Aunt Mattie's place one night and bragged about it to one of her girls. When she tattled on him, he got arrested right away and ended up getting a death sentence. One thing I knew for sure was that I'd never run my mouth about no crime I'd commit-ted. Another thing was, I didn't believe in using guns except for hunting. I didn't believe in knives neither. If I had stuck to my plan to burn down Yvonne and Milton's house, I would have made it look like a accident. The law wouldn't have thoroughly investigated the cause of the fire in a colored neighborhood, so they'd never have known it had been deliberately set with kerosene. Besides, this was the time of year a lot of folks lighted certain rooms in their houses with kerosene lamps and left them burning all night. Last year, a house on the lower south side caught fire in the middle of the night because the family cat knocked over a kerosene lamp in the living room. That family was lucky enough to get out alive. If I changed my mind and decided to burn up Yvonne and Milton anyway, it could mean trouble. That nosy-ass Buddy had seen me taking all that kerosene. He didn't have no reason to suspect I was going to do something devilish with it. But he could still run his mouth to the wrong person, and they'd make something out of it. Then it hit me, something I should have thought of before I got that flimsy house-burning idea: *rat poison.* We always kept some in stock. Poisoning Yvonne and Milton would be a lot more humane than burning them up. I felt much better now.

Right after I got up out of my seat to go see how much rat poison we had, somebody knocked on my door. My first thought was that it was that damn Yvonne, coming to see me for the same reason Milton had. I snatched the door open so fast, I almost pulled it off the hinges. It was Sadie.

"Odell, I'm sorry to bother you," she said in a edgy tone. She started wringing her hands and blinking like a owl. I treated my employees with respect, but my presence still made them nervous from time to time. I was firm and gracious, but I never let them forget who was boss. When Mac and Millie was running the store, they'd let Buddy and Sadie, and every stock boy they hired, walk all over them. They had never disciplined them for being late, lazy, or uppity. I'd never had no problems like that. Buddie and Sadie gossiped way too much. I didn't know any colored folks in Branson who didn't run off at the mouth, so I overlooked that. If I kept them happy, I knew they'd keep me happy. "I . . . I came to ask you if it was all right to let Earl have another pig foot?"

"Who the hell is Earl?" I boomed.

"Earl Griswald, the stock boy you hired last month."

I had hired so many stock boys since I took over, I couldn't keep up with their names. They came and went for one reason or another. Usually it was because they couldn't get to work on time, or we'd caught them stealing merchandise. "Oh," I said in a gentle tone.

"Earl is such a sweet boy. He was so anxious to get here this morning, he forgot to bring a sandwich from home like he been doing." I was glad to see that Sadie was more at ease now.

"Let him have all the pig feet he can eat. If he want to make a sandwich, give him a couple of them hoecakes you brung from home, and a bottle of RC Cola to wash it all down with."

"Why, thank you, Odell. Earl will be so pleased." Sadie's face lit up like a firefly. "I'll let you get back to work now."

I waited until she had returned to her workstation before I went to the aisle a few feet away where we kept the pest control products. I glanced around to make sure nobody was lurking about, the way Buddy had done when I'd took the kerosene, which I had never used to burn weeds in Daddy's backyard. I was going to keep it on hand just in case he did ask me to do that.

When I seen that the coast was clear, I snatched one of the biggest bottles off the shelf. I needed to be prepared in case Yvonne and Milton needed more than a few doses. All I had to do now was figure out how I was going to get it in them devils' vile bodies.

■ ■ ■ ■

When I got home from work, Joyce was in the kitchen cooking fried chicken, macaroni and cheese, mustard greens, and hush puppies. "Hi, honey," she said when I kissed the back of her neck. When she spun around, I kissed her on the lips. "I'm cooking enough in case Yvonne and Milton decide to come back this evening."

My chest and stomach got tight and I moved a few inches away from her. "Why would you think they'd be coming back over here this evening? They told you that?"

"Not exactly. After I got supper started, I decided to go sweep off the back porch. Yvonne was in her backyard hanging clothes on the line. I tried to get back inside before she saw me, but I didn't make it. First, she wanted to know if she could borrow some clothespins. When I brought them to her, she told me they might see us later. I told her we wouldn't be coming over tonight. Before I could stop myself, I said how sorry I was we hadn't been able to keep company with them when they came over Thanksgiving evening."

"Why did you apologize? She should have apologized to you for them showing up

294

uninvited when you had already told her we wanted to be alone. Shoot."

"Odell, don't make a big deal out of nothing," Joyce insisted. She wiped her hands on her apron and started walking toward the living room with me close behind. "I'm really looking forward to that supper they offered me. If we upset them, they might change their minds."

We plonked down on the couch. Before either one of us could speak again, the telephone rung and Joyce grabbed it. While she was chatting with her mama, I went to use the toilet.

When I got back to the living room, she had hung up. "Baby, that was Mama. Mervis and Jubal got back home from visiting their son in Mobile. They want Mama and Daddy to come to Lexington this evening to eat supper with them."

"That's a long drive," I commented, sitting back down on the couch. "The way your daddy drags along, it'll be pitch-black by the time they get there. Why don't they wait and go in the morning?"

"Mervis is cooking ribs, collard greens, and spoon bread for supper. Mama and Daddy are afraid everything will get gobbled up if they don't get over there this evening. They're going to spend the night."

"You going with them?"

"Mama asked me if I wanted to go, but I told her we might be having company for supper. I wouldn't mind going with them, though . . ."

"Then go. Call your mama back and tell her. And hurry up before they leave."

"What if Yvonne and Milton come over here this evening? I'd hate for you to have to deal with them alone."

"They don't bite, so don't worry about that." I laughed.

While Joyce was on the telephone with her mama again, a thought jumped into my head that almost made me do a cartwheel. If Yvonne and Milton came over for supper this evening, I could lace their food with the poison. But within a split second, that thought jumped back out of my mind. I didn't want them to get sick in my house while they was having supper with me. If they did, it might look suspicious that they got sick and I didn't. And if they died on the spot, I'd really have a mess on my hands. I had to get them to take the poison some other way.

CHAPTER 32
ODELL

Joyce apologized so much about leaving me on my own for the night, I was scared she'd change her mind. "Baby, your folks is already on the way to pick you up. I'd rather you disappoint me than them. I'll be fine by myself. You coming home tomorrow morning before you go to work?"

"Uh-uh. I'm going to take some work clothes with me, and I'll have Daddy drop me off at the school when we get back to Branson. If you don't want to be bothered with Yvonne and Milton over here this evening, don't answer the door if they come. If you decide to go over there, that's fine. I think you should. After all you went through with your daddy this weekend, you deserve to have some fun."

"I probably will go next door for a little while. Just to get out of the house." Milton wanted his four hundred bucks earlier, so I would have to alter my plans. The same day

297

he'd first demanded this huge payment, I'd started swiping a few extra dollars out of the cash registers each evening when I closed. I'd also been withdrawing some from my checking account every other day. But I was still fifty dollars short. Now that my in-laws was going to be away from home overnight, I could sneak into their house and take the rest from the stash in the pantry. The next thing I knew, I got a notion that almost knocked me off my feet. It would make more sense to take the whole four hundred from the pantry and keep the other money I had saved up. That would be more money for Betty Jean and my boys. I scolded myself for not thinking of this sooner.

Ten minutes after Joyce's parents picked her up, I drove to their house. I was in and out within five minutes with four hundred dollars in my pocket. Swiping money from the cash registers, fudging the invoices and all the other tricks I had to do to keep up my lifestyle wasn't so bad. That didn't even faze me. But looting such a big amount at one time from their home made me feel a little jittery, and more like a common crook. I had to do what I had to, though. Besides, I believed that any other man in the fix I was in, would probably do the same thing.

And they probably wouldn't be as subtle about it as I was.

When I got back home, I gulped down a shot of whiskey to calm my nerves. Twenty minutes later, I went next door. The whiskey had made me more mellow and I hoped it would help keep me from getting too ugly with Milton or Yvonne if they said something to set me off. I actually smiled when he opened the door. "Odell, my man. Good to see you." He looked over his shoulder for a split second, and then turned back to me, speaking in a lower tone. "I didn't expect to see you tonight, especially after our little meeting today. What do you want to drink?"

"I ain't drinking nothing tonight." I shook my head as he waved me in. As soon as he closed the door, I leaned closer to him and whispered, "Can we go somewhere to talk?" He raised a eyebrow, but he didn't say nothing. He just motioned for me to follow him to the kitchen. I had spent so much unpleasant time in this room lately, I was glad them walls couldn't talk.

I didn't like his tone when he started talking. "Listen here, if you came to try and weasel out —"

I held up my hand and cut him off as fast as I could. "I got your four hundred bucks."

Milton's eyes got so big and bulgy, it

looked like they was going to pop clean out of the sockets. "Thank you, Jesus. Thank you for blessing me and Yvonne with a friend like Odell." The way he was bouncing up and down on the balls of his feet, I thought he was going to rise up to the ceiling. "Where is it at?" He rubbed his palms together and then held one out. "Give it here."

I pulled the wad out of my pocket and handed it to him. "You don't need to count it."

His eyes bulged out even more and his lips formed such a big smile, you would have thought I'd just handed him the keys to Heaven's pearly gates. Even his tone of voice was blissful now. "Odell, you just made my day. I'll give this to Willie Frank before he leaves, and he can take it to Lamar first thing in the morning. Or drop it off on his way home tonight." Milton slid the money into his pocket and shook my hand. "My man, I just love doing business with you."

I snatched my hand away as fast as I could and glared at him. "I ain't your 'man' and this ain't hardly 'doing business,' " I blasted. "I wanted to get this over with as soon as possible so I can move on with my life and get my peace of mind back."

He gave me a weary look and whined, "I need my peace of mind back, too. You don't know how worried I was about us not paying Lamar back." He suddenly smiled again. "You sure you don't want a drink? Tonight you can have as many as you want on the house."

"No, but thanks for offering. I can't stay. Listen, I . . . uh . . . was wondering if you and Yvonne was going to be available tomorrow evening?"

He turned his head and looked at me from the corner of his eye. "For what?"

"Well, I know y'all like to fish. I was wondering if y'all wanted to go with me for a little while. We wouldn't stay long so you'd be back in time to entertain your guests."

"Taking off a couple of hours wouldn't be no problem. Willie Frank always covers for us when we can't be here." He was still gazing at me from the corner of his eye. "What brung this on? We been friends almost six months and you ain't never invited us to go fishing before."

I shrugged. "I just wanted to do something to show y'all that I ain't got no hard feelings toward y'all. I'll bring some of that beer from the store y'all like."

"That would be sweet. Let me talk to Yvonne. She probably won't want to come,

301

but maybe I can make it."

"Well, I was hoping she'd come, too. Since you and her plan on taking Joyce out to supper, I'd like to do something nice for y'all."

"Is Joyce going fishing, too?"

"She went to Lexington this evening with her folks to visit some relatives, and they'll be spending the night. She's going to go to work straight from there in the morning. I won't get a chance to ask her until I either call her sometime before she leaves Lexington, or when she gets to work. I'm sure she'll say yeah, though. But if she don't, me and you and Yvonne can still go."

I had never seen such a skeptical look on Milton's face. He cleared his throat and rubbed the back of his head. "Like I said, I have to check with Yvonne first. If you can slide through here again for a minute tomorrow evening, I'll let you know then. If we can't make it tomorrow or any other day this week, how about next week?"

"I might not be in the mood then. The weather is starting to get too cold to go fishing."

"I can't see how it could get too much colder in a week. Anyway, we'll shoot for tomorrow. Now before you go, there is just one more issue we need to conversate about."

302

"What?" There was no telling what Milton was going to tell me.

He licked his lips and gave me a tight smile. That made my chest tighten. "Me and Yvonne want to have a little leeway, so we'll need another lump sum."

I held my breath and glared at him. I was so stunned and enraged, I could barely stand still. "How much of a lump sum, and when do you need it?"

"I want another five hundred and I need it no later than next week on Friday."

It took a few seconds for his words to sink in. When I realized what he was saying, I was furious. "Milton, you can't be serious. And you want it by next week?"

"I'm as serious as polio. That don't give you much time to get the money, but I *know* you will. I'll come by the store to pick it up on my lunch break, so you won't have to be late going to visit your daddy that evening."

One thing I had promised myself was that I would never lose my temper and grab Milton or Yvonne by the throat during one of our encounters. But his new demand almost made me do it. Somehow, I managed to keep my cool. I didn't even bother to protest no more. Because as soon as Yvonne and Milton was dead, I'd steal the five hundred dollars back. That meant I had

303

to kill them the same day I gave them the money before they spent it. "All right then. Come to the store any time after noon next Friday and I'll give it to you." I was so elated knowing that them motherfuckers' days was numbered, I actually smiled. "Now will you excuse me? I have to get going."

Before I could even turn around, Milton grabbed ahold of my arm, narrowed his eyes, and shook his head. "Odell, I declare, you never cease to amaze me." He grinned.

I pried his hand off my arm before I replied. "I can say the same thing about you."

"True. I have to admit that I didn't know it would be this easy to get more money from you. If I had known it was —"

I cut him off immediately. "Milton, it ain't easy. But I'll do whatever it is I have to do."

"Bless your soul, Odell. That's what I wanted to hear." He reached out his hand for me to shake again. I ignored it. The only thing I wanted to do to it was bite it in two. The scowl on my face made him stop grinning and pull his hand back. That bastard stood in the same spot, looking confused, when I rushed to the living room.

I could barely breathe now. A couple of other folks attempted to conversate with me, but I ignored them and scurried out the front door. My head felt so light, I had to lean against the porch wall to compose myself before taking another step.

When I got home, I paced back and forth in my living room like a caged tiger, trying to decide if the fishing plan was a smart one or not. If I got them out to one of the isolated lakes where very few folks fished, I'd ply them with the tainted beer right away. Once they got weak enough, I'd drag them back to the car and drive further into the woods to the nearest pool of quicksand and dump them in. When they didn't come home, Willie Frank would no doubt come to my house and ask where they was. I'd tell him that they had decided not to go fishing with me when they ran into a old friend from the neighborhood they used to live in, and had gone off somewhere with him. I'd also tell Willie Frank that I'd tried to talk them out of going because the man was one of the bootleggers who was still pissed off about losing business to them. I wasn't concerned about nobody stumbling across their bodies because everything that went into quicksand and sunk to the bottom, stayed there. If Willie Frank didn't bring up calling the police to report them missing, I would. Sheriff Potts wouldn't spend too much time trying to locate them, though.

CHAPTER 33
YVONNE

Right after Odell left, Milton headed toward our bedroom. Just as I was about to follow him, a guest asked for another drink, so I had to tend to him before I went to see what Milton was up to.

Before I could get out of the living room, Sweet Sue came up to me. "Girl, everybody is raving about them fried chicken wings. I just ate the last one," she said. "Can you go cook some more?"

"Um, you know where everything is at. Can you do it for me?"

"I guess I could. You know, I do so much when I come over here, I feel like the help," she grumbled.

"You can drink for free the rest of the night," I assured her.

"That suits me just fine." As soon as Sweet Sue headed toward the kitchen, I whirled around and took off before anybody else could hem me up.

Milton had locked our bedroom door. That didn't sit too well with me. I pounded on it with my fist, and he opened it right away. "Why did you lock the door?" I asked, wagging my finger in his face.

"I didn't want to be disturbed," he muttered, blinking like he was nervous.

"Milton, I live here. And ain't nobody else got no business coming in this bedroom unless we ask them."

"I know, baby. But you can't predict what drunk folks will do. The bathroom is right across the hall and somebody might make a wrong turn."

His explanation was flimsy, and it wasn't what I wanted to hear. "I want to know what you and Odell was talking about in the kitchen a few minutes ago?"

"Close the door back," he ordered. I did so and locked it. I'd caught a glimpse of Aunt Mattie heading into the bathroom. If somebody was going to stumble into our bedroom by mistake, I didn't want it to be a nosy busybody like her.

"Now answer my question. And don't you try to —" I stopped talking when Milton went to the dresser and opened the top drawer. He reached in and pulled out a wad of money thick enough to choke a mule. "W-what's that?"

"Our early Christmas present." He grinned. "Odell brung our three hundred bucks tonight." He fanned the money, sniffed it, and then kissed it.

"Bless his heart," I mouthed. Milton held the money up to my nose and I sniffed it. "Ooh-wee. There ain't nothing in the world that smells as good as money."

"I don't know about that now. You smell pretty good." He winked and chuckled. "And you taste good too."

"You behave yourself," I scolded, slapping the side of his head. I exhaled and reached over and caressed the money.

"I was putting the money in this drawer until later tonight. After everybody leaves, I'll give it to Willie Frank to give to Lamar." Milton put the money back in the drawer under a stack of my socks.

"Did you tell Odell we'll need another three hundred?"

"Uh-huh. He said he'd give it to me next week," he told me as he closed the drawer and draped his arm around my shoulder.

I gasped. "Just like that?"

"Just like that."

"Damn. This turned out to be easier than I thought."

"Tell me about it. But it ain't going to get him off the hook." Milton took his arm from my shoulder, narrowed his eyes, and stared at me. "W-why you looking so sad all of a sudden?"

"I ain't sad. I just wish we didn't have to hurt Joyce so much in the process. She looks down on us, and says things that hurt. But she ain't a bad person. Just snooty and insensitive and out of touch with real folks like us. I don't think she can even tell when she's hurting our feelings. Other than that, she's been nice to us. It's a shame we'll hurt her when we tell her about Odell and Betty Jean."

Milton snickered. "Pffft. That's her problem. If we don't tell Joyce what her Prince Charming is up to, somebody else might catch him with Betty Jean and tell her. If that was to happen before we got that other lump sum, he won't have no reason to pay it. We done come this far, it would be foolish for us to stop now. I can't believe you having second thoughts this late in the game. Even if we don't get that money from him, we still have to punish him for lying to Sheriff Potts about us."

"I ain't having no second thoughts. I just made a comment. And there's something else I been thinking about. Joyce is going to be hurt sure enough, but *we'd* be hurt even more if Odell was to do something to get

310

back at us some other way before we chastise him, and before we tell Joyce. We been pushing our luck for a long time. Sooner or later, we'll push him so close up against a brick wall, he'll snap."

Milton gave me a serious look. "Baby, believe me, I know what you mean. That's crossed my mind, too. I think Odell is already up against a brick wall. He said something tonight that threw me for a loop."

"Humph. He's pretty good at throwing us for loops."

"I'm serious, Yvonne. I think he's cooking up something else to get back at us."

Milton's words gave me a jolt. "Oh? What did he say?"

"He wants me and you to go fishing with him tomorrow evening."

I shook my head. "Fishing?" I shook my head harder. "That's mighty suspicious to me. Odell must hate our guts by now, so why would he want us to go fishing with him?"

"There ain't no telling. After all we done did to him, I wouldn't feel safe going to church with him these days."

"And how come he wants to go tomorrow evening — before we get the other money you told him we want? I hope you told him we don't want to go."

"I told him I'd check with you first. But I had already made up my mind not to go. I just wanted to stall him. I told him if we couldn't make it tomorrow, we'd go next week."

"Everything will be over by next weekend. That Friday will be the beginning of the end." I sighed and looked toward the window. "Uh, you know it ain't too late for us to back out. We don't have to tell Joyce nothing, and we'll still get that money from Odell."

Milton's mouth dropped open. "Yeah, we'd get the money from him, but if we don't stop him from getting back at us again, we might not live long enough to spend that money. Remember Willie Frank done warned that as long as Odell is alive, he's a threat. Now if you don't want to finish this project with me, I'll do it by myself . . ."

"Hush up. You know I would never let you handle something this serious on your own. We been working together too long, and everything we do is for the both of us. But . . ." I paused and gave Milton a thoughtful look. "Do you ever wonder how things would have turned out for us if you hadn't caught Odell with Betty Jean?"

"Nope. I'm just glad I did." Milton tickled

my side and gave me a quick kiss. "I'm glad you did, too."

CHAPTER 34
MILTON

Business had been pretty good for a Monday night. While guests was finishing up their last drink, I pulled Willie Frank into the kitchen. "What's going on?" he asked, looking me up and down.

I didn't say nothing at first. I just reached into my pocket and pulled out the three hundred dollars we owed his uncle. "Paid in full," I said as I stuffed the bills into his shirt pocket.

He looked puzzled for a few seconds. Then his eyes got big. "Uncle Lamar's money? It ain't due until Thursday. I seen him this morning and he told me to remind y'all."

"I know it ain't due yet. But me and Yvonne was so anxious to get it over and done with, we decided to pay it off early. Um . . . I was able to borrow the whole amount from Odell and he said I could pay it back when I can. Under the circumstances, it's the least he can do."

"That's nice. This'll sure impress Uncle Lamar. If y'all need to get money from him again, I got a feeling he'll look at how prompt y'all settled with him this time and be glad to lend more."

"Well, I hope we won't get in a fix this big again."

"You still going to try and hit up Dr. Patterson and Mr. Cunningham? Y'all still need to make up for the time you missed work. You can delay your next two payments to me for your alcohol orders until February. And I'll float y'all fifty bucks next week after I collect from some of my customers. I'll give you more if and when I can afford it. My offer to borrow from Aunt Mattie is still open, too."

"Thanks for allowing me to pay for my orders in February. And you know we'll be glad to get them fifty bucks from you next week." I suddenly had a change of heart. "Uh . . . Yvonne don't need to know about them fifty dollars you going to give me. After you, she is my other right hand. But she is a woman. It's her nature to get greedy and try and get me to get even more from you."

"No problem. I believe that the 'other right hand' don't never need to know what the left hand is doing."

"I'll decide later if we want to borrow from Mr. Cunningham and Dr. Patterson. Hold off on Aunt Mattie for the time being, too. We don't need to eat all our apples at the same time. We'll let them be our back-up plan, in case we need one. But this money from Odell don't change nothing. We still need to punish him. Me and Yvonne is trying to decide what's the best punishment for him. As soon as we do, we'll let you know that, too."

"I done told you before, don't put it off too long. He could be brewing up something else."

I had to come up with something to stall Willie Frank until after I got that five hundred dollars from Odell. Since I was such a fast thinker, I came up with what sounded like the perfect plan right away. "Okay. We'll take care of him next Sunday."

"Why then and not before?"

"Well, we can't do nothing until after me and Yvonne take Joyce to that supper we promised her. She said she can't go until next Friday. Odell will be at his daddy's house that whole weekend. We'll get him on his way home on Sunday. Bring your shotgun."

Willie Frank looked at me with his eyes

316

stretched wide-open. "So, you want to kill him after all, for sure, huh? You don't want to do none of them other things we talked about?"

"Naw. Sinking his car in the quicksand, and all that other stuff we talked about won't be enough. We definitely need to kill him. And I don't think we need to worry no more about none of them agitating politicians making a fuss about somebody killing a prominent man like Odell." The murder plan I came up with at the spur of the moment seemed reasonable enough to me. "We'll run him off the road and force him into the woods on foot. We'll do him there and take all his money. It'll look like a robbery, and ain't nobody got a reason to suspect us. There is a heap of ex-cons and other lowlifes operating on them roads near Odell's daddy's house."

Willie Frank scratched the top of his head. "Well, I'll bring my gun if you want me to. But I'd better bring a rope, too. We already talked about stringing him up, remember? A shotgun blast would be too noisy, not to mention messy. Besides, a hanging would look like typical Klan activity. They've been busy raising hell all over the South this year, including two lynchings in the same week. They'll no doubt get blamed."

"Hmmm. Yeah, bring a rope in case we decide to take him out that way."

"All right then. One more thing, how do you know what time he'll leave his daddy's house?"

"Um . . . we'll have to go out there at some point and hide somewhere until we see him leave."

"All right, buddy. I can't wait to see his face when we let him know we know he made that call to Sheriff Potts."

"I can't wait neither."

I hated deceiving Willie Frank, but I didn't have no choice. I still didn't think it would be a good idea to let him know about our plan to tell Joyce about Betty Jean — or that Betty Jean even existed. For one thing, I didn't want him to feel left out if he found out we'd known about Odell's secret life all this time and didn't share that information with him. But he was the one who told me it wasn't a good idea to let the right hand know what the left hand was doing. Even when he was the right hand in question.

After I collected them five hundred dollars from Odell and took Joyce to Hartville next Friday, there was no telling what would happen next. Me and Willie Frank wouldn't be hiding nowhere on that road that led to Odell's daddy's house so we could ambush

318

him next Sunday like I'd told him. But this was the best way I could stall him for the time being by letting him think we would.

If Joyce forgave Odell and things went on as usual between them, I knew he would come after me and Yvonne. We wouldn't give him a chance to do us in, though. As soon as we found out our plan to ruin his life with Joyce didn't work, *then* me and Willie Frank would ambush him somewhere and take him out in the woods and put him down. There was no telling how many new lies I'd have to come up with to tell Willie Frank so he would never suspect we kept him in the dark about our involvement in this mess. One thing that gave me hope was the chance Joyce would kill him, or he would take hisself out. But for now, I wasn't going to count on that happening.

Time was going by so fast. The clock in my head was ticking so loud, you would have thought it was a time bomb. Odell didn't come back to the house on Tuesday to see if we was going fishing with him. I didn't think he would nohow. There was something "fishy" about his invitation. I had a feeling that after he thought about it a little more, he realized I'd suspected something was up. With everything that had happened, there was no way me and Yvonne was going to go off somewhere alone with him. The fact that he had done something as unspeakable as lying to the white folks about us, was proof that he was dangerous. And so was we.

Odell showed up Wednesday night a few minutes before eight. Right after he got in the house and greeted a few folks, he motioned for me to go into the kitchen with him. When we got there, Sweet Sue and Tiny, the cute midget prostitute who worked for Aunt Mattie, was standing by the stove giggling about something with Willie Frank. I beckoned for Odell to follow me to my bedroom. The way he was dragging his feet, you would have thought he was on his way to his execution. When we got inside, he kicked the door shut. "I just came to give you your eight dollars." I couldn't believe the evil eye he gave me when he pulled a five and three ones out of his pocket.

"Thank you very much." I snatched the money, folded it in two and slid it into my back pocket. "What drink do you want me to get for you?" Despite the mean way he was looking at me and his harsh tone, I was still able to behave like a gentleman.

"Nothing." His tone was so snippy, it sounded like he had spit out the word. He was already walking back toward the door.

"Hold your horses," I ordered, grabbing his arm. He looked at me like he wanted to cut my head off. "In case I don't see you no more this week, I need to know if we still cool for next Friday?"

Odell looked puzzled for a few seconds. "Yeah. If you can't get to the store before I leave for the day, you'll have to wait until Sunday night when I get back home."

"Oh, you ain't got to worry about me not getting there before you leave," I assured him. "I want my money. And, if it ain't asking too much, give me small bills."

"I will. Is that it?" he said with a smirk.

"Well, since you asked, I'm a little curious." I cleared my throat and narrowed my eyes. "How come you ain't making a big fuss about giving me another five hundred dollars? It don't bother you?"

"Hell yes, it bothers me. But what good would it do for me to make a fuss? It didn't make no difference none of them other times."

I narrowed my eyes even more. "How do you know I won't come back for more after you give me that five hundred?"

"Look, Milton. I'm sure you'll have more demands in the future. I'll deal with them as they come up."

My breath caught in my throat and my

eyes got wide. "Do you mean to tell me I can keep this up as long as I want to?"

Odell nodded. "That's about the size of it."

I didn't know what to make of Odell. He was one of a kind. Not only was he a complete *fool,* he had to be one of the wimpiest men alive to let me and Yvonne take advantage of him in such a big way. But I had to admire him for being sly enough to keep two women happy and lead two separate lives. I would never try to pull off hanky-panky that extreme without the help of Aunt Mattie's hoodoo black magic. Yvonne was way too smart to let me get away with a on-going story like his "sick daddy" tale, without doing some serious investigating. Anyway, I was glad Odell was *our* fool. It was a shame I hadn't caught him with Betty Jean sooner. If I had, me and Yvonne would be eating steak on a regular basis instead of pig ears, and we'd be sleeping up under eiderdown quilts. "I declare, we sure do appreciate your generosity."

"I'm sure y'all do," he snapped. He gave me one of his usual mean looks and stormed out of the room. By the time I got back to the living room, he was gone.

■ ■ ■

Joyce came to the house Friday and Saturday. Odell didn't come again until the following Wednesday. And he only stayed long
enough to give me my weekly payment. He
never mentioned us going fishing with him
again and I sure as hell wasn't going to
bring it up.

CHAPTER 35
MILTON

I was glad the big Friday had finally rolled around. This time I borrowed Mr. Cunningham's truck to drive to Odell's office. There was a lot of customers in MacPherson's when I got there shortly after noon, so Sadie and Buddy didn't notice when I whizzed past them.

Odell didn't even look surprised, or mad (yet), when I strolled into his office and closed the door behind me. When he held up his hand, I stopped in front of his desk. "Don't bother to sit. You won't be staying long," he said in a flat tone.

"That's fine with me. I don't want to stay nowhere I ain't wanted." He gave me a dirty look as he reached in his pocket. He pulled out a wad of cash and handed it to me. "Damn," I mouthed. I looked at him and blinked. "Goodness gracious, Odell. You really been on the ball lately, my man. I'm impressed. Yvonne will be tickled to death when I get home. I don't think she believed you'd give us more money again so soon."

"She'll believe it when you show it to her. Now please get the hell up out of here." He pointed toward the door.

"I'm going, I'm going, I'm going," I chanted, still standing in the same spot.

"Go faster, damn you."

"You ain't got to be such a bully. I didn't come here to get my feelings hurt," I pouted.

Odell's jaw dropped. "I can't believe what you just said. Every time you come here you hurt my feelings. Now get your disgusting black ass out of my sight!"

"I said I was going. But there is something else I want to say before I leave." I swallowed hard and shifted my weight from one foot to the other. Odell glared at me even harder. "I never thought things would turn out the way they did. I almost wish I hadn't caught you with Betty Jean."

His gasp was so loud it sounded like a fart. "Milton, how can you say some mess like that with a straight face? You jumped on this opportunity like white on rice. So don't be trying to lighten up what you and Yvonne been doing to me. Now get!"

I started walking backward toward the door. "Okay, I'm leaving." I whirled around, snatched open the door, and skittered out before he said something that would make me lose my religion. But the thoughts bouncing around in my head about what was coming up this evening with Joyce, was hard to process. I was a little nervous about it. But at the same time, I was anxious to get it over and done with.

I took my time walking back through the store, glancing around at all the nice new stuff laid out. Me and Yvonne had swiped hundreds of dollars' worth of merchandise from this store, and we'd charged our credit account up to the limit. We didn't plan on paying it off now. With all the stuff we had on Odell, he wouldn't be stupid enough to sue us.

When I got outside, I stood in front of the store and stared in the window at the Christmas decorations next to the new frocks Odell had put on display. There was a black-and-white striped suit with a double-breasted jacket that would have made me look as sharp as a tack. I was tempted to go back inside and tell Odell to give it to me so I could wear it at the Christmas party me and Yvonne was think-ing about hosting. But that five hundred dollars felt so good in my pocket, I didn't want to go back and take a chance on him saying something else to upset me and ruin my mood even more. This was probably going to be the last time I visited MacPherson's, so I focused my attention on that suit for another minute. I wanted to savor the moment.

Willie Frank picked me and Yvonne up after work and drove us home. We was going to use his truck to take Joyce out, and he was going to stay at the house and hold down the fort for us.

Me and Yvonne took turns peeping out the window until we seen the car that belonged to the lady Joyce rode to and from work with. After she piled out and went in her house, we didn't waste no time going over there.

"I'm sorry I'm running late," she said as she beckoned us in. "Just as Patsy and I were leaving the school, she remembered she had hung some clothes on the line yesterday evening and forgot to get them off this morning and bring them inside. She tried to call her husband to tell him to do it, but he didn't answer the phone. Anyway, she had to rush to her house before she brought me home and take them down before they got too stiff. I told her she shouldn't be hanging clothes on the line outside this late in the year in the first place. It's way too chilly, and it looks like rain is on the way. This time of year, I hang my clothes on the lines Odell hung up in the attic."

I was in no mood to listen to her mundane comments about laundry details, so I prodded her along. "Um, me and Yvonne didn't eat much lunch, so we'd better get going before we get too weak," I said with a grin as I rubbed my belly.

"Oh, okay. I ate one sandwich for lunch so I'm pretty hungry myself." Then she started grinning. "Y'all have a seat while I run in the bathroom and splash on one of my smell-goods and change into the outfit I bought just to wear for this evening." She abruptly stopped talking. "Are we still going to an out-of-town restaurant?"

"Yes and no. But not the one we told you about. We had to change our plans a little bit."

"Oh? Why is that?"

"Um, one of our customers at the grill told us that they was doing some remodeling at that place in Mobile. We decided to go to a place we heard about in Hartville," Yvonne said as we plopped down on the couch. "Folks say they serve some world-beating food."

"Hartville? Hmmm. I haven't been to that town since I attended a revival over there eight years ago. It's such a countrified hick town, I can't see them having too many nice places to eat. And they got grasshoppers as big as shot glasses hopping all over the place."

"Joyce, I'm sure you'll love the restaurant we going to, and you ain't got to worry about no grasshoppers this late in the year. Now I don't mean to rush you, but the sooner we get going, the sooner we can eat and get back home," I said.

She darted out of the room and came back ten minutes later. "I didn't take too long, I hope."

"Don't worry about it. We'll still have plenty of time to enjoy our meal," Yvonne said.

"Joyce, you look so nice in that pink flowered blouse and that matching pink skirt," I commented. She looked like a pink giraffe and smelled like she'd been dipped in a bowl of rose sachet. "And you smell so good."

"I know," she said with a sniff. "Odell loves to see me in this color. He says it makes me look like a film star. Yvonne, you need to add a few pink pieces to your wardrobe. I'd be glad to help you pick out a few."

"I'd like that, Joyce. I'll come over one day and we'll go through your Sears and Roebuck catalog." Yvonne snuck a glance at me and rolled her eyes.

"Uh-uh. I think we'd be better off going shopping in town. The stuff in the catalog is too sophisticated for you. Besides that, it's out of your price range."

If we had to listen to this kind of talk all the way to Hartville, I was scared I'd be stir-crazy by the time we got there.

CHAPTER 36
YVONNE

The comments Joyce made before we left her house didn't ruffle my feathers no more than none of the other stupid stuff she'd said to me since we met. That was the reason I'd been able to stay calm and not say nothing to drag her down during the ride to Hartville. I had a feeling that when the trip was over, she'd be feeling so low, she'd never low-rate me again. Couldn't nothing bring a person down quicker than them finding out they been played for a fool. Especially in Joyce's case.

She was so excited about us taking her out, you would have thought it was the first time she'd ever ate in public. Before Milton even steered the truck onto the main highway, she started spewing more trash talk than a junkman. "I was flabbergasted when y'all invited me to go out for supper. I have to admit, and I hope y'all don't take this the wrong way, but I thought y'all would choose one of the chicken shacks or rib joints on the lower south side. I'm so glad we're not going to a restaurant in Mobile. That city scares me. A lot of the convicts end up there when they get out of prison." Joyce glanced out the window for a few moments and then she shifted in her seat next to the passenger window. She looked around inside the truck cab, frowning and shaking her head. I was not surprised when she ran her finger across the dashboard before she went on. "I sure wish we could have ridden in something better than this dusty, tobacco-smelling old truck. I thought y'all were going to borrow Mr. Cunningham's truck."

"We was, but he had some relatives show up unannounced on foot today. He had to keep his truck in case he had to haul them around," I explained.

"Oh. The next time we go out to eat, we'll have to make sure it's when Odell is available. That way we can go in a decent vehicle. He keeps his spotless and fresh smelling. Just like everything else he owns."

I didn't feel like listening to this cow complain about anything else, or brag about Odell. I decided to take the conversation in another direction. "At first, we even talked about cooking supper for you at home. Them restaurants can be so expensive. And, as you know, we been having some serious money problems lately."

"We don't have to go out. I'd be just as happy if y'all treated me to a home-cooked meal," she said. "Oh well. It's probably too late to do it for this evening, but some other time would be okay. The only thing is, I'd like to choose what y'all cook. Odell and I eat enough possum and squirrel meat at my parents' house."

"No, no, no," I chanted. "After we thought a little more about cooking something at home, we decided to do something more personal. With all the traffic in and out of our house, a supper there wouldn't be as much fun. Other people would want to eat, and it wouldn't be as special as eating out. Besides that, me and Milton cook every day. It's a treat to us when somebody else do all the cooking."

"All right then. I just hope this raggedy old jalopy doesn't break down before we can get to Hartville and back. I'd hate to be stranded on a dark gravel road in my new clothes." Joyce looked at the plain green-and-white dress I had on. "Girl, you must love that dress. I've seen you in it at least a dozen times in the last couple of months. I wonder why it hasn't fallen apart at the seams by now. When it does, it'd make some

333

good quilt pieces and dust rags. Where in the world did you find it?"

"At a secondhand store."

"I figured that. They stopped making that style years ago."

I was seething, but I managed to bite my tongue. "Well, you know me. I ain't half as good as you when it comes to keeping up with what's in fashion. But this dress is so sturdy, I'm pretty sure I can wear it at least a dozen more times before I wear it out."

"I'm sure you will." Joyce shifted in her seat again. "It's been months since Odell took me to a restaurant other than Mosella's, or one of the chicken or rib shacks in Branson or Lexington. What's the name of this place in Hartville?"

"It's Po' Sister's Kitchen. A lot of our regular customers at the grill told us about it," I replied. "Some of the folks who come drink at the house mention it all the time. They claim that them folks serve the best deep-fried, buttermilk-marinated catfish in the world."

"If I like it, Odell and I will treat y'all to supper there some day," she gushed. "He doesn't like to drive, and he probably won't be too eager to go because it takes about an hour to get to Hartville. I'm sure I can talk him into it, though."

I had to hold my breath to keep from laughing at her last remark. Odell put at least a hundred miles a week on his car going to and from Hartville.

"Joyce, feel free to take a snooze if you want to. We don't mind," Milton piped in.

She giggled. "Oh, I'm not sleepy. I'd rather chat. Talking to y'all is a lot less complicated than it is with most of the other folks Odell and I know; teachers and other professionals. With them, I have to keep my guard up so I won't say anything ignorant or offensive. I can say whatever comes to my mind around y'all."

There was no end to this happy heifer's petty put-downs. Instead of showing my disgust, I forced myself to act normal. I detoured the conversation by saying how happy and grateful me and Milton was to be out of jail. He made a few comments about how shocked, mad, and disappointed we was that somebody would go so far to get us in trouble with the law.

Joyce clicked her tongue and went on to say things that really ruffled my feathers. "Well, with all the enemies y'all got, something bad was bound to happen sooner or later. Odell said, and I agreed with him, that they'll more than likely try something else eventually. I hope your aunt and uncle don't

335

hear about the arrest. If they do, I doubt if they'll ever let you have your kids back. I advise y'all to pray every day and be more careful who you let in your house. The same culprit that fingered y'all might still be coming around and might try something else."

I was itching to tell Joyce that we *knew* who the culprit was. We planned to do that when she asked us why we was blowing the whistle on Odell. I was a little concerned that she might have a heart attack and drop dead before we could get the whole story out. But at least she'd die knowing what a deceitful, fake, Goody Two-shoes, adulterous snake she'd married. If she didn't die and was still sane afterwards, then we'd tell her that Odell was the one who had called Sheriff Potts on us. And we'd add that he'd been robbing her folks' business blind to support his other family. We'd tell her as much as we could before she shut down, or shut us down. I decided to mute up for a while and keep my face pointing forward. That way I could focus more on the road and she wouldn't see the disgusted look on my face.

After a few silent moments, Joyce started praising Odell again. "I wish every woman could know what it's like to be blessed with a man like mine." She went on and on until

I couldn't tell where one sentence ended and another one started. The picture she had painted of that asshole would make the Prince Charming in the fairy tale books I read in grade school look like a troll. I felt like I was going batty, and from the grimace on Milton's face, I could see that he was, too.

By the time Milton turned onto the street where Po' Sister's Kitchen was located, he couldn't take no more of her gabbing. "Joyce, Odell ain't the man you think he is," he blurted out. It wouldn't have seemed so harsh if he hadn't slapped the steering wheel when he said it.

Joyce jerked her head around and looked at Milton with her mouth hanging open. She let out a gasp that was so sharp, it sounded like somebody was letting the air out of a tire. "Say what?" she wheezed. I nudged him with my elbow. When he glanced at me, I shook my head. "Milton, what did you mean by that?" Joyce asked.

"Nothing. Come on, ladies," he mumbled as he parked the truck across the street from the restaurant. He piled out before she could say anything else.

When Joyce got out, there was a confused look on her face. But she didn't question Milton again as he ushered us across the street. "Good Lord. There must be two dozen folks in the line waiting to get in," she wailed. I sensed some tension in her tone, and in the awkward way she was moving. She was walking on them high heels of hers like she was stepping on eggshells. "We'll probably spend more time standing in line than we will eating."

"Don't worry. I know somebody that works here, so we can bypass the line." Milton started inching his way in as soon as we got to the door. I hoped that the same waitress we'd spoke to before about Odell was working today. If she wasn't, he was so well-known in Hartville, I knew we'd be able to get the same information from one of the others. One thing was for sure, we wouldn't leave this town until we had accomplished what we'd come to do.

338

CHAPTER 37
MILTON

The people waiting in line to get inside Po' Sister's Kitchen was grumbling and giving us dirty looks as I brushed past them. One joker cussed and tried to block my path. I went around him, guiding Yvonne and Joyce along like sheep to slaughter.

When we got inside, the smell of fried fish, greens, hush puppies, and every other thing I liked to smack on, made me wish we really was going to stay for supper. After everything was over and done with, I'd bring Yvonne back some day to enjoy some of the scrumptious food these folks served.

"My goodness. It sure smells good in here," Joyce commented. If she was still bothered by what I'd said about Odell in the truck a few minutes ago, she was hiding it good. "I can't wait to sink my teeth into some of that fish. Do they give big portions, Milton?"

"Yup. I guarantee when you leave here,

you won't never be the same again." When I added a snicker, Yvonne kicked the side of my foot and gave me a stern look.

The restaurant folks had put up a Christmas tree by the front entrance. It was so big, it blocked the view of the tables in the middle of the room. I had to step around it to see the main dining area better. I scanned the place for a few seconds and didn't see the waitress I was looking for. What I did see made me do a double take. As brazen as could be, there was Odell sitting at a table with Betty Jean and them three little boys. And it was the same table I seen them at when I busted him. I couldn't believe my luck. Joyce wouldn't have to hear no second-hand story from none of them waitresses. All the evidence was right in front of us. I stepped a little to the side so she and Yvonne could move forward and see what I seen.

Joyce froze. She stood in her spot as stiff and straight as a bean pole. "W-who are those people with my husband?" she asked in a raspy tone. She looked from me to Yvonne and back at Odell's table. I didn't have to answer her question. Odell draped his arm around Betty Jean's shoulder and leaned over and kissed her on the lips.

It was what he said loud enough for us to

hear that put the nail in his coffin. "Boys, y'all better stop fussing and finish your supper before you make Daddy go out and break a switch off one of them trees."

While Odell was wiping snot off the youngest boy's nose, the middle boy asked, "Daddy, you still taking us Christmas shopping tomorrow?"

Joyce didn't wait long enough to see or hear nothing else. She backed out the door with me and Yvonne moving right along with her. The people in the line had stopped grumbling and was just giving us curious looks now. "Joyce, where you going?" I tried to grab her hand, but she slapped mine away and gave me a hot look.

She stopped moving when we got to the sidewalk. Me and Yvonne stood a safe distance away. We didn't want to get punched in the nose if she broke loose and took out her anger on us. "W-what . . . what the hell is . . . is all that up in there?" she stuttered, nodding toward the restaurant entrance. "Is this supposed to be a joke?"

"Girl, what you just seen was the *real* Odell," I said. "I tried to tell you in the truck that he ain't the man you think he is."

Her lips quivered, her eyes blinked, and her voice dropped to a whisper. "Then how come when I asked you about it, you said

341

'nothing'?"

"Because I wanted you to see it up close instead," I explained.

Joyce swallowed hard and shook her head. She looked so miserable, I wanted to give her a hug. But I had a feeling that was the last thing she wanted from one of us. "What in the hell is going on?"

"You need to go in that restaurant and ask Odell that question," Yvonne advised.

"How long have y'all known about that woman?" Joyce narrowed her eyes and looked directly at me. "Milton, I know how some men like to boast to their male friends when they're involved with another woman. Sadie and Buddy told me how often you and Odell spend time in his office with the door closed. I don't believe you didn't know what he was up to before now."

If she thought I had been covering for Odell, there was no telling what she would do to me. "No, I didn't. I just found out a few weeks ago one Saturday evening when I accidentally stumbled up on him and Betty Jean and them kids at this same restaurant. I didn't shame him then because I didn't want to make a scene. Well, that Monday, I went to the store and told him to his face that I didn't like what he was doing! I couldn't let him give the rest of us married

Christian men a bad name!" I boomed.

"Not only that, he been stealing money left and right from your folks' business to support that woman and them kids. Part of the money he is using, is probably coming out of your paycheck," Yvonne tossed in. "We couldn't keep listening to you praise him knowing he was making a fool out of you and your parents."

"Yvonne, you knew about it and wasn't friend enough to tell me?" Joyce wailed, choking on a sob.

"Odell had enough wool to make a blanket pulled over your eyes. If we hadn't brung you over here to see it, would you have believed me if I told you?" Yvonne asked with her hands on her hips.

Joyce gave her a blank stare. "That biggest boy looks pretty old," she commented. "He must be at least four . . ."

"Yup. Which means Odell started up with Betty Jean right after he married you," I pointed out.

Joyce inhaled suddenly, with her mouth hanging open. "Betty Jean? Y'all even know her name?" She looked so miserable now, I was surprised she wasn't pulling her hair out and cussing a blue streak.

"Yup. He told me the whole story," I admitted.

343

"Joyce, I don't know how you want to handle this. If I was in your shoes, Milton would be mincemeat by now. You need to let Odell know you here. You want me to go ask him to come out here and face the music?" Yvonne said in a harsh tone of voice.

Instead of answering, Joyce mumbled gibberish for about five seconds. When she cleared her throat, so many tears started rolling down her cheeks, it looked like somebody had threw a bucket of water in her face. Then she started sniffling and moaning like a dying cow. Next thing we knew, she stumbled out to the street and ran down the middle in the opposite direction. A truck and two cars had to swerve to keep from hitting her. She was howling and waving her hands like a windmill. The people towards the back of the restaurant line turned around and yelled for somebody to catch her before she got run over.

We ran after Joyce, determined to get her back inside the restaurant. That wasn't going to happen because she was moving so fast, we couldn't catch her. When she got to the end of the block and turned the corner, we stopped in our tracks. Yvonne's face was as red as a cherry and she was huffing and puffing like a overworked mule. She leaned against me, panting so hard I had to clap her on the back until she caught her breath and could stand up on her own. I wasn't in too much better shape myself. I held my breath and looked toward the restaurant door, thinking Odell would come running out. When he didn't, I realized how wrapped up in his other woman he really was. Even after all the noise Joyce had made and the reaction of the folks standing in the line, Betty Jean had him so mesmerized, he hadn't noticed or heard nothing.

"Milton, we got to find her before she do something crazy, or get run over," Yvonne wheezed as she tugged my sleeve.

"The way she was running and screaming like a banshee, it might be too late. Come on, sugar. Let's go hunt for her." We went back to the truck, climbed in, and sped off down the street. I drove in the same direction Joyce had run in, but she was nowhere in sight. "Let's go back home."

"Hell no. What's the matter with you, Milton?" Yvonne blasted. "We can't leave that poor woman alone in this strange town. She don't know nobody over here. How will she get home?"

"What do you want to do then?"

"We have to keep looking for her."

I drove up and down several more streets

for another half hour. We still couldn't locate Joyce. By then, Yvonne was so wore out, she was ready to go home with or without her. And that was what we done.

346

CHAPTER 38
YVONNE

The way Joyce had reacted when she seen Odell with that woman told me that she was not going to forgive him and stay married. I was glad to know that we'd got the results we wanted. Well, at least it looked that way. I didn't want to jump the gun, though. Yeah, Joyce had exploded and disappeared. But after she calmed down, she could still forgive Odell and stay with him. That was my biggest fear. Because then all our plotting and planning would have been for nothing.

Willie Frank's truck chugged along, rattling like it was on its last leg. Or wheel, I should say. Every time we hit a pothole, the cab trembled, and smoke seeped from under the hood. Willie Frank put a lot of money into getting repairs done on this piece of junk. But it still broke down every now and then anyway. I hoped that didn't happen to us. Especially today when so

347

much was happening. The last thing I wanted to deal with was us having to find another way home. Like Joyce was going to do.

Milton gazed at me from the corner of his eye and let out a weary sigh. "Say something," he grunted.

I exhaled and rubbed the side of my neck. My head was aching, and my chest felt like a elephant was sitting on it. If I was feeling this bad, I couldn't imagine how Joyce was feeling. "What if she can't find a way home?"

"Well, we can't do nothing about that now. We tried to find her. And even if we had found her, how do you know she would have got back in the truck with us? There ain't no telling what went through her mind when she realized we had set her up. Don't worry about how she getting home. Shoot. Joyce got a lot of friends and a daddy with wheels. She might have already called one of them by now. Besides, there's probably bus service between Hartville and Branson. Put Joyce in the back of your mind. We need to be thinking about what *we* going to do when things explode."

"What do you mean?"

"Yvonne, Odell is going to go stark-raving mad when he finds out we let the cat out of the bag."

"We'll deal with that when it happens. But there is something else I been worried about. How do we know Joyce wasn't involved in Odell making that call to the sheriff? She could be just as conniving as he is, but better at hiding it."

"Pffft. You talking way out of your head. Joyce? She ain't the kind of woman who would do nothing like that. She is so ditzy, I don't think she'd even know how to be evil. If she had been involved, I don't think she would have kept coming to the house."

"Odell kept coming to the house, and he was the one that done it, Milton."

"Yeah, but we know what a snake Odell is. We been blackmailing him, so he had a damn good reason for trying to destroy us. We ain't done nothing to Joyce. If he did try and drag her into his plan, she'd want to know why. Do you think he'd tell her?"

"No, but he could have told her some other story without mentioning Betty Jean."

"Yvonne, let's drop the subject. Why don't you rear back in your seat and take a nap? We got a long ride."

"I'm too jittery to take a nap."

"Then hush up about Odell and Joyce."

"What do you want to talk about then?"

"Nothing. I just want to get us home as

349

fast as I can."

I reared back in my seat, but I didn't take no nap.

Milton took a few shortcuts and drove down some back roads so we'd get home a little sooner. I stayed quiet for about fifteen minutes. "Baby, what if Joyce went back to that restaurant? If Odell left before she got there, she could have asked some of them folks about him. What if she got enough information to track him down before she left Hartville?"

"I thought I told you to get off this subject."

"Milton, you might not want to keep talking about it, but I do. She might pick up a stick and beat him and that woman to death," I wailed.

"That would be bad for him, good for us. Then we wouldn't have to worry about him coming after us. At the end of the day, we got his money. If Joyce don't kill him, and you worried about him getting back at us, we can haul ass."

"Where would we go?"

"Well, my brother in Louisiana been trying to get me to move over there for years. The church he pastors is known for helping folks start new lives. He'd find a job for me, and I'm sure he'd find something for you.

350

There is still white folks with money that need help. I'm a damn good cook. I know I'd be able to get on at another restaurant or do farm work again. And if you can't get no waitress job, you wouldn't have no trouble getting hired as a mammy."

My mouth dropped open and I looked at Milton like he'd lost his mind. "I don't want to be nobody's mammy. And I know you don't want to be no farmhand again. You hated that kind of work."

"Look, I'm just talking about temporary jobs until we can get something better."

I sighed and softened my tone. "I never thought you'd give up bootlegging."

"I ain't said nothing about giving up bootlegging. We can do that business any-where. But if we move to Louisiana, we'd have to do some other kind of work to keep us going until we got situated in the bootleg-ging business again. Remember how it was when we first got started? We had to struggle to succeed. Drumming up business, finding the right location, and all."

"Milton, if we move to another state, we'd have to find a new alcohol supplier. Willie Frank ain't about to leave Branson and go with us. All the colored folks I know that run stills, only make enough booze for their personal use. In a new location, we'd have to do a lot of asking around to find some-body to fill Willie Frank's shoes. And them is some mighty big shoes. Doing business with anybody else wouldn't be half as enjoy-able as it is with him."

Milton gave me a dismissive wave and a weary look. "Hush up. I'm tired. We'll be just fine, even if we relocate. And I don't care how successful we get, we'll stay as humble as we is now. I'd hate for our new customers to start calling us Prince Charm-ing and Queen of Sheba behind our backs." He laughed, I didn't.

"Humph. We could never behave as hoity-toity as Joyce and Odell, not even in a nightmare." I let out a loud breath and shook my head. "I know you trying to do what's best for us, and I'm with you all the way. But I need to let you know that I really don't want to move away from Alabama. And I sure don't want to get involved with your preacher brother's church. He'd be all up in our business, trying to get us to come to Jesus."

"What's wrong with your memory, girl? We done already went to Jesus. We just ain't as close to Him as we should be. We'll get there, though." Milton chuckled.

I blinked back a tear threatening to ooze from my eye. "If we move to Louisiana, there ain't no telling how often I'd get to see my children then. You know Uncle Sherman's truck won't make it that far. And him and Aunt Nadine ain't got the kind of money to be traveling over there on the bus or the train. It's bad enough my babies think I'm their cousin."

"Yvonne, your folks is going to tell them kids you their real mama when they get grown. You done waited this long, what's a few more years? Be glad you ain't in Joyce's shoes. She ain't got no kids at all. After tonight, she probably never will have any — at least not by Odell." Milton laughed, and after thinking about his last comment, I laughed, too. But I could tell from his tone and body language that he was just as exasperated as I was. Laughing lightened it up a little bit. "Let's concentrate on our future."

"All right then. You know, I never expected Joyce to take off running away from that restaurant," I said. I didn't care how tired Milton was about this subject. I was going to keep harping on it as long as I wanted to.

"Why not?"

"I thought the least thing she'd do was go up into that place, pick up a chair, and bash it over Odell's head. That's what I would have done. I bet every other woman would have done the same thing, or something worse. It would have been nice to see Joyce show some gumption."

"Yvonne, something just came to me." Milton cleared his throat and slapped the steering wheel. "If we don't know nothing about what happened to Joyce by morning, let's drive back over to Hartville."

I looked upside his head, wishing I could see inside it. Maybe I could figure out what made him come up with such a outlandish notion. "Why would we do that?"

"We got this ball to rolling, and we need to find out where it went. We'll talk to them waitresses and find out where Betty Jean live at."

"Milton, what good would that do?"

"If Odell don't know Joyce was there, or us, he don't have no idea what's going on. We can go to that woman's house —"

I cut him off right away. "Hell no." I couldn't believe my ears. Milton said a lot of stupid stuff from time to time, but this was way over the top. What he'd just suggested shocked me so much, my heart almost busted out of my chest. "We can't go to that woman's house while Odell is there and rub in his face what we done. I say we should wait and see what happens when we see them again. *If we ever do . . .*"

"You right," he agreed.

By now I was so exhausted, I reared back and went to sleep.

Chapter 39
Milton

Even though I had tried to discourage Yvonne from talking about Joyce, I still done a lot of thinking about her on my own. Some serious questions was coming at me. Had we done the right thing by exposing Odell's misconduct? I hoped it wouldn't force us to leave town, because I wasn't ready to give up some of the friends we'd had for years, our lovely house, our jobs at the grill, our bootlegging business, and having Willie Frank nearby.

But I was realistic. Our lives would never be the same, no matter what. If Joyce stayed with Odell, they would never want to socialize with us again, and vice versa.

Odell's deception was deeper than the Red Sea. But Joyce's folks was as crazy about that sucker as Joyce was. It wouldn't surprise me to hear that Mac and Millie forgave him when and if they found out about Betty Jean. I seriously doubted that they would let him off with punishment that didn't fit his crimes, though. He'd be out of a job for sure, and they'd never trust him again. That was the least I expected. Even folks as gullible, forgiving, and stupid as Joyce and her parents, had to draw the line somewhere. If they didn't, every colored person in Branson would talk about them like dogs. They'd be known as the town fools. All the folks who had thought Odell was such a great husband and a role model would drop him like a bad habit. When I turned onto our block, I pushed all of them wild thoughts out of my head. They had made my head hurt enough. "Yvonne, wake up. We'll be home in a minute."

She opened her eyes and sat up straight. "It's about time."

"This been one hell of a day," I griped. "As soon as I walk through our front door, I'm going to get one of the biggest jars in the kitchen and fill it to the brim with the strongest booze we got, and drink every drop nonstop."

"I'm going to do the same thing," Yvonne said with a yawn.

We walked into our living room a few minutes after eight p.m. I was pleased to see that Willie Frank had been tending to a dozen-and-a-half guests. "Did Joyce enjoy the supper y'all treated her to?" he asked.

"Um, we had a unexpected mishap and didn't get to eat nothing. I said something Joyce misinterpreted, and she got upset," I replied in a low tone. We was standing by the end of the couch. There was a bunch of other folks around and I didn't want them to hear us. "Anyway, before I could explain what I'd said, she took off running down the street and disappeared. We drove around for the longest time, but we couldn't find her."

Willie Frank gasped. "Do you mean to tell me y'all left her in Hartville?"

"We didn't have no choice." I put my arm around Willie Frank's shoulder and led him into the kitchen, and Yvonne was right beside me. We didn't stop walking until we got to the back of the room.

"Did what you say that upset her have anything to do with Odell making the call to Sheriff Potts?" Willie Frank wanted to know.

I had a lie already formed in my head. Yvonne answered before I could get it out. "Yup. She almost fainted."

"Hell's bells. Did she admit he was the one that done it?"

I still didn't think it would benefit us if we came clean and told Willie Frank everything

358

yet. He'd feel slighted if he knew we'd been keeping Odell's other woman and them kids a secret from him, and that that was the reason we'd cooked up a phony supper invitation for Joyce. Telling him the whole story eventually depended on how this mess played out in the end. If Joyce broadcasted the news about Betty Jean, then me and Yvonne would come clean with Willie Frank. We'd tell him we hadn't wanted to drag a God-fearing man like him into such a unholy mess unless we had to.

I didn't waste no time replying. "Uh-huh. When we laid out the facts, she didn't have no choice. She swore to God she didn't realize what he'd done until we brung it to her attention."

Willie Frank blew out some air and raked his fingers through his hair. He was red with anger, and there was a scrunched-up look on his face. "I hope this don't get too out of hand." He shook his head and continued. "I advised y'all not to waste too much time before confronting Odell."

I glanced around the kitchen. "Let's discuss this later. I want to get back out there and entertain our guests."

"All right then. I got a lot more to say about it," Willie Frank said, sounding dog tired. This mess had drained him and he didn't even know the half of it.

I hadn't told Yvonne that me and him had "finalized" Odell's punishment. The main reason was because I had to wait and see what happened with him and Joyce.

Ten more guests had come since we got home, and we got really busy. But every few minutes I peeped out the front window at the house next door. Just before nine p.m., I seen a light come on. Less than a minute later, Joyce started closing all her living room curtains. "Joyce made it back home," I whispered to Yvonne when she walked up behind me.

"Good. At least we know she ain't dead, or in the crazy house," she replied.

Folks usually stayed with us well into the early morning hours on weekend nights. And even though we was making a nice piece of change, by eleven p.m. I was ready for everybody to leave. I couldn't be rude and tell them that, so I done what I always done when I wanted people to skedaddle: I yawned and started cleaning up. Within twenty minutes, everybody except Willie Frank was gone. Five minutes later, he started yawning, too. When he put on his shoes and got up to leave, he stopped on his way to the door and turned back around. "I won't see y'all again until Sunday. I have to drive my mama to Huntsville in a few hours to visit her sister. I hope everything will be all right until I get back." There was a worried look on his face. He nodded toward Joyce and Odell's house.

"Willie Frank, don't you worry about us. We'll be fine," I declared.

"I sure as hell hope so. Look-a-here, I'll be back Sunday no later than noon." For some reason, he cocked his head and stared at me so long it made me uncomfortable. "I just hope I don't get back too late . . ."

"Too late for what? You think noon is 'too late' to come over?" I waved my hand and laughed.

"That ain't what I meant —"

I cut Willie Frank off because I didn't need to hear what he meant. I knew it had something to do with us chastising Odell. If Joyce was home alone, that meant she probably hadn't confronted him. So, if he was going to do something to us, it wouldn't be until he got home on Sunday. "Uh . . . when you come back, bring your shotgun, just in case. Now go home and get some sleep. It's a long drive to Huntsville."

CHAPTER 40
JOYCE

I stopped crying when I noticed how many folks were staring at me as I stumbled down the street. I pulled a handkerchief out of my purse and dried my eyes and blew my nose. I had a lot more tears to shed. But first I had to figure out what I was going to do next, and how I was going to get back to my house.

I kept seeing Odell and that woman and those children in my head. What I'd heard him say was ringing in my ears over and over. At one point I covered my ears and closed my eyes. But I could still see and hear him in my mind. They looked like the perfect American family. That woman was living the life I'd been cheated out of. She'd been blessed with three children, and I hadn't had one. What could I have done for God to let this happen to me? I regretted that last thought immediately. One thing I didn't need to do was blame God for Odell's actions. I still had enough faith left to believe that something positive would come out of this nightmare.

My mind played tricks on me as I wandered up and down streets I'd never been on before. My head was spinning, I was seeing dots in front of my eyes, and my insides felt like somebody had tied them in knots. If all that wasn't bad enough, I felt like I had fallen into a black hole that didn't have a bottom. With so much going on, I was still determined not to let Odell's behavior destroy me. I had to pull myself out of that hole now. That thought was enough to jolt me back to reality. I suddenly felt stronger.

However, despite the fact that I was feeling better, I still roamed around until my legs started cramping.

When I finally came to another restaurant with colored people going in, I went in, too. It was a dreary-looking rib joint with dingy windows, a gummy floor, and mismatched tablecloths. There was a small Christmas tree loaded down with ornaments and tinsel sitting on a table in a corner. With all the satisfied-looking patrons gobbling up their ribs so fast, I knew I couldn't have picked a better place to hole up in until I felt relaxed enough to make my next move. "Merry Christmas, ma'am," a cute young waitress greeted at the door.

"Um . . . the same to you." I was in such a daze, I almost tripped over my feet. Christmas — and no other day — would ever be "merry" for me again.

"Sit wherever you want. I'll get you a menu."

"I don't need a menu. I just want a glass of water." I dropped down into a metal chair at a table with squeaky legs a few feet away from the door.

"I'm sorry. You have to order something if you want to sit at this table. Otherwise, I can give you some water, but you'll have to take it to go."

"I'd like a rib sandwich."

"You want potato salad or coleslaw? And mild, medium, or hot sauce?"

"Mild. And I don't need any salad or coleslaw."

"You have to pay for it anyway so you might as well take it."

Somehow, I managed to smile. "Okay. I'll take some coleslaw."

After the waitress finished scribbling my order on her notepad, she looked at me and squinted. "You ain't from around here, huh?"

"No, I'm not."

"I didn't think so. This is a small town. I

know almost every colored person in it."

Her last sentence really got my attention. "Oh? Do you know a light-skinned woman with long hair named Betty Jean?"

She tilted her head to the side and gave me a pensive look. "I know three Betty Jeans. They all light skinned and got long hair."

"This one has three little boys."

"Hmmm." The waitress pressed her lips together and scratched her head. "All three of them women got kids, but the only one with three boys is Betty Jean, Odell Watson's wife. How do you know her? Is she kin to you?"

"I'm kin to Odell. He's hard to keep track of. I thought maybe I'd catch up with Betty Jean and leave a message with her for him."

"Well, he's usually home by this time every Friday, so you can tell him yourself. They love to entertain company. I know they'd be pleased to see you. What's your name?"

"Uh . . . Lula."

"Well, Lula. If you don't see them today, I'll let them know I talked to you when I see them at church on Sunday."

"Okay."

"Betty Jean is such a lucky woman to have a man like Odell. You wouldn't believe the fat, sloppy, clumsy ox I'm married to — dagnabbit. Odell makes such good money, she don't have to work, so she stays home puttering around the house every day waiting for him to come home. He brings her roses several times a month — sometimes three whole dozen at a time." Roses had been my favorite flowers until now. I sniffed and listened as the waitress went on. "A lot of folks visit her, but she will rarely go out unless it's with him. I tease her all the time. I tell her that if she ever dumps Odell, I'm going to snatch him up." The waitress laughed and to my surprise, I laughed, too. "You going to go visit them?"

"Um . . . I'd like to. But there was a mix-up with the friends I came over here with. We got separated, so I need to try and find them first. Besides, I'm not sure about Odell and Betty Jean's address."

The waitress waved her hand. When she started talking again, the words poured out of her mouth like water. "Pffft. Their house ain't hard to find. I'll give you directions. And let me tell you, the one they live in now is a lot better than that last place they had. Odell and Betty Jean spent oodles of money decorating this one with nice ruffle-edged curtains, and furniture you'd expect to see in a white family's house. Betty Jean had a big Thanksgiving celebration this year. Me and my husband and our two kids was there, along with our preacher and his wife. The only thing is, she had to have it the day after the holiday because Odell couldn't be there until then. He's a traveling salesman and spends most of his weekdays on the road. Anyway, he was back home bright and early Friday morning. Just like he'd promised Betty Jean he would be. Matter of fact, she told me he ain't never let her down. Every time he tells her he is going to do something, he always come through. I love reliable men."

"So do I," I muttered.

"And that Friday after Thanksgiving, like every other Friday, he brung all kinds of nice things for Betty Jean and the kids. This time he even brung me some face powder and a corset. That company he works for let him take anything he wants. Every weekend when he gets back in town, his car is loaded down with boxes and boxes of clothes, food, smell-goods, and household items. His bosses must really be crazy about him."

"I'm sure they are," I hissed. I cringed and my head started throbbing when I tried to imagine how much money and merchandise Odell had stolen from my family over the years. No wonder that devil had left me so early the Friday morning after Thanksgiving. Just thinking about our "romantic" night the day before made me sick to my stomach. I couldn't even wrap my brain around the things I'd heard about Odell so far. But his claiming to be a traveling salesman and entertaining his preacher and other folks took the cake. "In case I decide to visit Odell and Betty Jean today, is their house close enough I can walk to it from here?"

The waitress looked at the heels I had on. Then she squinted at the blouse and skirt I had spent so much time picking out for my special supper with Yvonne and Milton. "Yeah, you can walk it. It might be hard on your feet in them shoes, though. But it ain't that far." She squinted again. This time she focused on my tearstained face. "Ma'am, you all right? I can see that you been boohooing. There is even tearstains on the front of your pretty blouse. Did somebody jump you?"

"Oh, I'm all right. A car almost ran me down a few blocks from here and it shook me up." I cleared my throat and put on as happy a face as I could. I even chuckled. "I feel like such a crybaby."

"I know what you mean. I got hit by a man driving a mule-wagon one day. I didn't get hurt. But it shook me up so bad, I squawked like a parrot. Now, every time I see a mule or a wagon, I panic."

"Um . . . now how do I get to Betty Jean's house?"

The waitress pointed at the door. "When you leave here, turn left and walk all the way to the end of the road until you get to a bait shop at the end of the block. Turn right. Walk all the way to the end of that road until you get to a church with a great big statue on the front lawn of Jesus holding a lamb. That's my church. Odell and Betty Jean and their boys belong to it, too. Odell is a usher and our treasurer, and Betty Jean sing in the choir."

Treasurer? There was no doubt in my mind that part of the money those people had trusted him with, was going in his pocket, too.

The more I heard about the secret life Odell had been leading, the angrier I got. My heart felt like it had dropped down to my feet, and there were other parts of my body I couldn't even feel. A lump that felt like it was the size of an apple was lodged in my throat. I was surprised I could still function.

"Since you didn't order no drink, do you still want some water, too? Or a bottle of

Dr. Pepper?"

"No, thank you. Now let me ask you one more thing. Is there a telephone here I can use?" I prayed that Patsy was home when I called and could come pick me up.

"Go to the back of the room. It's right next to the toilet. Is it a local call?"

"Yes, it is." I was lying but I didn't care. I had been basically honest all my life and look what it had got me. It seemed like the folks who told the most and biggest lies always got what they wanted. It was too soon for me to know how I was going to live the rest of my life. One thing I did know was that I'd never be the same fool twice.

When the waitress left to go get my order, I went to use the telephone. Patsy had gone out for the evening, so I called up two of my other coworkers. They had company and neither one knew how to get to Hartville. I couldn't call up Daddy because I'd have to explain to him what I was doing in Hartville without a ride. I knew it was going to be hard enough on him and Mama when I told them about Odell, and I wanted to spare them as much misery as possible for as long as I could. If I was on the verge of a nervous breakdown, I couldn't imagine how all this was going to affect them.

A few minutes after I returned to my

table, the waitress came back with my order. "Okay. Now do you need anything else? We have pecan pie for dessert."

"No, this is enough. But I need to ask you something else. In case I don't find my friends and have to get home another way, is there a bus that goes to Branson?"

"Yeah. You can catch it a few blocks from here on the same side of the street. Go left when you leave here. The last one going out of town today will be leaving in about six or seven minutes, if it's on time. If you don't catch it, the next one won't come until eight o'clock tomorrow morning, if it's on time."

I immediately paid the waitress and had her wrap my order to go. It was a good thing I left when I did; and ran all the way. The bus was just about to leave when I got there.

I was so overwhelmed and exhausted I almost accidentally sat down in a vacant seat. It was in the front of the bus, where colored folks were not allowed to sit. I caught myself before the driver and the white folks in the front had time to make a fuss and flag down a policeman. I claimed the last empty seat in the back and set the bag with my food on the floor because I had no appetite. Within minutes after the bus pulled away from the curb, I closed my eyes and dozed off. A dream of myself running toward Mobile Bay to jump in, jolted me awake. I had slept almost all the way home. When I got off at the corner of my block, I felt like a zombie and probably looked like one as I walked toward my house.

Willie Frank's truck was parked in front of Yvonne and Milton's house, so I knew they had made it back home. I had no idea what I would say when I saw them again. And only God knew what they'd say to me.

When I got inside my house, I dropped my purse and the bag with my ribs onto the living-room coffee table. I made a beeline for the kitchen and poured myself a large glass of the strongest whiskey we had in the house.

I returned to the living room, kicked off my shoes, and stretched out on the couch. I gulped down half of my drink in one pull. I couldn't relax because my mind was all over the place. I wasn't just angry with Odell, I was so mad with myself I wanted to kick my own behind. How had I been so naïve and stupid? Was I so blindly in love with that devil I couldn't see what other women would have seen with their eyes closed? What woman in her right mind would have believed he was spending so much time with his daddy and not checked it out? Was it because I was not in my right mind? On top of everything else, now I was worried about my mental state. The wonderful life I'd had until a few hours ago was over. Without Odell and no children, what did I have to look forward to now? The answer to that question came to me right away. I still had my parents, my job, my health, and some good friends. What I was going through was enough to drive any woman insane. But I had too much to lose to end up drooling and spewing gibberish in the state asylum. I was determined to stay well-grounded and focused for as long as I could.

"Joyce, be strong. You'll get through this. The situation could be a lot worse," I told myself out loud. I had to laugh to keep from crying some more because I couldn't think of any situation that could be worse.

More disturbing thoughts entered my mind. Odell had taken up with a woman so beautiful, I wondered what he thought each time he made love to a plain Jane like me. And those kids. Lord have mercy. I hadn't been able to give him even one, and he'd found a woman, a younger one at that, who had given him *three.* I wondered why he hadn't divorced me and married Betty Jean so he wouldn't have had to lie and sneak around. I answered that question myself, too: money. Without his job, he'd be as poor as a church mouse.

I wanted to cry some more. But I was so angry, I couldn't squeeze out another tear if I tried right now. Questions kept bouncing around in my head. How would I be able to live next door to Yvonne and Milton now? Why had they taken so long to tell me about Betty Jean? Just thinking about how they and Odell had kept me in the dark made my blood boil. What had Odell said or done to make them finally tell me? I had no idea what was going to happen to those two lowlifes, but Odell was going to go down like a lead balloon. My life had been turned upside down. However, I was not going to let this setback set me back. I knew that if I worked and prayed hard enough, and kept my guard up, I could still have a future worth looking forward to.

I finished my drink in one gulp. My head felt like somebody had batted it with a mallet. Now that I knew how to get to Betty Jean's house, I'd be paying her a visit — maybe even tomorrow while Odell was still there. I couldn't wait to see his reaction when he realized the jig was up for him. His suffering was going to be of biblical proportions.

CHAPTER 41
ODELL

This morning, a few minutes after I got to Hartville, me and the boys took a walk out to the woods about a mile from our house and chopped down a Christmas tree. We decorated it as soon as we got home. Betty Jean hung up garlands in every room and put a wreath on the back of our front door.

On the way to Po' Sister's Kitchen to eat supper this evening, we decided to sing some Christmas songs in the car. The kids loved "Jingle Bells," so we sung it two times in a row. Then we sung my favorite, "Joy to the World." After that, Betty Jean insisted on us singing "Silent Night." She even cried when we finished. "I declare, Odell. Every time I hear that song, I get emotional." She sniffled.

"Baby, this is the time of year when almost everybody gets emotional about something," I said with a heavy sigh.

We enjoyed our supper, and conversated

375

with some of the staff and a few of our other friends. By the time we left, the place had so many customers, we had to push our way through the crowd to get back outside.

When we got in the car and pulled away from the curb, Betty Jean gave me a curious look. "Odell, I wonder what all them folks in line outside was buzzing about when we came out?"

"I heard a man say something about a woman stumbling out of the restaurant, hollering and screaming and running down the middle of the street. Probably just one of them slow-wit retarded souls having a fit," I replied, cranking up the motor.

"That poor woman. I bet it was because of a man."

"I bet it was, too. Even retarded women can be fools when it comes to men. I'm glad we didn't witness it. Something like that would have gave the boys nightmares and I —" A commotion in the back seat interrupted me. "Boys, stop kicking and punching one another or I'm going to get back out of this car and go get a switch," I scolded. The chaos stopped right away. I rarely had to whup my boys, but I was the kind of parent who believed in chastising kids whenever it was necessary. Usually, a warning about a switch was all it took for them to act right. They was as quiet as mice now, and that made me beam with pride on how well we was raising them. Another thing I believed in was rewarding good behavior. "Y'all want to sing some more songs, or want me to tell a Christmas story?"

"Daddy, tell us the one again about the three wise guys that came to bring presents to baby Jesus when he was born," Daniel said with a anxious look on his face.

Me and Betty Jean laughed.

"What's so funny?" Daniel asked.

"Son, it's not 'wise guys,' it's the three wise men," I corrected. All three boys sat still and didn't say another word until after I finished telling the story. It was one of their favorites and I enjoyed telling it.

When we got in the house, the boys ran to their room. Me and Betty Jean took off our coats, hung them on the hook by the door, and eased down on the living-room couch. "Baby, thanks for picking out such a nice tree."

"Thank you, sugar. And the best thing about it is that it was free." I laughed.

"Now all it needs is some presents under it," she hinted, giving me a hopeful look.

"Don't worry about that. We'll get some of our shopping done tomorrow and next weekend. This year's Christmas will be our best one ever," I assured her.

After tucking the boys into bed a couple of hours later, me and Betty Jean got back on the couch and drunk some lemonade. Right after I finished my first glass and kissed up and down her neck, I slid a few inches away from her and crossed my legs. "Listen, baby . . . uh . . . I know you don't like to fish at night, but I been hearing how good the carps been biting after dark. Tonight would be a good time to go." I prayed she wouldn't want to go with me. To discourage her, I went on. "I'd hate to get the boys back up to go out on that lake, though."

Betty Jean clicked her tongue and rolled her eyes. "Odell, I'm not getting my babies up to go fishing — especially as cold as it is tonight. I done already told you not to ask me to go no more. Shoot. The last time, it took me a whole hour to pick all them briars off my socks, not to mention all them creepy bugs crawling up my legs. And it's danger-ous to be on a fishing bank in the dead of night with quicksand all over the place."

"We won't have to worry about it being dark. I'm going to carry the kerosene lantern you gave me for Father's Day."

"You carried your lantern the last time and still stepped on three different snakes."

"I won't step on no snake tonight."

"I won't neither, because I ain't leaving this house." Betty Jean pinched the side of my arm. "Besides, I thought we was going to work on making our baby girl tonight," she cooed.

"I'll be back in a few hours, and we got tomorrow and Sunday to take care of the baby-making business."

I couldn't stop thinking about the five hundred bucks I'd swiped from my in-laws' pantry last night and gave to Milton when he visited me on his lunch hour again today. I had gone to Mac and Millie's house after they went to bed, and while Joyce was at home talking on the phone with a coworker. They slept like dead folks, so I didn't have to worry about waking them up when I let myself in. Now I had to get that money back and return it to the pantry as soon as possible. I couldn't keep pushing my luck. My biggest fear was that one day Mac and Millie would suspect something and set a trap for me. The thought of getting caught stealing probably would have caused me almost as much heartache as them finding out about Betty Jean. In either case, my life wouldn't be worth a dime no more.

I couldn't stand to go another day knowing Yvonne and Milton was still alive, so I *had* to kill them tonight. And since I'd never killed nobody, I didn't know what to expect. What if they put up a serious fight? We could scuffle for a long time before I brung them down. Even more disturbing thoughts was them getting the better of me, escaping, and me not getting my money back. But I wasn't going to let them possibilities stop me. The bottom line was, when I left their house, they would be dead.

I had originally planned to sneak out after Betty Jean and the boys went to sleep. When I gave it more thought, it didn't sound so smart, though. They was heavy sleepers and rarely woke up during the night. But there was always a first time for everything. If they woke up and found me gone, I would claim that I'd went out to get some fresh air. I often done just that. This time, fishing seemed like a better alibi.

I would need about two-and-a-half hours to get the job done, which was how long I normally stayed out when I did go fishing at night. Yvonne and Milton usually had guests up until at least midnight on Friday, and sometimes even later. It was already close to that time now. If I drove faster than usual, I could make it to Branson in forty or forty-five minutes, take ten or fifteen to do them in, and another forty to forty-five to get back to Hartville. But that was only if everything went according to my plan. I would find out soon enough. I prayed that they'd gone to bed by the time I got there. If not, I'd lurk around outside in the bushes until they did.

"You want a couple of sandwiches to eat while you out there fishing?" Betty Jean asked.

"Um, no. That big supper we ate at the restaurant this evening will hold me until tomorrow." I gave her a quick kiss and stood up. "Well, I'm going to use the toilet, get a drink of water, check on the boys, and then I'll be on my way to the lake."

"All right. You just be careful, baby."

I left Betty Jean's house at 11:25 p.m., dressed in the shabby dark clothes I usually wore when I went fishing. The minute I hit the road, my heart started beating twice as fast as it should have. Then my hands started shaking and sweating. Even though I was a nonviolent Christian, I was convinced that I was making the right decision about killing Yvonne and Milton. I figured that if Moses could kill somebody and stay in God's grace, so could I. I had already laid out a plan for my atonement: I'd do a lot of good deeds for Joyce and the community when the dust settled, and I'd never commit another murder.

During the ride, I prayed out loud that things would go off without a hitch. I'd changed my mind several times about how I was going to do the killings, but the one I had in mind now seemed like the best one. First, I'd knock Milton out because he was the biggest threat. Then I'd force Yvonne to give me my money back. As soon as she did, I'd put her lights out. I wasn't sure if I should strangle her, or beat her to death. When I got done with her, I'd slap Milton's face until he regained consciousness and then kill him. If things got real messy, I'd get their blood on me. I had thought about that ahead of time so I'd put a change of clothes in my car that I planned to put on before I returned to Hartville. My blood-stained clothes would get tossed in a creek along the way. I had it all planned out down to the last detail. Nothing could go wrong.

After I got to Branson, I parked two blocks away from my house and started walking toward my destination. I was pleased to see that all of our neighbors had turned off their lights. That meant I didn't have to worry about none of them looky-loos peeping out their windows and seeing me.

When I got to my house, I crept along the

side to the backyard and got the claw hammer I had hid in the grass at the base of our pecan tree. Then I sprinted to Yvonne and Milton's house. One of the kitchen windows was open a few inches, just like I knew it would be. I raised it up as far as I needed to, gripped the sill, climbed in.

I was glad their house had the same layout as mine. So, even in the dark, I was able to feel my way to their bedroom with no trouble. Before I even reached it, I could hear Milton snoring like a ox. When I opened the door, it creaked, and that scared the bejesus out of me. I almost turned around and left. But that was a option I couldn't consider. I wanted my five hundred dollars back and I wanted them devils dead.

The noisy door didn't wake them up. But when I stepped into the bedroom, the squeaky floorboards did.

CHAPTER 42
ODELL

Milton sat bolt upright and immediately turned on the lamp next to him. "Odell? What the hell you doing here — dressed like that?" he asked when he seen me standing at the foot of the bed. I had never seen a man look so stunned before in my life. I had on a black sweatshirt, black pants, and a black jacket. Milton had only seen me in casual clothes three or four times since we met. Him seeing me out of a suit must have threw him for a loop.

I didn't give him time to say nothing else. I lunged at him and held the hammer up to his face. "I came to get my money back! Where is it?" I growled. As loud as our voices was, I was surprised Yvonne hadn't woke up. All she did was mumble some gibberish and stir a little bit.

Instead of answering, Milton leaped off the bed and grabbed my arm. I held on to that hammer like my life depended on it —

and it did. There was no way I was going to let this short-legged, pot-bellied pig overpower me. The next thing I knew, we was punching each other and scuffling around the bedroom. When his fist went upside my head, it dazed me. I stumbled a few steps backward and dropped the hammer. It gave him enough time to get out of the room. I picked up the hammer and followed him to the kitchen. When I got there, he had clicked on the light. "Have you lost your fucking mind, man?" he yelled, waving a butcher knife like it was a magic wand. There was a wild-eyed look on his face. What he said next made me stop dead in my tracks. "I'm going to kill you! But first, I want you to know the reason why! *We know it was you that called Sheriff Potts and told that lie on us!*"

"W-what?"

"What my ass! There ain't no way you could have known Sheriff Potts got the call at his house unless you called him! Only the sheriff and his wife, and Willie Frank and his uncle, knew that. Willie Frank done already verified it with Sheriff Potts."

My heart just about dropped down to my toes. There was no use in me lying, not that it mattered anyway. Milton and Yvonne was going to die regardless, so I wouldn't have to worry about them telling nobody else. And I wasn't going to worry about Willie Frank spreading that information right now. If it came up, I'd figure out a way to deal with him. For now, it was more important to take care of the main source of my problem. "Who told y'all I made that call?" I asked with my voice cracking.

"Your dumb ass told on yourself when you mentioned it to Joyce. She blabbed it over here one night."

"My wife told on me?" I was so stupefied, I almost lost my train of thought. Shoot. Now I had to wonder what else was going on in Joyce's head.

"You ain't got to worry about her, though. All she done was repeat some information you shared with her. She didn't have no idea what she was saying. And Yvonne heard you tell Dr. Patterson exactly how long it took for the sheriff to get over here after he got the call. Eight minutes? How did you know that, too?"

I was shaking like a sumac leaf. The hole I was in was turning into a bottomless pit. I wondered how Milton and Yvonne had managed to keep this information to themselves so long. "All right. What if I did make that call? It didn't work and that's why I'm here now. How long did you think I was going to let you and Yvonne keep taking my money?"

"Well, breaking into my house will be your last mistake." He stood wide-legged and waved the knife some more. "Yvonne, Yvonne, wake up!" He roared so loud, I was surprised the windows didn't shatter. With his eyes narrowed, he sneered. "Listen up, *Romeo,* I got another humdinger of a thing to tell you that you —" I didn't let him finish. I didn't want to waste no more time. He'd already said enough to make my blood boil. I threw the hammer at his hand holding the knife, and it fell to the floor. I shot across the floor, picked up my hammer, and bum-rushed him so fast he didn't have time to react. I bashed his head until he fell and stopped moving.

A few seconds later, Yvonne stumbled into the kitchen. "What — Odell, what in the world did you do to my husband?"

"The same thing I'm fixing to do to you, bitch!" I shouted. She snatched a sugar bowl off the table, threw it at me and missed. I ran up to her and slapped her face as hard as I could. She took off running toward the living room, and I was right behind her.

There was enough moonlight coming through the front window to see she was heading for the front door. The clash with

Milton had almost wore me out. It took every ounce of the strength I had left for me to catch Yvonne before she opened the door. She screamed, grabbed my hand, and we started tussling from one end of the room to the other. She got distracted when we knocked the Christmas tree over, and I gained more control. I repeatedly clobbered the top of her head with the hammer. She screamed again and stumbled around like a headless chicken. I pinned her against the wall and hit her head much harder this time. It cracked open like a rotten egg. Blood and brains oozed out like lava, and she toppled to the floor. If I hadn't had such a strong stomach I would have puked.

I was doubly disgusted now because I'd killed them devils before they'd told me where my goddamn money was. I ran back to the bedroom and ransacked every dresser drawer. I looked under the mattress, in the closet, and couldn't find nothing. While I stood there panting and wiping Yvonne's blood and brains off my face, I heard footsteps running toward the room. I almost fainted when I whirled around and seen Milton coming at me with that butcher knife. I thought I'd killed that fool. I knocked him to the floor with a sucker punch to the face. Then I headed back to the living room where I had left the hammer, and tripped over Yvonne and fell. When I grabbed the hammer and stood back up, Milton stormed into the room with that knife. He charged at me and plunged the blade into my chest so hard, it felt like I'd been split in two. I was so enraged, the pain didn't stop me from doing what I done next. I raised the hammer and whacked his head until he fell and stopped moving. Since he'd played possum on the kitchen floor, I wasn't taking no chances. I hit his head some more until I was sure he was dead this time. Yvonne wasn't moving neither, but when she started making gurgling noises, I realized she was still alive, too. What kind of superhumans devils was I dealing with? With that knife still in me, I squatted down and hit her head some more until I was sure she was dead, too. I dropped the hammer and wobbled up. Then I gently pulled the blade out of my chest and flung it to the floor.

"I can't believe that motherfucker stabbed me," I mouthed, covering the hole in my chest with my trembling hand. I was losing blood and in indescribable pain, but I needed to try and find my money. I had no idea where else to look. Besides that, I was so weak, I couldn't climb the steps up to their attic and see if that was where they had stashed it. I couldn't stay around too much longer, in case one of the neighbors had heard the commotion and called the law. And I was getting too woozy to stay focused. I had no choice but to leave.

Somehow, I made it back to my car where I had parked a couple of blocks away. By then, my head was swimming and my vision was blurry. The pain was even worse, and I was bleeding too much to try and make it back to Hartville.

I drove to my street with the driver door open, parked in front of my house, and literally fell out of my car. I got up and staggered to my front door and fell against it, too disoriented to root around in my pocket for my key. But when I turned the knob, the door opened. For the first time, I was glad Joyce had a habit of forgetting to lock up when she went to bed.

Our Christmas tree lights was off, so it was pitch-black in the living room. When I stumbled over the threshold, Joyce clicked on one of the end-table lamps. She'd been sitting on the couch in the dark. "Joyce, thank God you here. Somebody just tried to rob me. Call for help." I was as frantic as I'd ever been in my life and she just sat there blinking so nonchalantly, I thought I was hallucinating. I was getting delirious. My legs suddenly went numb and I hit the floor. "Please . . . please . . . help me."

Joyce finally stood up. The way she was walking toward me, you would have thought she was taking a casual stroll in the park. "Odell, who did this to you?" I couldn't believe how blasé she sounded. Was this woman crazy, or just plain mean? With her husband dying right before her eyes, she was acting like she was discussing what to cook for supper.

"I don't know. Some thug. He tried to take my wallet. He got away before I seen his face," I rasped. My voice was getting weaker by the second. "He . . . he stabbed me." While I gasped for air, she stood over me with her arms folded. "Woman, what's the matter with you? Can't you see I'm bleeding to death?"

"Yup," she replied in a low tone. Then she cleared her throat. "Odell, Yvonne and Milton brought me over to Hartville not long after you left to go visit your daddy." Joyce looked and sounded as cold as a block of ice.

Good God! I was busted again. "W-what?" was the only word I could get out.

"I saw you with that Betty Jean woman and those kids in that restaurant. And

391

Yvonne and Milton told me how you've been robbing my family blind for *years* to support them."

I couldn't believe my ears. This had to be the other "humdinger of a thing" Milton tried to tell me before I hammered him. After all the money I'd gave them blackmailing motherfuckers, they'd still tattled on me. With demons like them on the loose, it was no wonder the world was in such a uproar. "Joyce, I can explain," I wheezed, spitting up blood. "Aaarrggh . . . please . . . please help me."

"You can lie your black ass there and explain all you want. And it wouldn't make any difference to me. I know all I need to know."

"I . . . I . . . declare, I'll make it up to you. Don't end our marriage."

"Me end our marriage?" She threw her head back and let out a sharp laugh. "Devil, you ended it. I'm just sorry it took so long for me to find out what a low-down funky black dog you really are. I loved you with all my heart and treated you like a king. But I wasn't woman enough for you, huh?"

"Don't put all the blame on me." My voice had dropped to a whisper that seemed to be crawling up from the bottom of my throat. "You knew how bad I wanted children and you couldn't make that happen."

"You didn't give me time before you started up with that woman. You got with her within *weeks* after we got married. And at the time I was pregnant!"

"Joyce, call for help," I begged. "You can kick my ass later. Let's work things out. I don't want to lose you."

She blew out a loud breath and went to the telephone on the stand by the couch and picked it up. Before she dialed, she started talking some more. "Lose me? Pffft. I'm not the only thing you'll be losing. You'll *never* work at my family's store again. You and that woman will have to scrape by the best way you can until somebody else hires your deceitful black ass." She paused and glared at me. "I'm going to find myself a man who deserves me."

I was so woozy, I didn't know what I was saying next until I'd said it. "I doubt that. If you do, he'll be some random slow-wit geezer. And that's if you lucky. A *beast* like you will never latch on to another man like me, unless you *buy* him like you bought me."

Words could not describe how horrified the look on Joyce's face was when she heard all that. But she still managed to respond in a gentle tone. "I'm glad you're *finally* being

393

honest with me."

"Joyce, please. If I don't go to the hospital, I'm going to bleed to death."

I couldn't believe what she did and said next. She set the telephone down and walked back over to me. "The only place you're going to go is hell. Have a nice trip." And then she casually clicked off the lamp and walked out of the room.

CHAPTER 43
JOYCE

The long, bumpy bus ride from Hartville, and sitting in my darkened living room crying nonstop ever since I'd got home, had worn me out. If Odell hadn't stumbled in when he did, I probably would have cried myself to sleep on the couch and stayed in the same spot all night.

I had no idea who had tried to rob Odell and ended up stabbing him. The way he flaunted how prosperous he was, I was surprised somebody hadn't tried to rob him sooner. But how did that fit into why he had come back home from Hartville tonight? It was possible that Yvonne and Milton had gone back into the restaurant and told him they'd brought me to Hartville and that I'd seen him. If so, maybe he'd come to confront them and one of them had stabbed him. If that was the case, how come he hadn't mentioned that as soon as he saw me? And why would he tell me that a would-be robber had stabbed him? If that was true, that person could still be lurking around outside and might bust into the house to finish him off. They could even attack me. But I was already in so much pain and feeling so ugly — and stupid — I didn't care if somebody came in and stabbed me, too. I never knew pain could be as severe as what I was feeling now.

On top of everything else, I would remember and be hurt by Odell's last words for the rest of my life. If he hadn't called me a *beast* and told me I'd *bought* him, it might have made all the difference in the world, and I'd have called for help. With the way he was bleeding, it probably wouldn't have done any good. Knowing how he felt about me now, I didn't feel the least bit guilty about not calling for help. Who would I have called anyway? The closest hospital that treated colored folks was thirty minutes away, and the ambulance service was for white folks only. Even if I had found somebody to drive him to the hospital, he wouldn't have survived that long anyway. So, technically his death was not my fault. I took a long, deep breath and decided to take a hot bath and go to bed.

I went into the bathroom, removed my makeup, and coated my face with moisturizing face cream. While my bath water was running, I went through different scenarios in my head that I had considered before Odell came home. Instead of getting somebody to drive me or taking the bus back to Hartville when I cooled off, I had thought about waiting until he returned home on Sunday and confronting him then. I had also decided to have his clothes packed so he could move out right away. Then I'd suddenly made the decision that it would hurt him more if I burned up all of his fancy suits and other nice pieces. That was what I had planned to do Saturday morning. Now I wouldn't have to do any of that.

I had been scared to death to let my parents know what Odell had done to me — and them. I wouldn't have to tell them after all. Whoever had killed him had done me a favor, and I didn't care if the law caught them or not. My parents had doted on Odell almost as much as I had, so they'd be devastated when they heard he'd been murdered. So would all the folks who'd looked up to him.

I cringed when I tried to imagine what Aunt Mattie would have said if things hadn't worked out the way they did, and I had to tell folks that I'd put Odell out because of Betty Jean. Aunt Mattie had been insinuating all along that I wouldn't be able to hold on to him. Now I wouldn't have to tell anybody about him and Betty Jean. But I was concerned about Yvonne and Milton blabbing that news to other people. I didn't know what I could do to stop them. When the time came, I'd get down on my knees and beg them to keep what they knew to themselves. I'd pay them to keep quiet if I had to. They were hoodlums, but they had cared enough about me that they couldn't continue to sit back and let Odell get away with his antics. He was the real villain in this horror story, not Yvonne and Milton. They were ignorant, greedy, and uncouth, but at the end of the day, they'd had more compassion for me than the man I'd put on a pedestal.

After my bath, I went back to the living room, clicked on the light, and checked on Odell. There was so much more blood on the floor around him, it looked like he was lying on a red blanket. His eyes were closed, and he was still breathing. But it was so slow and shallow, I knew it was just a matter of minutes before he took his last breath.

I made sure the front door was locked before I turned off the lamp. And then I went to bed.

Before I'd left to go have "supper" with

Yvonne and Milton, I had started reading *Wuthering Heights* for the second time. The first time I'd read it, I'd felt so sorry for Heathcliff and Catherine. I had enjoyed how happy they had been in the first half of the book, and I had compared their relationship and devotion to each other to Odell and me. But by the second half of the story, Heathcliff had gotten bitter and vengeful because of all the bad things he'd endured. I was disappointed that Emily Brontë had done a turnaround on such a beautiful love story. Being a Christian, I had wanted Heathcliff to forgive the people who had hurt him. Well, I was still a Christian, but in less than twenty-four hours I had been betrayed and hurt beyond belief. I could *never* forgive Odell. The fact that Yvonne and Milton had known about his cheating and thieving ways and kept it from me, made me almost as mad at them.

I got out of bed a few minutes before seven a.m. Saturday, and immediately went to check on Odell again. He looked dead, but I poked him with my foot to make sure. He was as stiff as a board. That flawless, coffee-colored skin he — and I — had been so proud of looked like it had been covered with grayish-brown paste.

I covered him with a sheet and called my parents. Daddy answered on the first ring. "What's wrong with you, gal? You know better than to be calling over here this early in the morning."

"Daddy, Odell is dead!"

It took him at least five seconds to respond. "S-say what?"

I started crying so hard and gasping for breath, it was hard to talk again. When I did, it was in a raspy voice that sounded nothing like mine. "Somebody stabbed him. I . . . I just got out of bed and found him on the living-room floor."

"Sweet Jesus!" Daddy yelped. "Lord up in Heaven! Millie, get in here! Somebody stabbed and killed Odell last night." He cleared his throat and went on. "Joyce, what in the world happened?"

"I don't know yet. Uh . . . somebody probably tried to rob him. That's all I know right now."

"Did you call Sheriff Potts?"

Before I could respond, Mama came on the line. "Joyce, what in the world is going on? You all right? Do you know who stabbed Odell?"

"I'm fine, Mama. I didn't hear or see a thing. It happened while I was asleep. My stomach was feeling queasy again last night, and I took one of those pills you brought over to help me sleep."

"Somebody broke in the house, killed your husband, and you slept through it?"

"Well, that pill put me into a deep sleep. The same way they do you when you take them."

"I thought Odell went to visit his daddy yesterday evening, like he been doing every Friday for years," Mama hollered.

"Um, he did. I guess he came home early, and somebody followed him. Everybody knows he always carries a heap of cash in his pocket."

"We'll be there in a few minutes. Did you contact Sheriff Potts?"

"Not yet," I sniffled. "I was waiting to talk to you and Daddy first."

"Call the peacemaker," Mama ordered. "Sheriff Potts needs to get on this right away."

I was so enraged by now, I didn't know what I was crying about the most: Odell's betrayal or somebody else killing him before I could do it. I suddenly started howling like a hungry baby.

"Joyce, calm down and take some deep breaths. You got to make sense when you talk to Sheriff Potts. No, don't you call him. You might say the wrong thing and complicate the situation. I'll call him myself."

"Mama, you don't have to do that," I whimpered. "If you make the call, he'll want to know why I didn't do it. I'll call him up right now."

It was no secret among colored folks, or the rest of the country, that when it came to crimes in the Deep South that involved only colored folks, the police "investigation" was sloppy, and half done at best. But I had to follow the law anyway. I ended the call with Mama and called the sheriff's office. One of his deputies answered and put me through to Sheriff Potts right away without asking any questions. "Yeah. This is Sheriff Potts," he answered, sounding like he'd just woke up.

"Hello, this is Joyce Watson."

"Mac and Millie's daughter?"

"Uh-huh." I was so jittery, I had to pause and catch my breath. "My husband was murdered last night."

I couldn't believe his casual response. "Well, blow me down with a feather. Who would want to kill a good egg like Odell? Did they kill him at the store?"

"No. It happened way after he'd closed."

"Hmmm. You know who done it, and where?"

"No. Somebody must have followed him

402

home last night. I found him on our living-room floor this morning. They stabbed him in the chest."

"Hell's bells. Now listen to me, gal. If you done it, you need to come clean right now. It'll make things a whole lot easier for you, and me."

The sheriff's implication was so ominous and out of left field, it made my head swim. "I didn't kill Odell! I wouldn't hurt a fly!" I exploded, clutching the telephone so hard it felt like it had become part of my hand.

"Calm down. I'm just doing my job. If you say you didn't do it, I'll have to take your word until I know enough to sort things out. I'll be there as soon as I can."

Fifteen minutes later, Mama and Daddy steamrolled in through the kitchen door. They rushed to the living room and stopped at Odell's feet. I had never seen them so wild-eyed and distressed. Mama was wiping tears off her face with a large white handker-chief and clutching her Bible. "Lord al-mighty," she wailed. She was fully dressed, but Daddy had on pajamas under his over-coat and mismatched house shoes.

"Joyce, you sure Odell is dead?" Daddy hollered, laying his two canes on the coffee table. With a groan, he squatted down and lifted the sheet off Odell's face and answered his own question. "Yup. He dead. The boy is stiff as a stalk of sugar cane," he said gently.

I had cried so much by now, my eyes were red and swollen. Mama hugged me and we eased down on the couch. Daddy started pacing back and forth, mumbling under his breath. After only a few minutes, he stopped pacing and marched up to the couch with a scared expression on his face. "Joyce, don't you hold back nothing! I know a couple of real good lawyers!" he boomed. "We'll get all the help you need." I was confused for a few seconds until I realized he was accusing *me* of killing Odell.

My mouth dropped open and I gave him the most incredulous look I could manage. "Daddy, you know I'd never hurt Odell, or anybody else. Like I already told y'all, I slept through the whole thing."

"Mac, don't you never say nothing like that again. Can't you see how upset Joyce is? She and Odell was the perfect couple. Everybody knows that!" Mama yelled.

"Well, I can't leave no stone unturned. Married couples have violent disputes all the time," Daddy said in a softer tone.

"If you don't come to your senses and stop upsetting this girl, the next married couple in a violent dispute will be me and you," Mama threatened.

I cried some more. Daddy hung his head and slunk into the kitchen. He made coffee and Mama and I stayed on the couch with our arms around each other. She was crying as hard as I was.

Three hours later, the sheriff showed up with a bored expression on his long, homely face. After I let him in, I glanced over his shoulder and saw two of his deputies standing on our front porch, looking like they were mad at the world. Mama was standing in the middle of the floor wringing her hands. Daddy was slumped on the couch. "Mac, Millie, Joyce. What's going on here?" Sheriff Potts growled as he crouched down on his lanky legs and lifted the sheet off Odell. "Woo-wee. Looks like a hog butchering. Smells like one, too." He let the sheet go, rubbed his beaky nose, and stood back up. "Now tell me, who done it?" I told him the same thing I'd told him when I called. He pulled a notepad out of his shirt pocket and scribbled on it for about ten seconds. After squinting at the blood trail on the floor, he opened the door. "I'll be back directly." When he left, I ran to the window and watched him and his deputies go into Yvonne and Milton's house.

Sheriff Potts came back about fifteen

minutes later, looking even more bored. "Well now, I got a mess on my hands. From the looks of things over there, a maniac is on the loose. Odell's blood trail starts next door, so that's where he was attacked." He snapped his fingers at Mama. "Millie, get me a glass of water." In the same breath he added, "I don't know if the perpetrator broke in, or if them bootleggers let him in. It was more than likely somebody who had been at the house drinking earlier and when things winded down, he lagged behind. Odell entered at some point or was already there when the mayhem started. I'll have to figure out them bootleggers' role in this mess."

"You think Yvonne and Milton killed Odell? Lord, Lord, Lord. They was some of his best friends. Umpossible. That's absolutely *umpossible,*" Daddy insisted, wobbling up off the couch. "They was heathens, but they wasn't killers. They didn't do it."

"Well, *somebody* killed Odell. From what I can make out based on the evidence I seen, I suspect some joker attempted to rob Yvonne and Milton and things got out of hand. The bedroom was ransacked, and the living room is a wreck. Things was knocked over, blood's all over the kitchen and living room floors. Odell managed to get out after he got stabbed and made it to his car, which for some mysterious reason he'd parked a couple of blocks down the street. I know that because he left a mess of blood leading to it, too. The culprit got away without leaving a trace. The only blood trail I seen leading from the house next door to Odell's car was his. He must have been out of his head and didn't know what he was doing. He drives his car home, gets out, and staggers into his own house."

I had never heard such a convoluted story before in my life. Nothing was making sense to me. "Well, what did Yvonne and Milton tell you, Sheriff Potts? If they were there, they have to know who stabbed Odell and why," I wailed. I had to be careful what I said. If I confessed to my actions after Odell got home, Sheriff Potts wouldn't waste any time putting handcuffs on me. I'd had enough bombshells dropped on me, so I was going to stick to my original story.

Sheriff Potts ignored my question and picked up the telephone and dialed. "Moe, it's a bloodbath over here. Don't send the ambulance. It's for white folks only. Get that telephone list out of my desk drawer and look up the number for that colored undertaker; Rufus . . . uh . . . Morgan. Give him a call and tell him I said to get his tail over to Odell Watson's residence lickety-split. It's the house next door to the right of them bootlegging darkies we recently dealt with." After all that had happened since yesterday evening, I didn't think there was anything else somebody could say that would shock me. What the sheriff said next did. "And tell the undertaker he'll have to make *three* trips." He paused and sucked on his teeth. "Naw. Odell is dead and so is them bootleggers." There was another pause, this one longer. "Yup. You right about that. I seen something like this coming, too. I been telling folks for years that colored folks are mentally limited, so them and alcohol don't mix. All right now. You go on and do what I told you, you hear?" Sheriff Potts hung up, adjusted his cap, and gulped down the glass of water Mama had just handed him. After a mighty belch, he set the glass on the coffee table and went on. "The undertaker will get here directly. He'll haul Odell and them other two corpses to the morgue so the coroner can do his job. After that, they'll be released back to the undertaker for funeral and burial purposes."

Mama and Daddy were standing side by side in the middle of the floor, looking like they were about to pass out. It was a miracle I hadn't already done that myself. "Sheriff, are Yvonne and Milton dead, too?" I asked.

"Yup. Somebody beat the dog shit out of them. There was a bloody hammer on the floor." Sheriff Potts took off his hat and used it to fan his sweaty face before he put it back on. "There was also a large butcher knife with blood all the way up to the handle, which is what I suspect Odell got stuck with. I don't want y'all to move his body. That'd be tampering with evidence." He pulled his watch out of his shirt pocket, checked the time, and then mumbled something I couldn't make out. After a loud snort, he started talking again. "Joyce, I'm sorry you lost your husband and your neighbors. Just be grateful the perpetrator didn't do you in, too."

"This is the devil's work. Who else could be behind something so evil?" Daddy said in a raspy tone. "There ain't never been no murder in this nice, quiet neighborhood. Now we got *three*?"

Sheriff Potts narrowed his eyes and shook his fist in the air. "Be glad it ain't no more than that. But don't y'all worry none, I'll straighten out this mess."

"I sure hope so," I mumbled.

"Now everybody relax and be patient. I got everything under control. Lock the doors and keep your eyes open in case the same maniac decides to come back. Hear me? Y'all have a nice day now." Sheriff Potts tipped his hat and shuffled back out the door, whistling like he didn't have a care in the world.

CHAPTER 44
JOYCE

The rest of Saturday morning went by in a blur for me. The queasiness and other minor discomforts I'd recently started experiencing, were more frequent now. I threw up three times in less than two hours. Neighbors and friends came to the house to check on me. But I was so miserable, physically and mentally, I didn't want to have company so I holed up in my room for a while.

After Odell's body was removed, a few minutes before noon, Mama and a lady from our church started cleaning up his blood. There was so much, some had seeped through the cracks in the wooden floor. Even after the area had been scrubbed, I could still see traces of blood. When Mama covered the spot with a blanket, I ran to the bathroom to throw up again. After that, I went back to bed. I cried some more and eventually went to sleep.

Three hours later, I got up and returned

411

to the living room. Mama was in the kitchen cooking supper. Daddy was stretched out on the couch. I went to the window and saw the same hearse that had transported Odell's body to the morgue parked in front of Yvonne and Milton's house. Mama walked up behind me. "They took Yvonne's body while you was sleeping," she told me. "They just came back for Milton's. I don't remember the last time three people died in Branson at the same time."

"I do," Daddy said with a groan. "During the War Between the States, when them Yankee soldiers tore through here, they killed dozens of folks at the same time. Some of them soldiers was used-to-be slaves that had run away to the North and joined the Union Army. I was a little bitty boy, but I remember it all like it happened yesterday. But they was killing white folks. It's a shame all this had to happen now to colored folks, with Christmas right around the corner." He sat up ramrod straight and coughed before he spoke again. "Baby, you can't stay in this house tonight. Go pack a few things and come home with us."

"Okay. Daddy, somebody needs to go out to Odell's daddy's house to let him and his wife know what's going on," I said.

"Don't you worry about that. Buddy came

412

by while you was sleeping, and I let him borrow my car to go out there to tell Lonnie and Ellamae."

I packed a few clothes and went home with Mama and Daddy. We were all feeling so beaten down when we got up Sunday morning, none of us wanted to go to church. After breakfast, they met with Reverend Jessup and the undertaker to make the arrangements for Odell's service. I called up some of my coworkers and our principal at their homes and told them I'd be off work indefinitely.

With Odell gone, I was going to manage the store until Daddy and Mama replaced him. But no matter who took over the job, I would do the bookkeeping for the rest of my life. Now that I knew Odell had been embezzling money and stealing merchandise for so long, I dreaded checking the inventory records and going over other paperwork that covered the last five-and-a-half years. I insisted on doing it so my naïve parents wouldn't have to. Because if they did it and noticed something suspicious, they probably would have come up with every reason in the book not to accuse Odell of any wrongdoing. I was going to do all I could to keep them from finding out the truth.

Odell's funeral was scheduled to take

place on Wednesday. To honor him, Daddy decided to keep the store closed the whole week. Buddy and Sadie balked about that, but when he told them they'd still get their full pay, they calmed down.

Monday morning, people came to the house in droves to offer their condolences. They couldn't praise Odell enough. Just hearing them talk about how "godly" and what a good "role model" he had been, made me sicker. I shuddered when I thought about how often and long I had praised him myself. Only a couple of folks, both from our church, mentioned Yvonne and Milton and it was only to throw out a few unflattering comments about how they had lived such a wicked lifestyle.

By afternoon, I felt well enough to go back to my house to get some more clothes. When I got there, I was surprised to see the old truck that belonged to Yvonne's uncle Sherman parked in front of her house. As I was about to unlock my front door, somebody hollered my name. I immediately turned around. It was Yvonne's thirteen-year-old daughter, Cherie. Her brothers, JJ and Ishmael, born ten months apart, were eleven. They were peeping out the front window. But they didn't come outside.

"Cherie!" I yelled. She was already running toward my house, so I ran to meet her halfway. When we got close enough, I wrapped my arms around her. "Sugar, I am so sorry about what happened to Yvonne and Milton. But you don't have to worry, they're going to catch whoever did this and lock them up for a long time."

"I hope so. I'm sorry Mr. Odell got killed too. My uncle went to the police station this morning. That skinny old peckerwood sheriff told him to wrap up his business here with the undertaker, and don't interfere with the investigation." Cherie's eyes were as red and swollen as mine. She looked so much like Yvonne. Her skin was light brown, but today it was so pale, she could almost pass for white. And her long, straight black hair was hidden up under a homely plaid scarf that made her look much older. Grief had such a powerful effect on people. If a girl as young and pretty as Cherie looked almost like a hag to me, there was no telling what I looked like to her.

"We'll have to leave it up to God," I muttered.

"I know. I just hope the sheriff can find out what really happened."

This poor child didn't seem confident that Sheriff Potts would solve the case, and I sure wasn't. Daddy and Reverend Jessup had gone to the police station earlier this morning to see if Sheriff Potts had made any progress. He'd told them basically the same thing he'd told Yvonne's uncle.

Cherie rattled on and my thoughts wandered. Even though the sheriff kept insisting that some "maniac" had killed Yvonne, Milton, and Odell, the colored folks didn't agree. And when Daddy went back to the sheriff's office half an hour after his first visit this morning and asked him if he'd checked the fingerprints on the knife that killed Odell, the sheriff got downright hostile. Daddy trembled as he repeated what Sheriff Potts had said, even imitating his annoying drawl: " 'An unknown maniac beat Yvonne and Milton to death with a hammer, and then they stabbed Odell. That's all the information I can reveal until a suspect has been identified and apprehended. My deputies jumped the gun and picked up the weapons, so the only fingerprints I would have found belonged to them. And who are you to be telling me how to do my job? Now you get up out of here. I'm going to arrest you and the next one of y'all niggers that interferes with my investigation!' "

"He told you all that?" I'd whimpered.

"Word for word," Daddy confirmed.

Sadly, there was no higher authority we could go to without provoking Sheriff Potts. The colored folks wouldn't stop talking about the murders. Nobody could figure out why Odell had been in the house that night in the first place. One neighbor suggested that Yvonne and Milton had fought over money, Odell had intervened, and got stabbed by accident. A few speculated that Milton had suspected Odell was after Yvonne and Milton had stabbed him in a jealous rage. Then Milton must have done or said something to provoke Yvonne and she'd battered his head with the hammer. He'd overpowered her, got control of the hammer, and killed her with it before he died from his injuries. "Joyce, you the best thing that ever happened to Odell, so he didn't have no reason to lust after Yvonne," another neighbor said. That almost made me throw up again. The only woman Odell had been fooling around with — that I knew of — had been Betty Jean. The same neighbor came up with the notion that Odell might have been there to commit a robbery. Everybody knew that all the bootleggers kept their profits somewhere on their property. But Odell robbing somebody was ridiculous. He already had more money than he could spend. The stories got more and more outlandish. The bottom line was, nobody knew what really happened.

One theory I had was that Odell had killed Yvonne and Milton because he'd found out they'd brought me to the restaurant while he was there with Betty Jean. That theory didn't stay on my mind long. If that had been the case, how come he hadn't mentioned it before he died? And he seemed genuinely surprised when I told him I'd seen him with Betty Jean. As hard as I tried, I couldn't figure out any other reasons why Odell would want to kill Yvonne and Milton. Random thoughts kept entering my mind. Had he said or done something they didn't like that was so offensive it had set them off? As flimsy as that was, it was a possibility. Another random thought entered my mind. Maybe they had tried to make him pay them off so they wouldn't tell me about Betty Jean. I dismissed blackmail right away. Even though they had criminal backgrounds, those two had been too stupid to commit a crime as sophisticated as blackmail. If they had tried, I knew Odell wouldn't have paid them a plugged nickel. I was convinced that we'd never know what really happened.

A few people hinted that Willie Frank was probably involved in some way. Either he was the "unknown maniac" Sheriff Potts claimed had committed the murders, or he knew who was. The only problem was, he was white and his uncle Lamar was in cahoots with Sheriff Potts. Nobody was brave enough to question him or ask Sheriff Potts to do it. Unless somebody confessed to the crime, we didn't expect anything more. I shook my head to clear my thoughts and returned my attention to Cherie.

"I'm going to miss her so much," she said, choking on a sob. It broke my heart to know that this poor child and her brothers would never know that Yvonne was actually their mother, not their cousin.

"Yvonne loved you and your brothers to death." It was a struggle to keep my emotions under control.

"We loved her, too. That's why I wanted to come today." Cherie paused and swallowed hard. "Me and my brothers picked out the dress for Mama to be buried in."

I gasped. "You called Yvonne 'Mama.' Who —"

Cherie cut me off. "Aw, shuck it, Miss Joyce. Me and my brothers knew all along she was our real mama. We heard Uncle Sherman telling it to some people right after they took us in."

"If you've known all these years, how

come you didn't let Yvonne know?"

"We didn't want her to feel no worse about not being with us than she already felt." Cherie let out a sigh that was so long and loud, and she looked so sad, tears pooled in my eyes. "I have to get back inside and help pack up stuff. Some of Milton's folks done already come and took what they wanted. His brother, who is a preacher in Louisiana, is on his way. He's going to help preach their funeral tomorrow."

"There's going to be only one funeral?"

"Uh-huh. Aunt Nadine said that Mama loved Milton so much, that's what she would have wanted. And they have to be buried in graves side by side."

"Oh. Well . . . I don't know if I'll be able to attend the funeral. It's going to be hard enough for me to get through Odell's."

"Don't worry about it, Joyce. I understand how you feel. I'd probably feel the same way if I was in your shoes." Cherie looked at the ground for a moment and sniffled. When she looked back up at me, there was a sudden twinkle in her eyes. "When things quiet down, can I come visit you sometime? You don't have to give me a bunch of gifts like the last time, I just want to stay in touch with somebody that meant so much to my mama."

"You and your brothers can visit anytime you want. I'm planning to move back in with my mama and daddy until I find a new house. You can always find out where to find me by checking with the folks who work at the store."

"Okay, Miss Joyce. I'm glad I seen you today. Do you want to come in and say something to Aunt Nadine and Uncle Sherman before we leave?"

I glanced at the house next door. It was the last place I ever wanted to set foot in again. I didn't think I could handle seeing the scene of the crime. "Uh, not right now. I'm sure they want to get things sorted out and get up out of Branson as fast as they can."

"Okay." Cherie gave me a big hug and kissed my cheek. And then she was gone. Just like her mama.

CHAPTER 45
JOYCE

The double funeral Yvonne's and Milton's relatives had arranged for them at the church they belonged to, was the Tuesday after the murders. Odell's was scheduled for Wednesday at our church. I couldn't bring myself to go pay my last respects to Yvonne and Milton, because I was still too overwhelmed with grief.

Buddy and Sadie went, though. They were so nosy they attended funerals for folks they didn't even know, just so they could have something new to talk about. After they left the church, they came to my parents' house while I was alone. The minute they entered the living room, they started bragging about how they had arrived at the church before anybody else and had gotten prime seats close to the caskets.

After mumbling a few complaints about the weather and their health, they removed their coats and plopped down on the couch.

I eased down into the wing chair facing them. Buddy didn't waste any time getting the conversation started. "I declare, that was the dullest, no-frills double-funeral I ever been to. I guess Yvonne and Milton was not as well liked as folks thought. Right, Sadie?" He looked like a grizzly bear in his dark brown suit.

"Sure enough," Sadie agreed, bobbing her head. She had on the same plain cotton black dress she'd worn to the last three funerals. "There wasn't enough flowers to make a bouquet, the choir sung only two songs, and a few folks didn't even show up until the closing remarks. Aunt Mattie and all of them floozies that work for her was there, dressed like harlots, crying like babies. A few bootleggers that had axes to grind with Yvonne and Milton showed up."

"Humph. Them bootleggers probably came just to make sure their competition is dead," Buddy commented. "Now they'll get back all the customers Yvonne and Milton had wooed away from them."

"You right about that. Poor Willie Frank cried up a storm. I ain't never seen a white man grieve over colored folks the way he done. Yvonne and Milton's house was his second home. He'll never get over this. A heap of his kinfolks came with him." Sadie was talking so fast, she had to pause and catch her breath. "They done a lot of boo-hooing, too. This was the first time I seen hillbillies dressed up in suits and ties. I didn't know they even wore store-bought clothes."

Buddy took off his stiff-looking black tie, wiped sweat off his face with it, and stuffed it in his pocket. "I wish I had ate before I left my house. My stomach is growling like a wolf," he complained.

"I wish I'd ate something, too. Joyce, would you believe the only food they had after the service was crackers, cheese, and a few overcooked chicken wings? They didn't have nothing to drink except water," Sadie complained, adjusting her wide-brimmed straw hat.

Buddy looked like he couldn't wait to make his next comment. "I ain't never had such a miserable time at a funeral. I wish I had stayed home."

"I feel the same way," Sadie admitted.

I couldn't stay silent any longer. "I don't know what to say about the way you two feel. I assumed y'all thought of Yvonne and Milton as friends!" I hollered. "Y'all drank with them as often as Odell and I did."

"They was our friends, but Odell was our boss," Buddy shot back. "Now what is me and Sadie going to do for money? Them was the best jobs we ever had. Nary one of Branson's farmers want folks our ages working in the cane and cotton fields again."

"Don't even think about being out of work. The store will stay open, so y'all don't have a thing to worry about," I assured them. They perked up so fast it made my head swim. The smiles on their faces reached from ear to ear.

"Whew. I'm glad to hear that. You don't know how I been fretting over being unemployed." Buddy shook his head and fanned his face with his hand. "Anyway, the undertaker told us there was so much damage done to Yvonne's and Milton's heads, he couldn't spruce them up enough to leave their caskets open. With them being bootleggers and ex-convicts, I was amazed at how Reverend Hayes and Milton's preacher brother stood up at that pulpit and made them sound like saints. But that's usually the case at most of the funerals I go to. I'm glad I live a righteous life. Reverend Jessup won't have to lie about me at my funeral. Oomph, oomph, oomph."

"And you should have seen the way Milton's brother's wife was dressed. She looked like part of Aunt Mattie's crew." Sadie paused and looked at Buddy.

He nodded and I braced myself because I knew he was about to start up again. The more I heard, the more my stomach turned. When I was able to get a word in edgewise, I excused myself to go throw up. When I got back to the living room a few minutes later, Buddy and Sadie had gone into the kitchen and helped themselves to some elderberry wine. Buddy had removed his shoes and propped his feet up on the coffee table, so I knew they planned to stay for a while. But they had already worn out their welcome in my book. Being sick made it easy for me to politely ask them to leave so I could go take a pill and lie down. They still didn't leave until they'd finished their drinks and made a few more unflattering comments about Yvonne and Milton's funeral.

Our church wasn't big enough to hold the crowd that came to pay their last respects to Odell. Before the service started, there wasn't one single seat left on any of the pews. Dozens of folks stood along the walls and in the aisles. At least three dozen more weeping mourners who hadn't been able to get in, stood outside in front of the church. I saw people I hadn't seen in years, including old folks in wheelchairs I thought had already died, and babies still in diapers. It was the most extravagant event I'd ever attended in my life.

The tuxedo and solid bronze, gold-plated casket with blue velvet interior that Mama and Daddy had picked out for Odell had set them back a pretty penny. Not to mention what they had shelled out for the numerous elaborate floral arrangements. They had brought in a well-known soloist from Lexington whose fee was one of the highest in the state. She sang eight songs back to back. But the carriage with four white horses that my parents and Odell's daddy had hired to transport his body to the cemetery took the cake.

Odell's daddy and stepmother were devastated. I hadn't seen them in several months and they'd looked sickly and decrepit back then. Now they looked even worse. They hadn't been able to get in touch with the brother and sister Odell had practically lost contact with who lived in Birmingham, or any other relatives. "I'm going to miss my boy. He didn't come see me but once or twice a month for a few hours at a time, but I enjoyed every one of his visits," Lonnie sobbed to me. I was glad nobody else heard his comment. They would have most definitely questioned me about it. Odell had so many people believing that he visited his daddy overnight almost every Friday and Saturday, most of Sunday, and sometimes a few hours during the weekdays, every week for years.

I got a lump in my throat when I saw the four-page program. There were so many philosophical quotes on it, you would have thought Shakespeare had written it. Somebody had submitted a corny poem that mentioned how sad it was that Odell had never fulfilled his dream to be a father. I shuddered when I thought of how all these well-meaning people would react if they knew about Betty Jean and Odell's three sons. Nobody would ever know about them, if I could help it.

I lost count of all the folks who went up to the pulpit to praise Odell. They described him as honest, God-fearing, generous, and loved by everybody he met. I didn't get upset about how he'd duped them, because he had duped me more than anybody else. A white farmer Odell used to work for came with several members of his family. During a break in the lengthy service, he gave me a hug. "Joyce, I wish I could have got to know you. Every time I went into the store and chatted with Odell, he talked about how lucky he was to have a wife like you. I know

God will help you bounce back from this unspeakable tragedy with your faith intact. Odell had done what God sent him to do, so it was his time to go. And, keep in mind that you were his whole world. You kept him grounded and humble," the distraught man told me. His comments made my stomach churn. So many other folks said things along the same lines, but I didn't believe it.

If I had been half the woman Odell had made everybody think I was, Betty Jean would never have been in the picture in the first place. Since nobody knew about her, she had no way of knowing Odell was dead. If she had shown up, it might have been another double funeral because I probably would have dropped dead.

I cried along with everybody else. But I was still so hurt by Odell's betrayal, his funeral was the last place I wanted to be.

When the service ended three hours later, the mourners gathered in the dining area. Aunt Mattie strolled up to me and gave me a bear hug and a quick peck on each cheek. "Joyce . . . I'm . . . I'm going to pray for yooooou," she sobbed, mopping tears off her face with a large handkerchief.

"I appreciate that. Odell thought so highly of you," I mumbled.

Aunt Mattie honked into her handkerchief, narrowed her eyes, and scrunched up her lips. "Joyce, did Odell ever tell you what I told him on the day y'all got married?"

I gave her a puzzled look. "I can't answer that until you tell me what you told him," I replied.

"Right after the preacher told him to kiss you, I got a cold chill. The same kind I got a month before my mama died, and a few months before my used-to-be boyfriend got bit by a snake and died. That chill was a sign. I told Odell there was going to be trouble down the road for you and him. I even offered to work a little hoodoo to help y'all avoid it."

"What kind of trouble?"

"Well, my psychic abilities relayed to me that it was going to be something really bad, but I didn't get no details. If he had took me up on my offer, I could have diverted whatever it was, and he'd still be alive."

"He didn't tell me anything about that conversation." I sucked in some air and gave her a guarded look. "I guess that was why you used to make all those comments about him leaving me, huh?"

"*Nobody* thought you was Odell's type. I reckon he did, because he married you." Aunt Mattie sighed and gave me a pitiful look. "Poor fool. He was confused, but he was still a good man. He just happened to be in the wrong place at the wrong time and it costed him his life. When you was with him, there was always a big smile on your face. I'm glad he made you happy."

"Yeah . . . he sure did," I muttered. And it was true. The Odell I'd fallen in love with had made me happy. The real one had turned me into a scornful shrew. I couldn't continue this conversation with a straight face. "Excuse me, please." I made a beeline for the restroom.

I was glad when we left the church. So many things had depressed, overwhelmed, and stunned me today, I didn't think there'd be any more. I was wrong. There was another one when we got to the cemetery. The gravediggers had dug a hole for Odell right next to Yvonne's. Milton's was on her other side. It was so ironic, but appropriate. The three devils were going to spend eternity together.

I slept less than two hours Wednesday night. When I got out of bed Thursday morning at seven, I tiptoed through the house so I wouldn't wake up Mama and Daddy. I had buried my painful past, but there was one more loose end I had to tie up: Betty Jean. I caught the first bus to Hartville.

I didn't have any trouble finding her house. I was glad it was only about half a mile from the bus stop. That waitress had told me Betty Jean rarely left the house unless she was with Odell. I hoped she was home today because I didn't want to make another trip. I was afraid if I had to put it off, I'd lose my nerve and never come back.

As I dragged my feet up her walkway, I prayed her kids wouldn't be present. I didn't want them to hear what I had to say, or even see me. Those babies were just as innocent as I was in this mess. They would be hurt enough when they heard the news about Odell's death.

A tricycle that looked new, stuffed animals, building blocks, and other toys were scattered all over the front porch floor. This was how *my* porch should have looked. Just thinking about that, made me feel even more cheated for not having the children I deserved. A fishing pole that looked exactly like the one Odell had at home, was propped up in a corner behind a glider. And the same exact Christmas wreath he had put on our door was also on Betty Jean's. If everything I'd seen so far wasn't bad enough, there was a plaque on the wall with big black capital letters next to the street address that read: THE WATSONS. *Just like the one he had nailed up on our front wall.*

I had to take a long, deep breath and count to ten in my head to compose myself before I could get up enough nerve to knock. While I was still knocking, Betty Jean cracked the door open just wide enough for me to see one side of her face. I felt like a giant standing in front of such a petite woman. She was much prettier up close, and at least ten or twelve years younger than me. "Can I help you, ma'am?" She had a husky voice for a woman her size.

"I'm Odell's wife," I blurted out.

She gasped and opened the door wider. I had never seen a person's eyes get so wide as fast as hers. *"Joyce?"* Her lips started trembling and she suddenly sounded as meek as a baby kitten. "W-where is Odell at? I been waiting for him to come home. I been worrying myself sick. He went night-fishing last Friday and never came back . . ."

"Well, you can stop waiting and worrying because he won't be coming back, period."

Her face went blank. "Say what? Is that what he told you? I want to hear it from him!" she hollered through clenched teeth.

I clenched my teeth, too. "Look, *Miss* whatever your last name really is. You won't be hearing that, or anything else from my husband."

433

"Humph. So you say. I don't know how you found out about me, but there ain't nothing you can do about it now. Why didn't you bring him with you? He could have at least been man enough to tell me, and not send you —"

I had to interrupt her before I exploded. "Odell is dead," I blurted out.

Betty Jean's mouth dropped open and she covered her heart with her hand. "W-what happened? Did he accidently fall in the lake and drown?" She was whimpering like a sick puppy now.

I shook my head. "He wasn't lucky enough to go out in a dignified way like that. Somebody killed him. That's all you need to know."

"How do I know you telling the truth? You scorned women will try every trick in the book to get back at your men. You could have made up this cock-and-bull story just to get rid of me so you can have Odell all to yourself. Well, he is my man, too, and I ain't going to let him go without a fight!" Betty Jean shouted at the top of her lungs. I could hear the kids talking and laughing in another room. She glanced over her shoulder and came out on the porch, closing the door behind her.

"Call the sheriff's office in Branson and

ask them. Or you can get in touch with the Branson newspaper and tell them to send you last Monday's edition. The whole story is on the front page."

"Who would want to kill a wonderful man like Odell? Everybody loved him," she sniveled.

"Humph. At least one person didn't." I sneered.

Betty Jean's mouth dropped open and she stared at me for a few seconds. "Uh . . . uh . . . y-you serious, ain't you?" she stuttered.

"His funeral was yesterday. He's buried in the colored section at the Branson cemetery."

"How come somebody didn't come tell me? Me and his sons should have been at his funeral. And Odell got a heap of friends in Hartville. I know they would have liked to pay their last respects."

"What's wrong with you, gal? Who do you think should have come from Branson to tell you he'd been killed so you could attend his funeral? Me? Pffft. You're lucky I'm here now. If I hadn't come, you might never have found out why he stopped coming over here. You and him had already made a big fool out of me. You think I'd have let y'all cause me even more shame and pain by seeing you at his funeral, and having everybody know how you and him made a joke of my life?"

"I . . . how long have you known about me?" she asked with tears streaming down her face. Her voice sounded so meek now and she looked so beaten down, I almost felt sorry for her.

"I just found out last Friday. All this time, I had no idea."

"Who told you?" she asked, choking on a sob.

"The same people who died with Odell."

Betty Jean's jaw dropped so low, her face looked as long as a lantern. "What —"

I held up my hand. "That's a story too long and painful to tell, and I don't have all the information anyway." I tilted my head to one side and squinted, glad to see that she was looking as miserable as I was. "You and Odell caused me a lot of grief. I hope he was worth it." I didn't wait around to hear anything else Betty Jean had to say. As soon as my feet hit the ground, I started walking as fast as they could carry me. When I reached the end of her yard, I stopped and looked back at her. Betty Jean was perched on her porch steps, crying like a whupped baby. I took a deep breath and started walking again and didn't stop until I got back to the bus stop.

Odell's daddy died of a massive stroke two days before Christmas. Ellamae managed to get in touch with his other children. They came and took his body back to Birmingham, where he would be buried. I didn't hear that news until Christmas Day, when Buddy came to my parents' house to eat Christmas supper with us. He also reported that Aunt Mattie had told him Willie Frank had found Jesus (again) and abruptly stopped making illegal alcohol. He offered to marry Sweet Sue if she would stop selling her body. She jumped at the chance (she'd found Jesus, too). Since it was against the law for colored and white to marry in Alabama, they boarded a train on New Year's Day and went to live with her sister in New York.

It was agonizing to think about everything I'd experienced in the past few weeks. I knew I'd still be thinking about it all for a long time to come. If Odell had lived, I probably would have forgiven him eventually. And I would have divorced his cheesy black ass as fast as I could. However, at the end of the day, I was in a much better place because of him. But that didn't make up for the indescribable pain he'd caused me.

EPILOGUE:
JOYCE

1940

When I'd experienced nausea and the other minor aches and pains the days leading up to the murders last year, it never occurred to me that I was finally pregnant again. I hadn't missed any periods or gained weight, so I had no reason to believe I was finally going to be a mother. When I missed my period in January, I went to the doctor. He stunned me with the news that I was three months pregnant. I hadn't drunk any neipee since the week Odell died. And I'd had so much on my mind the past few weeks, I had stopped asking God to bless me with a baby. I didn't know if the neipee had helped me become pregnant or if nature had finally come through for me — with God's help, of course. The important thing now was: I was going to have a child.

The first week in July, I gave birth to Odell's daughter. I named her Estelle. With

God's help, I would do my best to keep her from being as gullible as I had been. I planned to tell her everything about how her father betrayed me, when she got old enough to understand. But I'd never tell her that I hadn't tried to save his life when he was bleeding to death.

My labor had lasted over twenty-eight hours. Mama and Daddy had stayed with me at the colored clinic the whole time, and several more hours after I'd given birth. When they got sleepy, they slept in Daddy's car.

My parents were pleased beyond belief to finally be grandparents. "It's a shame Odell ain't around to see what a magnificent gift he helped create," Mama blubbered, with tears pooling in her eyes.

"Well, that sweet boy is in Heaven looking down, so he know he finally got a child of his own," Daddy added. They stood over my hospital bed beaming like flashlights.

I didn't like to think ill of the dead, but if everything I'd been taught in church was true, Odell was burning in hell. I was still mad at him, but my anger had eased up a little. Now when people praised him in my presence, it didn't disgust me as much when I smiled and agreed with them. Despite his actions, my life was still moving in a positive direction. I had a much better life now because of what he'd done.

I ran into Aunt Mattie last month at Mosella's while I was having lunch with some of my coworkers. She'd followed me to the restroom and told me why Odell had been fired from his handyman job at her place before I met him. She'd caught him attempting to rob one of her most important tricks. Her prostitutes had confessed to her that Odell would pressure them to have sex with him for free behind her back, two and three times a week. Another man, who'd worked at the house the same time as Odell, blabbed that he used to steal food and liquor from her pantry and sell it to rival madams. If I had known all that before I met that low-down, conniving, greedy, funky, black dog, I never would have gotten involved with him. Then he, Yvonne, and Milton would still be alive. My worshipping and praising him like he was a god, had made him even worse. Just as I was about to excuse myself and go back to my table, Aunt Mattie said something that almost made me faint. "I seen your baby girl. Your mama showed her off at the church bake sale last week. I done good, didn't I?"

"What's that supposed to mean?"

"That neipee ain't never failed yet . . ."

I didn't know what to say. While I was trying to find the right words, Aunt Mattie gave me a sly look and went on. "Clarabelle told me you sent her to me to get some help so you could have a baby. I wish you had come to me yourself. I would have given you a discount."

I gasped so hard I choked on some air. My face felt like it was on fire. I hadn't seen Clarabelle since the day she'd picked up the neipee for me, so I had no idea she had blabbed after all. I made a mental note that if I needed help again from a hoodoo, I'd go to one who didn't know me. "I . . . I hope you don't go around broadcasting my business. I don't want folks, especially my mama and daddy, to think I believe in all that . . . um . . . what you do."

Aunt Mattie laughed. "Girl, you ain't got to worry about me blowing the whistle on you. I declare, that kind of tattling would be bad for my business. Folks would stop trusting me with their secrets. But if you had come to me sooner, you would have been a mama yourself a lot sooner."

I sighed. "I still give the credit to God," I insisted.

Aunt Mattie nodded. "I do too. He sent Clarabelle to me for you." Aunt Mattie smiled and patted my shoulder. "Have a

441

nice life, Joyce. You deserve it."

"You too." We hugged for a brief moment. When I reared back and looked in her eyes, I was surprised to see tears.

"I liked Milton, but Yvonne is the one I really miss." She sniffled.

"Me too," I admitted. I left the room because I didn't want Aunt Mattie to see that I had tears in my eyes, too.

Despite the fact that Yvonne had betrayed me, too, I actually missed her. She'd been the closest female friend I'd ever had. I was sorry I had said so many unflattering, patronizing things about her to her face. I'd talked down to her because I was jealous of her good looks. Making her feel inferior had made me feel better about myself. I promised God that I would *never* treat another woman that way again, no matter how pretty she was. Yvonne had said things to hurt my feelings, too. But I think it was only to get back at me for putting her down. Odell had also said things to her and Milton that were unflattering. But I had no idea if it had been jealousy on Odell's part, too.

I returned to my job at the school in September and talked Mama and Daddy into letting Buddy and Sadie co-manage the store. They were so elated, you would have thought they'd just landed jobs at the White

House. Daddy also hired a couple of dependable folks Reverend Jessup had recommended to work the cash registers. The same stock boy who had been employed when Odell died, was still on the job. Even though Buddy and Sadie were co-managers, I delivered the profits in brown paper bags to my parents every Friday.

"These bags sure is a lot bulkier than the ones Odell used to bring," Mama commented after I'd made the first few deliveries.

Daddy responded before I could. "Hmmm. I guess them bags he brung didn't look as full because he folded the bills up neater so they'd take up less space."

"He must have folded them real neat," I threw in. I was glad my folks were too naïve to realize I was being sarcastic. The bags I dropped off were bulkier because I never skimmed money off the top the way Odell had. "Did y'all ever count the money after he left it?"

"Pffft. We didn't have to. We trusted Odell as much as you did. With the cash in the pantry and what's stashed in the attic, we set for life," Daddy said.

"After me and Mac pass on, you won't never have to work again if you don't want to. It's a shame poor Odell ain't going to be around to help you enjoy all that money." When Mama started crying, I left the room.

We never discussed the money again. But at least two or three times a week since his death, "poor Odell" was my parents' favorite subject. They'd even had one of our wedding pictures enlarged and framed. It was on their living-room wall. Every time I saw it, my blood boiled. I threw out the wedding pictures I'd displayed all over the house I had shared with him. When Mama noticed, I told her that the clumsy men who had helped me move had accidentally destroyed them. My lie went on to say that they hadn't secured the boxes on the back of their truck. The one with my wedding pictures had tumbled off, and the truck had backed up and run over it. When Mama had duplicates made of her copies and gave them to me, I was horrified. My explanation that it was too painful for me to look at pictures of Odell satisfied her, and she stored them in her attic. I didn't want anything in my house that would remind me of that man. Estelle didn't count. It helped that she didn't look anything like him.

Buddy and Sadie were still gossiping busybodies, but they were managing the store so well the money was still rolling in.

A week and a half after Odell's funeral, I had decided to go over the books that covered the last five years, with a fine-tooth comb. There was evidence that Odell had started embezzling and stealing merchandise *two months* after he started managing, around the same time Betty Jean entered the picture. Not long after that, he had set up some phony accounts. Two of the businesses he'd been "paying" invoices for each month had gone under the year before. Three others had never existed in the first place. I'd keep this information and his affair with Betty Jean to myself until the day I died. However, there was the possibility that somebody who knew Odell might end up in Hartville some day and hear about him and Betty Jean from one of his former friends over there. It was a slim possibility and I'd already decided if it came to that, I'd dummy up and claim complete ignorance of it. Acknowledging it would have caused a lot of people too much pain.

Sheriff Potts, and none of his family members or deputies, had shopped in the store again since Odell's death. One of the white vendors who had been close to Odell, told me that he'd run into the sheriff at the barbershop and had asked about the "investigation." He'd been informed that there were still no leads, but the case was still open. I had accepted the fact that nobody would ever be arrested. And I was sure that everybody else felt the same way. People eventually stopped talking about the murders.

Three months after Estelle's birth, I started a relationship with a man I'd met at a funeral Buddy and Sadie had dragged me to. Fred McGinnis was just as handsome and dapper as Odell. He had a great job supervising colored workers at Branson's turpentine factory, and he was from a fine Christian family. His first wife had died of a heart attack two years ago and left him with two little boys and a little girl, all under the age of five. They took to me like ducks to water and I adored them. Fred brought them to visit me frequently at the new house I'd moved into. It was in the same neighborhood where I had lived with Odell, but several blocks away so I never had to go near the "scene of the crime." After all the years I'd been praying for children, now I had four. I could never thank the Lord enough.

Fred didn't drink alcohol, so he had never visited a bootlegger's house, or a jook joint. I hadn't drunk any myself since Odell's death. Even though I had always drunk in moderation before I met him, and Yvonne and Milton, I believed my excessive drinking with them had had a lot to do with the foolish things I'd said to Yvonne and Milton. And I was convinced that alcohol had had something to do with me being so naïve about Odell. I was glad I'd given it up.

I had been seeing Fred for several weeks before he confessed that he was in love with me. I told him I cared about him, but "love" was too strong a word for me to be using again so soon. But I did love him . . .

Fred owned his house and it was only a few blocks from mine. I was surprised I had never run into him before. Everybody told me he was a good catch. Mama and Daddy loved him to death, but they admitted that they didn't think he'd ever be as good a catch as Odell. I agreed with them to keep them happy. Fred was a much better catch than Odell. It pleased me that a man with so much to offer wanted me. When he asked me to marry him in November, I wanted to accept his proposal right away. But I told him I needed time to think about it. I didn't want to jump into another marriage so soon.

As fond as I was of Fred, I would *never* trust him completely. If our relationship fizzled out and I got romantically involved with another man, the same thing would apply to him — and every other man who entered my life.

Things were going so well between Fred and me. Two years after his first proposal, he asked me again to marry him. I said yes because I loved him, and I was pregnant with his child.

■ ■ ■ ■

Reading Group Guide: Across the Way

MARY MONROE

■ ■ ■ ■

About This Guide

The suggested questions that follow are included to enhance your group's reading of this book.

DISCUSSION QUESTIONS

1. Since the anonymous call Odell made to Sheriff Potts accusing Yvonne and Milton of setting up a white female to be gang-raped backfired, Odell immediately planned to do something more drastic. Were you surprised that he decided to kill them?

2. Even the smartest criminals are too dumb for their own good. Sooner or later, they say something to someone about their crimes. Odell carelessly mentioned to Joyce that the person who'd made the call that implicated Yvonne and Milton, had called Sheriff Potts at his private residence, not his office. Joyce innocently repeated this information to Milton, and he suspected Odell was the culprit that got them arrested. But he was not quite sure. However, when Yvonne overheard Odell mention to Dr. Patterson the *exact* num-

ber of minutes it took the sheriff to arrive on the scene, she and Milton were convinced that Odell had made the call. Do you think he revealed enough information with his loose lips for them to come to this conclusion?

3. Instead of confronting Odell right away, Yvonne and Milton wanted to hold off and get as much money from him as possible, which was a dumb move on their part. Odell could have easily made another attempt to get rid of them first. Was Yvonne and Milton's greed their downfall?

4. Were you surprised when Milton demanded an additional lump-sum payment from Odell after he'd already collected one?

5. At the same time Odell was plotting the demise of Yvonne and Milton, they were plotting their revenge. Instead of killing him, they decided to destroy him by telling Joyce about his secret family. Did you think it would turn out the way it did?

6. Joyce loved Odell so much, she believed everything he told her. When she found out about his secret family and how he'd

been embezzling money from her family to support them, she did a complete turnaround. Do you think if he had not called Joyce a "beast" and accused her of "buying him" as he lay dying, she would have attempted to save his life?

7. Joyce's parents adored Odell and thought he could do no wrong. Do you think she should have told them that he was an adulterer, a thief, and a con man before they planned such an elaborate funeral for him?

8. Joyce was basically a good person. She had never committed a crime or hurt another human being. Odell's betrayal was so massive, was Joyce justified in reacting the way she did when she saw him bleeding to death?

9. Do you think Joyce "got away with murder" because she refused to get Odell medical assistance? Even if she had called for help, he still would have died. Therefore, she didn't think she had done anything wrong. As a matter of fact, Joyce was pleased that she had been able to "punish" him in some way for hurting her, and she didn't feel the least bit guilty. Do you

think Joyce should have felt some remorse? If your answer is yes, why? If it's no, why?

10. What did you think about Joyce going to Betty Jean's house to confront her after Odell's funeral?

11. Joyce decided not to tell anyone about Odell's secret family and his other crimes because then they would know how gullible she had been. She had convinced herself that this was the only way to save face. Did Joyce make the right decision?

12. Were you surprised when it was revealed that Joyce was pregnant?

13. When Joyce fell in love with another man, she also fell in love with his three children. Now instead of having one child to love and raise, she will have four (and her second is on the way). Do you think that because Joyce had been betrayed so severely, she deserved to be blessed so abundantly?

ABOUT THE AUTHOR

Mary Monroe is the award-winning and *New York Times* bestselling author of over 20 novels, with over one million books in print. She is a three-time AALBC bestseller and winner of the AAMBC Maya Angelou Lifetime Achievement Award, the PEN/Oakland Josephine Miles Award, and the J. California Cooper Memorial Award. The daughter of Alabama sharecroppers, she taught herself how to write before going on to become the first and only member of her family to finish high school. She lives in Oakland, California and can be found online at MaryMonroe.org.

The employees of Thorndike Press hope you have enjoyed this Large Print book. All our Thorndike, Wheeler, and Kennebec Large Print titles are designed for easy reading, and all our books are made to last. Other Thorndike Press Large Print books are available at your library, through selected bookstores, or directly from us.

For information about titles, please call:
(800) 223-1244

or visit our website at:
gale.com/thorndike

To share your comments, please write:
Publisher
Thorndike Press
10 Water St., Suite 310
Waterville, ME 04901